Peas and Carrots

ALSO BY TANITA S. DAVIS

Happy Families

Mare's War

A la Carte

Peas and Carrots

TANITA S. DAVIS

ALFRED A. KNOPF
NEW YORK

Visit us on the Web! randomhouseteens.com

Educators and librarians, for a variety of teaching tools, visit us at RHTeachersLibrarians.com

Library of Congress Cataloging-in-Publication Data
Davis, Tanita S.
Peas and carrots / Tanita S. Davis. — First edition.
p. cm.
Summary: After her mother is arrested, fifteen-year-old Dess is sent to live with the foster family that took in her baby brother several years before, and although she and her new foster sister, Hope, clash immediately, they soon realize they have much in common.
ISBN 978-0-553-51281-6 (trade) — ISBN 978-0-553-51282-3 (lib. bdg.) — ISBN 978-0-553-51283-0 (ebook)
[1. Foster home care—Fiction. 2. Brothers and sisters—Fiction. 3. Prejudices—Fiction. 4. High schools—Fiction. 5. Schools—Fiction. 6. Conduct of life—Fiction.] I. Title.
PZ7.D3174Pe 2016
[Fic]—dc23
2015002086

The text of this book is set in 13-point Granjon.

Printed in the United States of America
February 2016
10 9 8 7 6 5 4 3 2 1

First Edition

To McFlea, Luigi, and Bug,
the babies who needed a family and found themselves in mine;

and to KP,
with thanks for the inspiration of Galadriel the Great

ODESSA MATTHEWS, AGE ELEVEN

• • • • • • • • • • • • • • • • • • • •

By the door, on the other side of the sheet that divides the room, Baby cries in his car seat. It sounds like the rusted-out springs on Trish's bed, a hoarse over-and-over squeal. The wall above my head vibrates as next door bangs on it, hollering at Baby to shut up.

Baby cries kinda hopeless, like he knows nobody's gonna pick him up.

I read on the Internet at the library about some babies that nobody ever picks up, in orphanages and stuff. It's not good for them. In orphanages, if nobody picks them up, they stop crying . . . for good.

Trish should have taken him out of that seat. She knows he doesn't like it if he wakes up all strapped down. She should have laid him down and given him a bottle and a kiss before *he* came. She should have left us in the car, instead of Baby in his seat and me on the floor in a corner behind a sheet tacked against the wall.

Trish isn't even *trying* to treat Baby right. Not like Trish ever treats anybody who isn't waving a Benjamin or a dime bag like anything but a crack in the sidewalk, something to step over to get what she wants. Her time for anyone who needs help or a favor, or a bottle and a dry diaper, is pretty limited. On the floor in the corner, I clutch my pillow against me and ball up tighter in my sleeping bag, which smells like old French fries.

Baby's still crying. And crying. And crying.

And I can't get him, not now. Not with *Eddie* here, with the spiderweb tatted between his thumb and his first finger, and all the letters in blue-black ink winding up his wrist and the back of his hand. I can't walk past and pick Baby up. I can't even crawl next to the wall, across the room, all the way to the door. I can't get in reach of those hands.

The pillow goes over my head, clamped down. I don't want to hear. I don't want to hear the springs of the bed. I don't want to hear Baby. I don't want to hear Eddie getting mad, yelling about *Why can't you make that kid shut up.* I can't hear any of that, because if I did, I'd have to get up, and *You'd better not get out of that bed*—that's what Trish said. She always says that even though I'm already eleven, and anyway, Granny Doris says a sleeping bag isn't a real bed, and—

Baby's breath stutters, and I hold mine. *Please stop, please stop. Please. Please.* For a moment I think he will, but he gets louder.

Inside, I feel a twist. It feels like my stomach is trying to jump up my throat. He sounds bad, so bad . . . like he can't even stop himself screaming. But I can't go.

I can't.

Once, Eddie caught Trish going through his pockets, and that's when I saw that web stretched tight, when his fingers locked around her throat and he held her, eyes watering, heels drumming against the floor. She arched up, and the whites of her eyes went bloodshot and spit foamed up in the corners of her mouth while he held her down, while he told her that was what happened to girls who stole. Only he said "bitches."

She'd grabbed his wrist, tried to talk, to beg, and I know she was promising him anything, *anything,* just to breathe. I know she was, because *I* was, too. He looked at us, begging and crying and clawing at him, and laughed. But it was me he was looking at when he let Trish up.

And every time he comes, I worry about that "anything" we promised.

Sorry, Baby. I'm sorry. I'm sorry. I'm sorry.

Baby's just whimpering now, probably all worn out. Maybe he'll fall back asleep soon. It won't kill him to miss one bottle. I guess it's the "one bottle" lots of times that adds up, though.

God. If Trish just did what she's supposed to, I wouldn't have to call the social lady. They're going to come and beat on the door like last time, and they're going to cuff her wrists and take her. He'll be gone by then. Those tats on his hands have eyes; they'll never catch him. But her—they'll find her, like they always do when she's wasted. She's going to be a mess—sorry and crying and promising anything, just like before. They'll take us to stay with Granny Doris, who used to pinch if I wiggled at Mass and hollered when I peed the bed or cut paper with her sewing scissors. She doesn't like little kids, and she doesn't like messes. I know she won't like Baby's diapers, and she'll holler at Trish, too, and Trish will be so mad. But I've got to call. I've *got to*.

Somebody needs to look after Baby.

. . . .

First Day

Just before the bell rang for third period on the first day of her sophomore year, Hope Carter realized what the looks were about. There'd been an intermittent buzz for the past half hour, with sidelong glances, while Ms. Mallory, the geometry teacher, was going on about congruent angles. Hope, who actually liked geometry so far, was squinting through her caffeine-withdrawal headache and taking notes like mad. She'd even gone to the board a couple of times. Ms. Mallory was one of the nice teachers, and Hope didn't actually *mind* all that much that she got called on.

But when she got back to her seat the second time, a square of folded notebook paper sailed through the air from behind and landed in the middle of her binder.

You've got a spot on your skirt.

Hope clutched the piece of paper and twisted in her seat. Natalie Chenowith, her usual lab partner in biology, was two seats behind her and was nodding hard, her green eyes wide behind her glasses. Hope frowned and pulled on the edge of her skirt. She'd wondered if she'd sat in something. It felt as if there was a little cold spot.

She was just considering raising her hand for a pass when the bell rang.

"Homework is due at the beginning of class tomorrow," Ms. Mallory said, raising her voice over the chaos of twenty-four sophomores pushing out of desks and hurrying toward the door.

Hope bent over and picked up her pencil before standing. She found Natalie next to her, her hand pressing down on her shoulder.

"Wait," Natalie hissed through clenched teeth. "Your skirt!"

"What?" Hope asked, craning to look at her own backside.

"Big spot," Natalie replied, barely moving her lips. "*Major*. Sorry I don't have a sweater. I didn't bring a PE uniform today, either. You might have to call your mom."

"It's that bad?" asked Hope, suddenly panicked. It couldn't be *that*, could it? She was two weeks away, according to the calendar, and she'd always been regular . . . usually.

She stood and awkwardly edged away from her seat. Carefully she picked up her backpack, then held it behind herself and hustled out of the classroom, head down, heart pounding. She headed for the nearest bathroom, where she yanked her skirt, twisted around, and . . . stared.

"Oh, *crap* . . ."

In the nurses' station, Ms. Jerston took one look at Hope's face and clicked her tongue sympathetically. "Is your stomach hurting? Looks like you need to lie down."

"No, thank you," Hope said. "Can I get a pass to sit here . . . until my mom comes?"

Ms. Jerston's brows climbed to her hairline. "You want to go *home*? Why don't you rest awhile—see if the pain will pass."

Wordlessly, Hope spun around and pointed to the back of her skirt.

"Oh, honey!" Ms. Jerston said, and patted her on her back.

Her mother's sympathetic sigh came down the line. "Oh, *honey*."

"Can you just come get me?" Hope begged, already tired of hearing "Oh, honey" in that particular tone.

"Sweet, I can't," Mom said, her voice tense. In the background, Austin, who was four, was singing to himself. "Jamaira's at the nursery, and I'm on my way to North Highlands, to the county offices. The Department of Children's Services just phoned with our placement. We're getting Austin's sister—now."

"What? *Nooo!*" Hope's voice was just short of a wail. Why did her mother have to have foster-parent stuff today of all days? North Highlands was nearly three hours away from Walnut Hills. Was she just supposed to sit here and ooze? "Mom, there's *blood* on my skirt, and it's a *yellow skirt*. What am I supposed to do?"

"Oh, Hope," Mom groaned. Through the phone Hope heard a crinkling sound and Austin's insistent "Mama. Look. Mama!" In a muffled voice Mom said, "Just a minute, Austin," then added in a louder tone, "I'm so sorry, Hope. Have you got supplies? Did you try to wash it out?"

"Of course I have supplies. I tried to wash it out, but—"

"Ma! Where's my car?" Austin's voice was louder.

"—Mom, it's a *yellow skirt!*" Hope bellowed.

Her mother spoke over Austin's voice and hers. "Well, see if the secretary has a stain stick—or ask Ms. Jerston. If that doesn't work, call Henry."

Hope recoiled. "Mom! I can't call Aunt Henry—"

Of course, he was really her *uncle* Henry, but it had made him laugh when Hope was tiny and she'd insisted on calling him "Aunt" Henry. Hope didn't have any aunts. Dad was a "lonely only," and Mom was an only girl, with four brothers. Mom's little brother, Henry, had agreed with Hope that *everybody* needed an aunt and had offered to be her honorary aunt forever.

"Oh, honey, I know Henry's not your first choice, but— *Austin, leave the seat belt alone.* Hon, the firehouse is right on Broadway. Your other choice is to ask if they've got something for you to wear from the lost-and-found."

Wear something out of the lost-and-found? Hope's skin crawled. "On the first day of school? Mom, I doubt there's anything in—"

"Maaaa-ma!" Austin's voice was getting louder. "I just want to get my car!"

Hope heaved a sigh and spoke louder. "Mom? Can't I take the bus and go home?"

"On the first day? Sweetheart, no. Absolutely not. *Austin Matthews, put your bottom on the seat right now. Do not touch that seat belt.* Hope—"

Hope ground her teeth. As usual, her mother's attention was divided between Hope and everything else, and as usual, everything else won and Hope lost. It felt as if she *always* lost. The foster kids were important, she knew. Austin had come to them as a tiny baby whose grandma was too old to take him and whose mother was in jail. Jamaira's mother had abandoned her in a gas station recycling bin when she was just a few hours old. Hope knew her family was doing a good thing for the community, giving back and making a positive contribution to society.

Giving back was important. Hope just wished sometimes that her mother would maybe give back to *her.*

"Fine, Mom. Whatever. I'll call Aunt Henry. Bye." She hung up, not even sure her mother was listening anymore.

DESS, AGE FIFTEEN

· ·

North Highlands County Services

This place reeks like coffee. Like coffee and old people, and I don't know which is worse. I packed my stuff this morning—one bag. Rena at the group home tried to get me to take some books and things, but I don't want things. If I don't own it, nobody can steal it. I can't lose what I don't have. So no things for me. I like my life to fit all in one bag. Only the clothes I chose and my sewing kit—and nothing more than that.

I've been waiting for almost forty minutes, but I don't care. There are no books, but I've got my music, and that's all I need. If I were at Stanton High with the rest of the sophomores, it would be study hall, last period before lunch, and I'd be more bored than I am now. Boredom's nothing. If you're bored, at least nobody's in your face, yelling at you, crowding you, or making you do what you don't want.

There's a desk with three chairs in front of it and a big office chair behind it. On a bookshelf in the corner there are magazines, and there's a little table with one of those wire maze things, with wooden blocks threaded on it. I wouldn't touch that for money; I read on the Internet at the library last summer that there are fecal coliform germs on computer keyboards and doorknobs and clothes people try on at the mall. Not even the pump bottle of hand sanitizer on the wall makes me want to touch anything. I hate the posters in here. What little kid smiles like that about an apple? Nobody gets that excited over apples.

The door opens, and it's not the guard checking on me this time, just some big old black lady with long cornrows and dangly earrings. Rena at the group home always says that each person we meet gives us "limitless new possibilities," but I don't pay any attention when the lady smiles. I know some black lady has not got "limitless new possibilities" for me.

Then I see the little kid with her.

She's talking, but it's just noise, my heart's beating so hard. With sweet, smooth skin like creamy peanut butter, in a striped shirt and jeans, he's a bigger version of the baby in the picture Rena got me when I first came to the group home. He leans against the lady's leg, staring at me like I'm staring at him.

It's . . . he's . . .

11

He's darker than he used to be, darker than he was when he was a tiny baby and only the skin around his fingernails was even a little bit tan. I don't even know how to feel, seeing his little Charlie Brown head, bigger now. Once it held just a fringe of baby naps, just a line of raggedy curls, but now it's covered in sandy fuzz. His big old head on that little scrawny neck is the same, though. Why do babies have such big heads?

I pull out my earbuds. The black Amazon lady's *still* talking.

". . . and, Austin, this is your sister. Her name is Odessa."

"Dess," I correct, stepping hard and loud on the end of her sentence, even while my heart pounds. Trish picked the dumbest name of the dumbest city she could find to have me in, and I'm not having some foster lady tag me with that forever. Trish is crap with names; she had another baby, Dallas, but he died. Dallas, Odessa, Austin. Three for Trish from Texas. Just as well that poor baby died. The state would have taken him, too.

"You prefer Dess? I'll remember." Baby's foster lady—I guess that's who she is—talks like some kind of teacher, using words like "prefer." Baby keeps staring, his little face solemn. He doesn't know me. He doesn't remember.

There's a roaring in my ears.

Foster Lady says something else, her deep brown face full of smiles, her teeth all white and straight. What's she got to look so happy about? So what if she's got good teeth? That wrap skirt looks like she stole it off a hippie and makes her fat butt a mile wide. She's a thick chick—thick and old.

I can see gray hairs sticking out of her braids. Trish would never let herself get all fat like that.

Well, okay, you don't get fat on meth and black coffee. But *still*.

"Hey, Defsa."

Little man can talk! His eyes are round like his head when he looks up at me, and his teeth are like tiny white Tic Tacs in his smile.

"Defsa, come on!" He grabs my hand and tows me over to the table in the corner that's stacked with chunky building blocks. I give the foster lady a look, but she's smiling like there's nothing wrong with it. My neck relaxes a little.

"Go ahead and play," she says, settling in a chair in front of the desk. "I've still got paperwork to get from Mrs. Farris."

Farris is my social worker, or she was until this morning, when she blew me off. They called the house last night, and this morning they're signing me out of North Highlands into Glenn County, which doesn't make any sense. They just transferred Trish to Ironwood Vocational Center, down near LA, so we're miles apart now. Not that I care or anything—it's not like I'm some kind of mama's girl or whatever—but what's the matter with North Highlands all of a sudden? Who knows. I've got to start over with some other social worker and, instead of the group home, foster care with some big black Amazon lady. Me! I haven't been in foster care since I was eleven, and the last people kicked me back. You get this old in the system, group homes are the only ones who will take you.

"You got lotsa hair." Baby lets go of my hand to pat at my ponytail. I need to lighten it again: it's gone back to dull brown at the roots. Rena helped me dye the tips red last year, but I cut them off.

"You've got lots of hair, too," I tell Baby, who has forgotten about my ponytail in favor of a bucket of those fitted blocks. I sit on a too-short chair, my knees jamming up to my chest. I don't talk to Farris, not usually, but she asked me at the beginning of the summer if I needed anything. I said I wanted to see Baby. I meant just once, on a visit, but . . . here I am.

Not a visit. They're going to let me live with Baby.

Maybe Farris is retiring. She's old, too—even thicker and older than the foster lady. Maybe she's getting Alzheimer's; maybe she's losing her grip. That's got to be it. That's why they're doing this.

We play for maybe five minutes before Farris comes in on a blast of perfume, her heels click-clacking against the hard tiles in the playroom, her multiple bangles clashing. She smiles at the foster lady before motioning me over. "Robin, Dess has been at Stanton High here in town, and she's a good student. You won't have any problems with her. Right, Dess?" She gives me a warning look, her over-plucked eyebrows arched high.

Please. Like Farris'll be there to say boo if we *do* have problems? "Whatever."

"Mrs. Carter has a daughter your age, and you'll be going to school with her. She can help you catch up on anything you might have missed."

Not likely. I say, "What about Trish?"

Farris frowns. "Visitations are going to be a problem. Normally, we don't remove a minor child from the placement county of a parent, but because of"—she hesitates—"extenuating circumstances, we feel it's best right now for your mother to finish out her term at Ironwood."

"Best?" The word is out before I can stop it, and I already hate the look on Farris's doughy face. I hate the jangly plastic blobs of her earrings; I hate the blue shadow caked into the wrinkles on her eyelids. Damn, my head hurts.

"Dess, we've talked about this. There was a possibility that your mother would be safer if removed from some of the negative influences—"

"You mean 'enforcers.'" Farris always uses big words to hide what she means, like I don't know.

She ignores me and continues speaking. "—at the North Highlands facility. The district attorney's office will accept her testimony in exchange for a reduced sentence, but they are also taking seriously any threats made against her and feel that Ironwood would be safest now. That means you won't be able to see her until Thanksgiving, after her court date. But the two of you can still write letters anytime."

Right. Like I need Trish's letters. They're full of sob stories and "Sorry" and words I can't use; promises she can't keep. I turn to the foster lady. "You live by a library?"

Her dark eyes get all wide and bright. "I've heard you like to read. We have a little library in the house, and the public library is two stops away on the bus—"

"You have Internet?"

Farris touches my shoulder. "Dess, stop interrupting. You'll have everything you need, and if there's anything you want, you can call your new caseworker, Mr. Bradbrook. Don't give Mrs. Carter a hard time."

"Please, call me Robin," the foster lady corrects Farris. "And, Dess, you and Hope will share the house computer. In a homework emergency, you can use my laptop."

Baby throws himself against the foster lady's knees. "Mama, I'm *bored*."

Mama?

"Dess, are you ready?" The foster lady's eyes are almost as light as Baby's hazel greens. "Do you have any more questions for Mrs. Farris?"

Mama. My jaw is cranked so tight, my teeth are grinding. *Mama.* Foster Lady better not hold her breath waiting for me to call her *that.* I don't even play the "Mama" joke with Trish, and she *is* my mother.

"Are you ready to go, Dess?"

Jeez, could she stop asking? I push past Mrs. Farris and grab the black plastic bag with my clothes from next to the door. I cross my arms and stare at her.

"I guess that's my answer," the foster lady says, and smiles. She crouches down and gives Baby a squeeze and holds on to his little hand. "Come on, Austin. Let's go get Jamaira and go see Hope at home."

Home. Ha.

Farris pats my arm. "Be good, Dess," she says. I shake her off. She needs to stop touching me like she's still my

16

friend. Nobody asked her to sign me off to some other social worker.

The foster lady swings Baby's hand, and he skips along beside her, babbling about a truck and some other stuff. I don't know how she can understand him. He's cute, but he doesn't *ever* shut up.

"Defsa, come on," he orders, twisting to look at me. He holds out his other hand, marked with blue ink from a marker somewhere, and waits.

A shudder works through me. His hand is dirty. No doubt he has those fecal coliform germs, and probably tons of other germs on top of those. Jeez, *kids*. Sighing, I hold out my hand and feel his tiny, sticky fingers curl around and grip. Germy or clean, he's Baby, and he's mine. I'm not letting go.

. . . .

Later That First Day

The school nurse could only hand out sanitary supplies—no painkillers—without signed parental permission. Which was stupid, since all Hope needed was to pop into any classroom and somebody would have something—legal or not—but Ms. Jerston probably wouldn't write her a pass. Hope sighed. Someone should have picked her up by now. If her cramps kept up, she was going to call her father's office and ask if someone could find him to give permission by phone. Hope knew better than to text her mother again—Mom would want her to have a cup of chamomile and do some yoga breathing. A moment ago, she'd felt as if someone had smashed into her lower abdomen with a brick. Last time she'd looked, yoga didn't fix being hit by a brick.

She sighed again and turned on her side, readjusting the

novel she wasn't reading. This wasn't supposed to happen, *ever*. In junior high, when her bestie Savannah had still been in the US, the two of them had planned for *every* possible scenario. When they'd started their periods, Sav had put two tampons and a stain stick in the pocket in her denim messenger bag where pens were supposed to go. Even into freshman year, Hope had carried her supplies wrapped up in a roll of socks. But then stupid Rob Anguiano had kicked Hope's bag during study hall, and the flap had come loose and the socks had rolled out. Hope had held her breath in horrified anticipation when he picked them up, asking, "Are you going hiking or something?" Fortunately, nothing embarrassing had been revealed, but as soon as she got home, Hope had taken the socks out and shoved them into her bottom drawer.

Savannah had assured Hope that she'd keep on carrying *her* stain stick, at least. And as far as Hope knew, it was still in Savannah's denim messenger bag—unhelpfully now at King George V School in Hong Kong.

Hope blew out a breath. At least it was peaceful, lying on a cot in the nurse's office bathroom. Ms. Jerston had sent the registrar an absence excuse, and her student volunteer had picked up Hope's assignment from Mr. Cochrane in her American history and governance class. Hope had only English, lunch, PE, and whatever homework to worry about, and she didn't much care. Yeah, Mom wouldn't be happy she was bailing to go home, but whatever. A girl had to handle her business, and this was an emergency.

There was a knock, and Hope sat up eagerly. Ms. Jerston stuck her head in the door and said, "Your uncle's here."

Hope gave a limp cheer. *Finally.*

"He brought a laundry stick," Ms. Jerston continued, holding up a little bag. "Do you want to try it or—"

Hope was already shaking her head. "I'm just going to go," she said, unwrapping the blanket from her lower body, folding it, and putting it at the foot of the cot.

"I don't blame you," Ms. Jerston said, standing out of the way. She hesitated. "You have everything you need, right?"

"Uh, yeah?" Hope said uncertainly. What did she mean, "have everything"? "I'll be fine with Aunt—um, Uncle Henry."

"If you're sure," Ms. Jerston said. The woman patted her hair and gave a little smile. "I just meant, if you need a female opinion and your mother's busy—feel free to call. Or you could have your uncle call—"

Her *uncle?* Ms. Jerston and her over-bright smile finally made sense. "Sure, Ms. Jerston. I'll tell my uncle to call you if you want, but his wife might have plans for him tonight."

Smirking, Hope slipped out of the door and headed into the corridor. Aunt Henry was as single as he could be, but Hope had just gotten her uncle back after a four-year overseas stint in the navy. He'd been an EMT and search-and-rescue guy with the local fire station for the last year, and Hope wasn't ready for him to be married off to anyone just yet.

She'd had enough of things changing.

The tall, dark-skinned man pushed off the wall where

he was leaning and slid his sunglasses down a little, scrutinizing Hope with his caramel-brown eyes. "H-bomb."

"Aunt Henry."

He had longer eyelashes than most girls. He wasn't wearing his firefighting uniform, but Hope got why Ms. Jerston had been all weird and eye-batting. Aunt Henry was pretty hot, even for an uncle. His muscled chest, arms, and abs were on display in the tight black T-shirt tucked into battered jeans. More than the ripped jeans, the silver earrings he wore in both ears told Hope he was off-duty.

"You okay, babe?"

Hope nodded and stumbled, a little off balance, as her uncle took her backpack and swung it over his shoulder. "Thanks for picking me up."

"No bother. Sorry it wasn't sooner. Captain called a meeting at the last minute." Henry shortened his steps to match Hope's. "Rob said she'll be home by five-thirty."

Hope shrugged. She really didn't care when her mother, Robin, got home, now that she had a ride. All she wanted was to try to salvage her skirt and grab a nap.

Aunt Henry dug out his keys, and Hope heard the little chirp as his alarm defused and the door to his shiny black pickup truck unlocked. He came around to her side and handed up her backpack as she slid across the warm cloth-covered seat. He kept his gravelly voice low. "You need the drugstore?"

"Nope, I'm good," Hope said, avoiding his eyes. This was an awkward conversation, even with her favorite uncle.

Aunt Henry came around to his side, got in, and then

fiddled with his keys. "You want . . . ice cream or something? Rob said we're supposed to 'celebrate' and be 'body-positive.'" Hope could hear the ironic quotation marks.

Jeez, Mom, really? Hope glared at her uncle, embarrassed and irritated. "I. Want. To. Go. *Home*." She bit off every word. "Mom can 'celebrate' and whatever by herself."

Henry's serious face was transformed by the width of his grin. He patted her shoulder and started the engine. "I hear ya, H-bomb. That's what I thought."

· · · · · · · · · · · · · · · · · · ·

Foster Family

"Dess."

Foster Lady's voice is just a whisper, but I wake up, fast, and lean away from her. I don't fall asleep in the car, ever, but Baby's talking must have driven me to it. Funny, he's passed out in his car seat next to me, head flopped to the side and little arms hanging slack. I used to sack out like that.

Foster Lady's van has one of those electronic doors that open and close real slow without making much noise. She pushes the button, and the door next to me slides open. I gently pull my bag out from under the seat, trying to quiet its crinkling, and climb out into the dim cave of the garage.

This is the neatest garage I've ever seen—although it's not like I've been in a whole bunch of garages. There's space for another car, a tennis ball on a string hanging

23

from the ceiling, and shelves all the way up to the top. On the shelves are boxes, and each box has a strip of tape across it, with words like "Xmas Tree Stand" and "Camping" written on it.

These people have *everything* in here. There's even a box that says "Emergency."

"Dess?" Foster Lady is looking at me.

I look at the van. Baby's still in his seat, still strapped in. Though I was going to be quiet, and learn what I could, words blurt out before I can stop them. "What, you're just going to leave him there?" You aren't supposed to do that shit to babies. Doesn't anyone know anything?

The lady's face twists up in a funny smile. "Trust me, Dess, Mr. Austin here knows how to take off his seat belt. He will when he wakes up, and he'll come inside when he's ready. I'm not going to wake him and have him whiny all afternoon because he missed his nap. We'll leave the door open while we get you settled. Later, you can go with me to pick up Jamaira, and we'll have a little talk. Okay?"

Yeah, she says "Okay" like I have a choice, but I've heard that voice before. Rena at the group home always likes to have a "little talk" with the new residents first thing. I shrug. If Foster Lady wants to flap her yap at me, I can't stop her.

She goes ahead of me and opens the door into the house. A pocket door to the right shows a sink and a toilet with a potty chair on the floor. Across the hall, a stacked washer and dryer sit next to a long white counter with piles of clothes and towels folded on it. The washer has something yellow flopping around on the wash cycle.

"Garage bathroom, laundry room, and the linen closet. Through here is the kitchen," the foster lady is saying.

I leave the door open behind me, giving one last look at Baby sleeping in the dim garage, and follow.

"Are you hungry? Would you like something to drink?"

I shrug. I might be hungry, but I don't know. I can't tell; my stomach is jumpy.

Foster Lady just nods. "Let me give you a tour, then. This"—she points to a pair of yellowish wooden doors under the oven—"is the snack cabinet. You're welcome to anything in it whenever you want a snack."

They've got ice and water dispensers in the gray metal refrigerator, like at the group home. A handful of magnets hold stick pictures on the double-wide doors, pictures Baby drew, I guess. Foster Lady walks through a doorway on the other side of the kitchen, but I make a note to come back to this room and look through *all* the cabinets, not just the one for snacks, when everyone's asleep. I don't hoard food till it rots, like I did at my first foster home, but I like to know what my options are.

"This is the dining area and the living room," Foster Lady says over her shoulder. I follow her into the room and stop. It's *huge,* and it goes on forever, and it looks like something from a decorating show on TV. Now I wish I'd been awake when we drove down the street. Houses in this neighborhood must be massive.

Closest to the kitchen is a polished wooden table with eight tall chairs scooted in. At the other end there are wide couches with cream and brown stripes in front of a big window, and a fat red chair with a footstool is next to a red brick fireplace. The room is tall, with a white ceiling, and half the wall is gray, with a piece of white wood dividing it. The bottom half of the wall has red wallpaper. The carpet on the floor is a kind of grayish white that makes me not even want to walk on it in my ballet flats. It's thick enough that I don't hear Foster Lady's steps as she walks away.

"We don't bring food into the living room," Foster Lady says as she continues her tour, "so we can keep it nice. We mostly use the front room if we have a family meeting or when company comes."

Company. Yeah, I'll be sure and use it when the president's girls drop by.

We cross from carpet onto tiled floor and pass by what I guess is the front door. Foster Lady goes up three stairs and motions to an open door on her left, with a baby gate across it. "This is the office. When my husband, Russell, is at home, he tends to be in here." I barely have a moment to peep into the room with the L-shaped desk and two computer screens before she's opening a door across the hall. From the soft-blue paint on the wall and the big tree silhouette in the corner, I know where we are before she even says a word.

"This is the nursery—right now it's Austin and Jamaira's room. It's almost always a mess." She turns to me and grins, and her whole face moves with the force of it. "You'll discover Austin loves to take things out of his toy box and books off his shelf. We're still working on putting things back."

"Jamaira?" I ask, looking at the plain white crib in the corner across from the little bed. It smells like baby powder in here—not diapers, even though there's a baby. How many kids they got in this place? "Where is she?" What I really want to know is, How old is she? Is she white or black? Does Foster Lady treat her better than Baby?

Foster Lady's smile fades a little. "Jamaira's at the respite-care nursery right now. We'll pick her up when Austin wakes." She pauses, and from the way she looks at me, I can tell she's saying something important. "Jamaira's a good baby, a sweet, sweet girl with some major physical challenges. Her brain is calcifying, and that gives her little seizures. That makes some people uncomfortable looking at her, or holding her. If you don't want to be around her or look at her, Dess, that's okay."

Rich as they are, don't they have medicine for that "calcifying"? My stomach is rolling again. I don't want to be around some sick baby, but I'm not going to say so. I shrug instead and wait.

Foster Lady doesn't say anything for a moment, then nods and keeps moving down the hall. "A bathroom," she announces, gesturing to her right. "My and Russell's bedroom," she says, tapping a set of white double doors to her left.

The hall continues, and there's another set of double

doors. "The family room," she says, and opens the doors with a silent "Ta-da!"

It's another big room, almost as big as the living room, except this has some kind of wood tiles on the floor, and the ceiling is made out of wood. There's another fireplace, with rocks up the wall instead of bricks; there's a narrow doorway that shows another toilet; and there's a mixture of futon couches and fat brown plaid things. They're the ugliest couches I've ever seen. So are the recliner chairs, ugly and battered, but this room at least looks like a room I can get comfortable with. In the corner near the bathroom is a sliding glass door with a little deck that looks over the backyard, which has a bunch of grass and—

"You have a swimming pool?" I practically press my face against the glass.

"Go ahead and open the door, Dess," Foster Lady says with a laugh, and I do. It's warm outside, warm enough for me to put my feet in the water. A pool! God, these people are rich—stupid rich. The group home was big, yeah, but it's a whole building for ten girls, plus an office for staff. I remember the motel me and Trish and Baby lived in. Nobody from this house ever lived like that, all jammed up in one room.

"Do you have a suit, Dess?"

I shrug. I never needed a suit. When did Trish and me ever go swimming, except in our clothes in the fountain in front of the mall?

"We keep two or three suits for guests. You can use one until we can get you a suit of your own. Our only rule about the pool is that either Russell or I need to be with you the first time you use it, and if you can't swim—"

"I know how," I interrupt. I didn't think black people could, though. Granny Doris took me to the city pool when I was little. There was a black kid there, screaming, 'cause he was scared to go in. Granny Doris said it's because they sink.

"—if you can't swim, you absolutely *cannot* be in the water alone. One of us must be with you. That's a serious hard-and-fast rule, Dess—for your own safety." Foster Lady waits a moment as I take in the yard, then turn and look at the room again. There are tall bookshelves stuffed with books on either side of the fireplace, and all around the edges of the room there are pictures on the walls, in frames, of people—old black people, and kids, black and white and brown. Tons of kids. There's a big table in the corner that might be for pool or something. For the first time since I got out of the van, I'm feeling something other than jumpy.

"Are you ready to see your room, Dess?"

I don't like how she says that—like it's really my room, *mine*, and not a room in *her* house. I roll my eyes and follow Foster Lady to a door on the other side of the family room. "This is it," she says, and gestures for me to go inside.

It's middle-sized, with plain white walls. The bed has a tall frame made out of wood that looks like bleached-out telephone poles. There's a nightstand made out of the same bleached-out wood. There's a lamp on it with a lampshade that looks like it was made out of an old globe. The window has white blinds and a green-painted windowsill. There's a short white bookshelf beneath the window and, on the bed, a pale green comforter with two pillows, each with a dark green stripe. On the wall above the bed there's a wooden shelf painted the same green as the windowsill.

"I hope you like green," the foster lady says.

I shrug. "Whatever." Inside, my stomach is knotting. This is nice . . . way nicer than any room I've ever stayed in.

My first foster mother was like this—nice. At least the first day, before she started whining all the time because I pissed the bed a little. She never put me in a room this nice, though. It makes my neck tight. My plastic bag crinkles as I clutch it closer.

Foster Lady shows me the closet, which has a towel-cloth bathrobe hanging from a hook. There's a tag on it—it's brand-new. She points out the white dresser at one end of the closet, and all the hooks and hangers and places to put a lot of clothes I don't have at the other end. "And this is your bathroom, which you share with our daughter, Hope," she says, and pushes open another sliding door I didn't notice, built into the wall. Inside the bathroom there's a plain white tile counter with two sinks and a mirrored medicine cabinet above each sink. A short wall made out of glass bricks divides a bathtub and a shower stall from the rest of the room, and on a rack next to the tub are shelves of yellow and green towels.

At the group home, our bathroom had two sinks, two

shower stalls, two toilets, and no tub. I had to share with three other girls, though.

"In this house, our bedrooms are personal, private spaces." Foster Lady is waving her arms again, her earrings jangling. "And there's a lock on this door, so you can use the bathroom in privacy. In the morning, you might be okay with brushing your teeth at the same time Hope is brushing hers—or you might not. You'll need to work that out."

She steps back into my room. "You and Hope are responsible for keeping your separate rooms and this bathroom clean. It might work for you to make a schedule about whose turn it is to clean the toilet and the shower and the tub—or it might be easier for each of you to clean it right when you get out. You'll have to work that out, or else I will—and I'm sure you'd much rather work it out yourselves." Foster Lady smiles, but there's a look of determination around those white teeth. Maybe it's not her husband who yells when someone makes a mess. She probably thinks I have trashy habits, like some of the girls in the group home. Rich folks always think the rest of us are nasty. How much you want to bet there are cameras up here, to make sure I don't steal anything?

Foster Lady stands and beams at me. I look away. I don't know what she's waiting for. Am I supposed to say thank you or something?

"Do you have any questions for me, Dess?" She just looks too eager, too happy to answer anything.

"Nope."

Foster Lady says, "Why don't I go check on Hope and Austin and give you a few minutes to yourself? Then we'll talk about the house rules."

I shrug. I don't need but five minutes to put my stuff in a drawer and find a place to put up my sewing kit. But I'm not going to unpack anything yet. As soon as she gets out of my face, I'm going to check on Baby myself.

"Afterward, I'd like to go over some of what Mrs. Farris told me, and we can talk about your new caseworker—"

"Mom?"

Foster Lady's face lights up. "Oh, good, *Hope,*" she says, and ducks into the bathroom. "Did we wake you? Feeling better?"

"I was just getting up. I'm fine." The voice is low and sleep-fogged. I shift to where I can see through the bathroom and into the bedroom on the other side. Foster Lady is all bent over, hugging someone.

I step back, throat closing. I'm not ready to meet Foster Lady's "real" kid. I'm not sure how to play this family thing.

I look away, concentrating on rubbing the weird burning feeling in the middle of my chest. I don't get this. If Foster Lady's already got a kid, why's she got Austin and me? Why's she got the sick baby? With this big old house, she doesn't need the money.

"Come and meet your new foster sister," Foster Lady says.

Oh, here we go.

The girl looks right at me, and her eyes get all wide. She's darker than Foster Lady and shorter, but thick like her, with a crinkly mess of puffy hair in a sloppy bun. She's all baby fat and big cow eyes, which I'm about to slap out of her damn head if she doesn't stop staring at me.

"What are you looking at?" I snarl at the same time that she blurts out, "Um . . . I'm Hope. Hi."

. . . .

Home Invasion

"Um, I'm Hope. Hi," Hope said, trying to rearrange her face to cover her surprise.

So this was Austin's real sister—his birth sister. This girl, with her pale-blue eyes and dragon-lady nails, looked nothing like Austin, whose skin was a sandy brown, whose eyes were a dark hazel, and whose hair was tightly furled golden-brown curls. Hope searched for any trace of resemblance to Austin's sharp-chinned, round-headed adorableness in the single wary eye, ringed hard with liner, that glared out at her from beneath the sweep of stiff, blond bangs. Half siblings could still look alike, but . . . no, nothing.

"This is Dess Matthews." Mom looped an arm around Hope again, as if she, too, could feel the instant arc of tension. "Dess, we haven't had foster siblings close to Hope's

34

age in our family before, but it turns out this is especially good timing, since one of Hope's best friends just moved out of the country. You can keep each other company for a few weeks." She beamed at them, and Hope responded with a tepid smile. Mom was being way too enthusiastic. "Dess loves to read, Hope. You two have that in common."

Reading? Hope glanced at Dess, at her perfect manicure and skinny jeans. *She likes to read? Probably only* Vogue. *I doubt she's into weredragons or nanobots and dirigibles.*

The brief, awkward silence continued as the girl studied Hope as well. Hope's eyes moved from the girl's cold expression to the black plastic garbage bag she was clutching to the pristine white canvas ballet flats on her feet. She hadn't expected Austin's sister to be white and blond—obviously bleached—or that she'd be so much older. Hadn't Mom said they'd be in the same grade? Maybe Dess had been held back, since she *had* to be older than fifteen. She was much taller and seriously built. Maybe she was wearing a padded bra?

Unfriendly eyes. Hope realized, with a twitch and a glance away, that she'd been staring, and now the girl's hostility was almost palpable. As usual, Mom was still talking, pleasant little nothings that both girls were ignoring. Hope felt her heart pinch a little as an expectation she hadn't even known she'd had faded and died. They wouldn't be instant best friends. Austin's sister wouldn't replace Savannah in the hollow space in Hope's heart. No matter what Mom said, they had nothing at all in common.

But Hope knew the drill: she'd been the foster sister to

an endless parade of scared, angry, confused little kids, and her job was to be friendly and open. She smiled as her mother reached a pause in her getting-to-know-you spiel. "Nice to meet you. You're from North Highlands, right?"

The girl shrugged, the jerky twitch her only movement, then said, "I'm from West Texas. North Highlands is just where my last placement was."

"Texas. Oh. Cool." Hope cleared her throat and smiled, then caught a sidelong glance at herself in the mirror above the sink and cringed. Way to make a first impression— hair rumpled, sheet-creased and shiny-faced, and not wearing a bra. Meeting anyone for the first time, standing in the bathroom, being squeezed to death by your mother? *Awkward.* Worse, Hope could feel a zit coming on right next to her nose. And now Mom was prodding her in the back, so Hope gave another polite smile and tried to find something to say. "Well, it's nice to meet you, Dess," she repeated lamely. "If you need anything, just knock on my door."

The girl ignored this and jerked her chin at Hope's mother. "You going to leave Baby in the car all day?"

Baby? Hope blinked. What baby? Did Dess have one? Or was she talking about Austin?

Hope's mother looked up and smiled, relaxing her grip on Hope's shoulders. "I promise, Austin can get out by himself, but if it makes you feel better, Dess, I'll go and un-belt him now." She checked her watch. "The little turkey should be just about ready to wake up anyway." She turned back to Hope. "Keep an eye on Austin for me while Dess and I go pick up Jamaira, please. He's just going to want his snack and his trucks."

"Okay," Hope said with a sigh. So much for finishing her nap. Oh, well, Austin was easy, as long as you weren't trying to get him to do anything except what he wanted to do. "Oh, Mom? Aunt uh . . . Henry said he might swing by after dinner."

Mom beamed. "Aw, sure he will. Henry's such a softie, checking up on you."

"No, he's my good auntie who promised me he'd be my ibuprofen hookup if my crazy mother"—Hope dropped her voice, but Dess was walking away—"tried to make me do yoga or something for cramps. I'm serious, Mom. Aromatherapy candles and meditation are *not* a cure for cramps."

Mom snorted, smoothing a hand over Hope's snarly bedhead. "Okay, let's compromise. How about a little something for the pain *and* this great primrose tea I found? Dess, would you like a cup of . . ." Her mother paused, then frowned at the empty doorway. "I guess she's gone to get Austin. Hope, come give the boy his snack, please. Maybe some apples and a cheese stick? And make yourself some tea. Odessa—Dess—and I need some time."

Hope smiled as her father came through the hallway from the garage, loosening his tie and pulling his shirttails out of his slacks. On hearing the door close, Austin barreled out of his room, sliding across the kitchen floor in his socks. "Hey, Dad!"

"Hey, big man!" Mr. Carter gave an exaggerated grunt as Austin threw himself against his legs for the catch-and-release type of hug he preferred. "How was school, Hope?"

Hope tilted her face for his kiss. "Meh."

Her father yanked his tie over his head and tossed it on the counter. "Just 'meh,' huh? No strong women? Good-looking men? Nothing above average? Just 'meh'?"

Hope shrugged. "I didn't really stay long enough to find out."

Dropping his neoprene lunch bag on the counter, Mr. Carter turned to his daughter with a worried frown. Rolling up the sleeve of his striped blue dress shirt, he put his bare wrist on her forehead. "You sick?"

Hope pulled his arm away and kissed it before wrapping it around herself for a hug. "No, and you know it's scientifically impossible to tell if someone has a fever by putting your arm on their head."

"It worked for your grandma," her father said, and looped his other arm around her. "What happened, sweet?"

"Just the usual school stuff plus . . . clothing malfunction. Woman stuff."

"Woman stuff? Eww." Her father peered into her face with a teasing smile. "You're on your own with that, babe."

"Thank you at least for not saying 'Oh, honey,' like Mom kept doing." Hope held out her hand for his change as he emptied his pockets and then began unbuttoning his shirt. "I'm surprised she didn't text you to pick me up. I could have used a lift."

"She might have, but she knew I had meetings. Sorry, but I was completely useless all day long," her father said, unbuckling his belt and tugging it from the loops on his slacks as he padded down the hall. "I hate meetings."

Hope trailed after him, as was her ritual, pocketing the change he'd given her while he disappeared into his bedroom, shedding work clothes as he went. He emerged a few moments later in a pair of ratty jeans and a long-sleeve T-shirt with the logo of a software company in orange and blue centered on the back. "Much better," he declared. "What's the news from Hong Kong? How's our old friend Savannah?"

"Fine, I guess. The prefect introduced her to everyone in assembly today, and it was eighty-four and she couldn't take off her blazer, because it's part of the uniform."

He shuddered. "Sounds horrible. Poor kid. You meet Odessa yet?"

"Yeah, I met her. I wonder if she and Austin are named after towns in Texas on purpose." Hope shook her head in disbelief. "Mom called her Dess, though."

"Hey, Austin," Dad said, poking his head into the land of trucks and trains. "You have Hope and Maira and now another sister, buddy. How about that?"

"Defsa's with Mama," Austin said, and smashed his truck into a pile of blocks.

"De*ss*a," Dad corrected him, coming down hard on the "s" sound. "They should be back soon," he said, and headed for the kitchen. "Is it too hot to eat out back?"

"Nah," Hope said, falling into her role as sous-chef. "I'm starving."

They were halfway through dinner prep when Mom came home. She carried her diaper bag on one arm and swung Jamaira in her car seat up onto the counter with the other. Dad gave Mom his usual greeting—"Hey, beautiful!" and a quick hug and a kiss—and leaned over the car seat.

"There's my baby princess," he singsonged, and Jamaira, half-asleep, smiled sweetly at his voice. Hope, as always, felt her heart twist at Maira's smile. Her attention, however, was on the doorway behind her mother as Dess slouched in, fists clutching the sleeves of her hoodie, arms crossed.

"Russell, this is Dessa Matthews," Mom said.

Dad looked up and smiled. "Hello, nice to have you. I understand the name Odessa possibly comes from the Greek word *odysseia,* from which we gain the word 'odyssey,' which is a long and eventful journey. Have you had one of those today?"

Oh, Dad. Hope hunched her shoulders. She tried to see her father through Dess's eyes—and winced. Dark, thin, and wiry, three inches shorter than Mom, with close-shaved hair and a graying goatee, Dad was wrapped in an apron that said "Just a Man with a Pan." Now he was spouting crap that made him sound like some super-nerd on college *Jeopardy!* Dess probably thought he sounded stupid. Sometimes some of the older foster kids were hostile toward Dad. Mom said they didn't trust men. Hope found her fingers tensing on her knife handle, wondering how Dess would react.

After staring for a long moment, Dess spoke. "You play that word app thing on your phone, huh?"

Her father's brows rose in surprised delight. "Dictionary Duel? As a matter of fact, I do like word games," he admitted. "Are you a wordsmith?"

Dess didn't smile back. "Maybe," she said guardedly.

"Well, plenty of time to find out. Welcome home, Dess. Are you hungry?"

Dess flicked a glance over the dinner preparations. "Uh . . ."

Mom piped up. "You're free to eat anything you'd like tonight and skip things that look a little unfamiliar. Normally, I'd ask that you at least try everything, but since it's your first night—"

"It's fine. Whatever. I'll eat," Dess said, cutting her off. She pointed. "What's that with the green stuff?"

Dad tilted his chin upward. "That's the quinoa salad— q-u-i-n-o-a. It's a South American grain. The 'green stuff' is avocado. There are oranges in there, too."

"Oh." Dess looked briefly ill, but only Hope noticed. Mom was responding to Jamaira's thin cry, and Dad, who had washed his hands, was collecting plates and glasses to go and set the table.

"I'm hungry," Austin whined. He was standing in the middle of the kitchen.

Hope rolled her eyes. He knew the drill—no toys at the table, wash your hands, and sit down—but since Mom was picking up Jamaira and Dess was standing there, looking lost, he was starting to act out. "Out of the way, Austin. If you stand in the middle of the floor being hungry, you might get run over before dinner. Go wash—"

The blond girl whirled to face Hope with narrowed eyes. "Hey, back off. *I* take care of Baby," she said, voice low and razor-sharp.

"Um, excuse me?" Hope looked toward her mother. Was she not supposed to even *talk* to Austin now that his "real" sister was here?

Jeez, his "real" sister. What the hell did that make Hope?

Mom winced and opened her mouth, but Austin broke in loudly. "I'm *not* a baby," he announced.

Dess looked as if she'd bitten something sour. She glowered at him. "Yeah, you are, kid. You're only three."

"I'm *four*!" Austin was indignant.

Mom said, "Austin, you *are* four. You can do a lot of things by yourself because you're a *big boy*." She smoothed Austin's mutinous expression with her cheery-mommy voice. "Big boy, why don't you show Dess where the bathroom is, so she can wash her hands, please?"

"Come on." Austin gave Dess an impatient look and stomped down the hall.

"Mom!" Hope whispered as Dess slouched after Austin. "What was that?"

42

"Let's give her some time, Hope." Her mother refused to whisper. She reached into the cupboard, pulled out a can of dry formula, and continued making Jamaira's bottle. "We've had first-night adjustments with every foster child, hon. Don't let a little tension bother you."

"But what about Austin?" Hope persisted. "Am I supposed to—"

"Are you done with that melon?" Hope's father breezed back into the kitchen, wiping his hands on his apron. "The chicken is almost ready. Let's go ahead and put everything on the table. It's nice out."

"Hope, it'll be fine—don't worry about Austin. We'll all adjust. Be sure and bring a pitcher of water to the table, please." Mom hurried her words, twisting to fasten the baby sling around her back, snuggling Jamaira's small body against her chest. "Russ, Dess might struggle a bit with that salad. Do you think I should—"

It'll be *fine*? Hope opened her mouth to protest, but her father interrupted. "She knows what it is. She'll cope," he said, reaching for another set of tongs and grabbing the plate of melon. "Sweet, get Austin one of his plastic cups, will you?" He raised his voice. "To the table, folks. Let's eat!"

DESS

· ·

Dinner with a Dime

Apparently nobody around here has ever heard of barbecue sauce. The chicken tastes weird and has little twigs on it—rosemary, Mr. Carter says. His tub-of-lard daughter—oh, right, her name is Hope, or really *Hopeless*—scraped it off. Foster Lady isn't even eating the chicken—she's a vegetarian, she says—and she's balancing a bottle against her wrist, feeding the baby. Every other bite or so, she strokes its throat, trying to make it swallow or something. It keeps choking. Right now, a dribble of milk is running down the side of its neck.

That is straight nasty.

In the van, Foster Lady never shut up. She talked about Russell—Mr. Carter—and she talked about school—she just wants me to do my best—and about what she's adding to my clothing allowance, and about Mr. Bradbrook, who's coming on Thursday. She told me how she knows this might not be easy, with a new school and adjusting to a new "family," and that she'll do her best to meet me halfway and be flexible. Blah, blah, blah—all the things that these foster people are paid to say.

Then she was all "Kindness is the only rule in this family," and I just rolled my eyes. Kindness? That's not even a rule. Kindness doesn't say shit about how late I can stay out and what time I have to get up in the morning. Kindness isn't nothing about when to do laundry or how long I can take a shower. I wanted to say that, but I didn't. No point pissing her off the first day.

"I can see by the look on your face that I might have lost you," Foster Lady told me, and then she laughed. "It's easier than it sounds, Dess—before you choose words or actions, think about kindness. Speak with kindness or choose not to speak. Act with kindness or wait to act. Just slow down and think of kindness. That's the rule we want to live by."

Huh. Well, nobody told *Baby* about that rule. I tried to hold his hands under the water and make him wash long enough to get off all the germs, but he wouldn't. He screeched and jerked his hands, and I got water on me everywhere.

Little brat. I thought he'd be, you know, *nice*. Like, cute, like all the kids on YouTube that dance and know their states or stuff. All Baby wants to do is yell at me that he's big.

Baby makes me feel like I'm stupid, like I don't know

how to be with him. He's my brother, and he won't let me touch him. He lets that cow of a girl, though. She wiped his hands—country cow Hopeless didn't think I washed them right—and sat him in his booster seat and gave him a piece of melon, which he is driving around his plate instead of eating. He asked for a corn dog, but Mr. Carter shook his head and said something like "You get what you get, and you don't pitch a fit," which I guess Baby understands, but I don't.

And, *jeez,* nobody would have kids if they saw them eat. Baby has melon juice on his face and, now that he's whining, maybe snot. Makes me want to puke.

"Dad-*deeee,* I want a corn dog," Baby says again, winding up for a good cry. *Shut up, Baby,* I want to say. Trish hates crying. If she were here, she'd belt him one like she belted me for whining, but skinny little Mr. Carter just says, "I heard you the first time, kiddo. Maybe next time," and pokes a tiny piece of chicken into Baby's mouth, which he chews and—ugh, finally—swallows. Now he's eating by himself, fork in one hand and picking through the mess on his plate with the other. I can't even look at him. He's *my* brother. How can he make me sick?

"Use your fork, Austin Matthews. You know the rules." Across the table, Foster Lady shifts the little one onto her shoulder, patting her back so she'll burp. I hope she doesn't—I saw her burp when we picked her up at the nursery, and she spit milk all down the nursery lady's shoulder. I can't deal with that crap at the table.

"Mom, I'll take her," Boring Girl says, and I'm surprised

when Foster Lady says thanks and hands her over, just like that. Nobody would give me a sick baby to hold.

Not that I want anybody's baby, sick or whatever. I don't need that drama.

Foster Lady gets more salad and talks to Mr. Carter while the girl cuddles the baby. The baby's little mouth is all pooched up, trying to suck at nothing, but when Hope tries the bottle again, she doesn't suck. "You all done?" Hope wipes the baby's mouth with the little burp cloth and shifts her elbow under her head, holding her like a newborn. The baby's muddy-green eyes roll back in her head. Her little back arches, and Hope holds her closer, rubbing a thumb across the baby's forehead. "Hold on. I've got you," she says. "It's okay, I've got you."

"You're supposed to make sure she doesn't bite her tongue," I blurt out.

The girl looks up at me, her eyes all wide. "What?"

"When people have seizures. You're supposed to make sure they don't bite their tongues and choke. Don't you know anything?" I can feel Mr. Carter and Foster Lady looking over at us.

Hope's voice goes really, really quiet. "She doesn't have any teeth, Dess."

"I know that," I say, feeling red creep up my neck. I did. I *knew* that, obviously. She's a baby, duh. But Hopeless was just sitting there, not *doing* anything. At least I would have *done* something.

Hopeless clears her throat and looks up at me with these quick little glances. "Um, her seizures are really short, and

47

you don't have to do anything. They . . . they don't hurt. Her brain isn't developed enough to allow her to feel much pain, so she doesn't know it's happening. Um, do you want to hold her?" Hope's voice is still that quiet.

I sputter. "Oh, eff *that* noise. I— Eww, she's puking."

Hope's mouth gets tight. She swabs up more strings of spitty milk that are leaking from the corner of the baby's mouth. "It's not puke—it's just dribble. She's not that good at swallowing."

My gut plunges. Well, hell. She's going to die, then. That's what Foster Lady was trying to tell me before. If her brain's "calcifying"—turning to calcium, like chalk or bones—and she can't even eat right, the baby's going to die. That is straight messed up. Why's Hope gotta sit with *a dying baby* right there at the table?

Why are these people so crazy?

"You're okay, Maira," Hope says in a singsong voice. "You're a sweet girl."

The smile is back. The baby's eyes are a little bit crossed, like she can't really focus, but she's smiling, big as anything, her little pink gums showing.

She likes Hopeless. And Mr. Carter. She likes voices, and she smiles whenever she hears them. Babies always think you're talking to them, and if you yell, they think you're hollering at them, too.

Baby used to cry every time the Felon—the man Trish says is my father, Eddie Griffiths—came over. The Felon straight hated Baby, since Baby wasn't his kid, and he was always yelling at Trish to shut him up. His tattooed hands never even touched him, but Baby knew even then that that man was no good. I bet he would have known if his own father was okay, if Trish had ever remembered who he was. Babies know stuff.

As I watch Jamaira, I suddenly remember being in a Laundromat with Trish. There was another little girl there, with metal fillings in her front teeth and a ponytail and little heeled cowboy boots. Her mother had a baby, too, just as brown as our Baby, but with a little shock of straight black hair. I remember Trish put Baby on the washer, and when it spun, he smiled big like that, with all his gums showing, like the washer was putting on a show, just for him.

Across from me, Jamaira's eyes roll up in her head again. I turn away fast.

Hopeless clears her throat. "Um . . . so, you have nice hair."

"What? Oh. Thanks." I glance over at Baby, who has actually cleaned his plate. I check out the grass and the little sandbox under the tree and the fence around the pool, making sure to look at anything but Jamaira. How long does a seizure take?

"Is that your natural hair color?"

I scowl. What does she care?

Down the table, Foster Lady is watching. She smiles.

"Mostly," I mutter, instead of *What makes it your business?* like I want to.

49

"It's a lot different than Austin's."

She has my full attention now. I narrow my eyes. "Yeah? What's your point?"

Hopeless looks away. "Um . . . nothing. I just was thinking, now that you've pulled your hair back, how much you two look alike, except for your coloring and your hair."

"Baby and me don't look alike."

She shrugs. "I can see you have the same eyes and the same shape of face."

Now I want to stare into a mirror and make Baby stand next to me until I can see it. Until I can tell. I always thought I didn't look like anybody—not Trish, not Granny Doris, not anybody. It makes me feel weird to think we could be alike. Me and Baby, with his soft brown skin and his Charlie Brown head.

A shout comes from inside the house. "Rob-*bee*! You guys out back?"

"Enry!" Austin bellows, wriggling down from his seat.

"Wait a minute, buddy. Wipe your hands," Foster Lady says, grabbing a paper napkin and dunking it in her glass of water. She barely gets the kid de-smeared before he's sprinting toward the house, little arms and legs churning.

"Enry! Un' Tenry!" he screams, and I don't know what that even means. And then, just before he gets to the sliding glass door, he trips over nothing at all and goes flying.

"Baby!" I'm up out of my seat and halfway across the lawn.

But Baby's on his feet again, body-slamming into an absolute god who looks like a cross between that guy on the Lakers—yummy tall—and a model from a magazine. "Tenry!" Baby shouts, and wraps his arms around the guy's legs. "I have a new sister."

Day-um. I take two wobbly-legged steps back toward the table.

"You do, huh?" Hottie picks up Baby and looks him over. "You all right, brah? You fall like a boss, man."

"Let me down," Baby orders him. "Come see."

"All right, man, all right," the god says, and he swings Baby back and forth before setting him on the ground next to the table. He thumps Mr. Carter's shoulder and leans across the table to kiss Foster Lady. A medal on a silver chain swings from his collar.

"S'up, Russ. Robbi."

Foster Lady pats him on the arm. "Dess Matthews, this is my brother, Henry Larsen, who somehow manages to show up every time there's food on the table. Henry, this is Dess Matthews, our new foster daughter."

"It's not like *you're* going to eat the chicken," Henry protests to Foster Lady while grabbing a drumstick and setting it on a napkin. He wipes his hands on his jeans and extends one to me. "Nice to meet you. Dess, is it?"

Henry. *Henry.* Wow. I'm standing there, still staring like a loser. I force myself to shake his hand and nod, unable to speak while looking at his beautiful eyes. He has earrings in both ears, and barely any hair; it's even shorter than Mr. Carter's. I look at his hands. No rings. Thick, blunt fingers. Scars on his wrist. No tattoos. Ripped.

He sits across the table from me, but even that far away,

I can smell him. He smells . . . kind of like soap and wood polish, all lemony and spicy, the way the cologne counter at the mall smells. He lifts the chicken to his mouth to take a bite, and I zero in on his arms—muscles clearly defined. The man is a dime, the full ten, smokin' hot, *hot*.

"Thanks for getting my girl," Foster Lady is saying, and Henry nods, chewing. Even the muscles in his jaw are amazing.

He swallows and says, "No problem, Rob," then says to Hope, "I came to see if you needed me to bust you out of here."

He and Hope laugh at their private joke; then Foster Lady says something, and they laugh some more. Hope's sitting so close, she's practically in his lap.

Not gonna lie, I'd be sitting that close if I could, too. The man is *ridiculously* fine.

Baby's playing with a car he found on the grass next to the sandbox, and then Hottie takes Jamaira from Hope. He props her on his knees and talks to her, his voice rumbly and calm. The baby smiles, Hope smiles, and even Foster Lady looks less like an uptight hippie. I can hear the music from an ice cream truck down the street, and across the back fence a set of wind chimes tinkles invisibly in the light breeze. This could be one of those Disney Channel movies, where everybody looks nice, wears good clothes, and makes some stupid joke right before the credits roll.

For some reason, that pisses me off.

I cross my arms, digging my nails in. The pain clears my

head and pushes reality onto the sunny little scene. I remember my rules: If I don't own it, they can't steal it. You can't lose what you don't have. I remind myself that I don't care how hot anyone is—I don't even care how cute Baby is—I'm not about that. I'm here to make sure Foster Lady takes care of Baby, then I'm gone. Period. I'm not some weak shorty who's gonna get all attached. This isn't a holiday in some kind of family paradise. I don't have time for that.

Everybody's talking or watching the babies—everybody but Hope, anyway. Across the table, she's looking at me, her head cocked a little. She's thinking. . . . Behind that fat freak face, she's thinking things, and I don't like it. I don't need her thinking about me.

"Whatcha gawkin' at, heifer?"

It's barely a whisper, but she still jerks, shocked. At the group home, they dock my points for use of profanity, so I mostly don't, at least not out loud. Here, though, I don't know. Foster Lady didn't say if she gave points for "kindness."

Just like I thought she would, Hope looks off to the side, all hurt. *Weak.*

But just when I've got her schooled, Hottie next to her stares me down. Crap, did he hear? I brace myself.

"So . . . Odessa and Austin, huh? Buddy of mine lives in Austin. Nice folks there."

Meaning what? That Austin is better than me? That there aren't nice people in Odessa? *Whatever.* "The only 'folks' I know in Austin don't answer to 'nice.'"

He's grinning—laughing at me. "I see. Do you answer to 'nice'?"

Oh, this feels better. I flip back my hair. "Nice? Who needs that shit?"

Deduct ten points for profanity. Rena's voice in my head sounds disappointed. Everybody hears—Foster Lady, Mr. Carter, probably even Baby—but nobody does anything. Hottie's brows rise, and Mr. Carter looks over for a minute. Foster Lady just says, "Language, Dess."

Funny thing, though—since everybody's staring, my head feels calm now, for the first time all day. With everyone looking at me crazy, it feels . . . familiar. Better, like the little fizz in my veins means things are all right. But even though nobody's tripped too hard over this and the adults have gone on talking, Boring Girl's all in a huff. That female's staring so hard, her eyes are about to pop out of her head.

I smirk and lean forward to whisper, "What's the matter, widdle munchkin? Haven't learned that word in school? None of the big kids talk to you?"

Hope's chin firms, and instead of matching my whisper, she tells me, "Maybe nobody said, but we have a kindness rule." I just stare at her as she recites, "Before we choose words or actions, we choose kindness—"

"Or we get *time-out*," Baby says emphatically, shaking his finger.

Hope gives Austin a dirty look while Foster Lady's brother lets out a snicker, and Foster Lady chucks Baby under the chin. Even Mr. Carter is smiling and patting

Baby's head. All of them but Hope are laughing—not at Baby, not really. At me.

Me.

Hottie sounds straight *stoopid* when he laughs, like a big dumbass donkey. I hate Foster Lady's ape-faced grin, her horsey white teeth and fat lips and her big stupid mouth. I hate Baby's big wide eyes and the little curl of a smile that lets me know he thinks he's done something smart. I hate the— No. Forget it. They're all just stupid. I hate them all.

HOPE

. . . .

Snoopy

Hope rolled onto her back in the messy tangle of blankets, scowling. She could still hear her good-little-girl voice telling Dess the house rules, like the most incredibly *lame* loser ever. Who even did that? Who prissed around, sounding like their *mother,* for heaven's sake?

Hope grunted, imagining her mother's input. She'd say, "Well, Hope, at least you *have* a mother around to sound like," and then Hope would have to think of "the less fortunate," blah, blah, blah. Fine, so Dess and Austin's mom was in "vocational rehabilitation" down south. It didn't sound like real jail or anything, and it didn't give Dess an excuse to call Hope a freak.

Why did everything always have to change? Couldn't Dess have just stayed where she was? Why did she have to come to *Hope's* house, to get in *Hope's* face and mess up *her* life?

And . . . *heifer?* Who was that skinny little stick calling a heifer? At least cows gave milk. What did stick insects do? Nothing but look like sticks, that's what.

Hope fluttered the covers, sending cool air to her feverishly warm body. She should be better than this, she knew—Mom would be shaking her head if she heard her now. But Dess was trouble, no doubt. She'd probably stolen something or mouthed off to a gang of older girls. Her social worker had probably had to move her to Glenn County to save her from being beat down by thugettes with names like Trina and Mel, girls who knew how to punch.

Hope savored this image of Dess's tight-lipped, scowling mouth swollen and misshapen, her raccoon-ringed eyes smeary and sad. She flung back the covers and sat up, her eyes narrow. Dess probably had some kind of a record. In all seriousness, it wasn't fair that Mom hadn't even said anything. This was the kind of stuff Hope needed to know if she had to share a house with her. Why not find out for sure?

Within moments, she was up and padding silently down the hall.

Mom would drop a brick if she knew what Hope was going to do. And it wasn't because Odessa had called her a heifer—no. Hope took after her mom in build and her dad in height. Unlike her classmate Jaswinder Singh, who had topped six feet over the summer, Hope was probably going to stay five foot three forever and always be, as Grandma Amelie put it, "sturdy." Hope wasn't just mad that Dess had insulted her or sneered at her or tried to boss her about Austin. What bugged her was that Dess *knew* things. Dess wore her street cred like a high-gloss polish made up of secrets, lies, and information—and she looked at Hope with know-it-all smugness, like Hope was this ginormous dim-witted child who knew nothing at all.

So maybe Hope *didn't* know everything, but she knew how to find out. . . . Knowledge, after all, was power.

The door to the nursery was half-open, and the night-light spilled a tiny pool of pinkish glow into the hall. Hope paused to peek into the little cave and heard Austin's sodden breathing and the whistle of his breathy snores. Out cold. Jamaira was lying on her back, eyes open, taking in the shapes the shadows made on the ceiling. Hope watched her for a moment and then stepped back, feeling the conflicted twist of love and pity she always did at the silent, floppy-limbed baby. Eight-month-olds were supposed to roll over. They were supposed to babble and reach for things and rock on their knees and think about crawling. They weren't supposed to lie there and just . . . be. Hope rubbed her face and sighed. Well, at least Maira wasn't seizing or crying. Unlike her big foster sister, Jamaira was content. Hope made herself keep moving.

The office seemed empty at first glance. The lamp was on, so Hope listened in the hallway, wondering if Mom had just popped into the kitchen for a cup of tea. Hearing nothing, she pushed the door open farther. Crossing to the desk, she nudged the mouse and saw that her mother had been the last on the computer but hadn't left any documents open. Hope leaned over the desk and poked around briefly in her mother's desktop files, searching for the reports Mom completed for Austin's social worker. If she could get the name of Austin and Dess's mother, she was sure she could find something. Arrests were a matter of public record, weren't they?

Hope ruthlessly squashed the voice in her head that argued that if Mom had wanted her to know details, she would have told her. Mom *had* told her a few things about the situations of the other kids they'd had stay through the years, and she'd told her about Austin. Hope knew that Austin's mother—Dess's mother, too—was in jail now, but she didn't know why. She knew Dess had been in a group home in North Highlands for almost a year. But why hadn't she been in a home like Austin? Had she been in trouble? Hope had to know more.

Unfortunately, the universe didn't supply her any answers. There wasn't anything to be found in her mother's computer files, and for the moment Hope was stumped. She killed time by going online and checking to see if any of her classmates were saying anything interesting. She answered a quick note from Natalie, who hoped she was okay, and deleted a forward from Kalista, who still sent kitten pictures and dumb jokes to the whole class. Finally, Hope reread Savannah's last two emails and clicked through her travel blog.

Leaning back in the office chair, the wireless keyboard pulled toward her, Hope made a comment on Savannah's latest post. She pulled out the bottom drawer of the desk to prop up her foot and heard the crinkle of paper. She looked down and saw a white envelope printed with the seal of the Department of Public Welfare of the State of California, Department of Families and Children.

Score.

The envelope was wedged down the side of the drawer, as if Mom had dropped it there accidentally. It had already been opened and the contents refolded and replaced. Hope smoothed the papers open and skimmed. The first was a cover letter from Terrie Farris, MSW, stating that this was the transfer paperwork for the minor child Odessa LeAnn Matthews, who was transitioning from the child residential facility to secured foster care, blah, blah, blah.

"Here follows a list of possessions and transfer of child funds," blah, blah, blah, "medical records," blah, blah, blah, "Individual Service Plan," blah, blah, blah.

So . . . it looked as if she'd been in *tons* of foster homes, short placements here and there, and— A police report! Hope wriggled happily as she scanned it. Arresting Officer, Isaac Tindley. Incident Report: *(1) Runaway delinquent c. 602, (2) Resisting arrest c. 148.*

Hope read further, and she blinked in shock. According to the missing persons report, Dess had been on the street for two months! Jeez, she'd only been—Hope quickly did the math—eleven! She shook her head and read on. No wonder she hadn't been in foster care with Austin. A three-month stint in Juvenile Hall after that, then two group homes in the last three years. *Huh.* Hope skimmed a few more papers, thumbing through them quickly. No parole officer was listed. There was something about a lawyer, though. But all foster kids had lawyers, even Austin and Maira. Hope frowned and flipped through some more papers, strangling on the legalese and wishing for something easier.

Transfer of guardianship of minor child, blah, blah, blah— Ah.

The words on the bottom of the page seemed to stand out in bold print:

> **The confidential transfer of the minor child Odessa LeAnn Matthews by order of the District Court of Los Angeles, Honorable J.D.D. Levins, at the request and for the protection of Trish Matthews, who is currently serving the remainder of her mandatory minimum sentence in segregation at Ironwood Vocational Center. Information may be released only upon request to the child's and to the parent's attorney, the court and court services, including probation staff, U.S. government agencies, and deputized agents of the Department—**

"Hope. Harmony. Carter."

Hope jerked so hard at her mother's voice that the envelope almost flew out of her hands. She folded the papers immediately. "Mom." She gulped, her throat suddenly Sahara dry. *Crap,* this was bad. "Uh, I was—"

"No." Her mother snatched the papers from her grasp and glared down at her, her wide mouth compressed with anger. "Don't even try, Hope. There is no way you could imagine that this was for you. *None whatsoever.*"

Hope licked her lips and talked fast. "Okay, no. But, Mom—"

"Was I gone too long today? Was I not available to you to answer any questions?"

Oh, here it came: her mother's "I'm-so-disappointed-you-didn't-come-to-me" talk. Hope heard it frequently these days. "No, Mom."

"Was your father unavailable? Was there no other option but to find information by snooping and poking through things that don't belong to you?"

"No." Eyes safely pointed toward the floor, Hope rolled them in disgust.

"I cannot imagine what I did or said today that would let you think that it was okay for you to come into the office and snoop through an obviously confidential file. This was not a kindness, Hope Carter. You now know things about Dess that you didn't need to know."

"Jeez, I wouldn't tell anyone," Hope mumbled. "Mom—"

"*That* is *beside* the *point,* and you *know* it!"

Hope jumped as her mother thumped the heel of her hand against the desk. Her mother's brown eyes were dark with emotion, and she was blinking rapidly. "I am disappointed, Hope. This dishonest, unkind behavior is beneath you. You know better. Just because Dess is your age doesn't mean she's not like any other foster child we've had in our home. She is your *sister.* Sneaking and spying won't win her trust."

"I'm not *trying* to win her trust," Hope said. She hated when her mother talked parenting-book talk. "She thinks

I'm a freak, and you heard what she said when I just *talked* to Austin. It's like she's the 'real' sister now." Hope made quotation marks in the air. "And I'm supposed to disappear. You don't know what she's like when you're not there. She says stuff when you can't hear her. I was just . . . I don't know."

Mom sighed. "You were just trying to get information on the enemy. In a war, that would make sense, Hope. But your life isn't a war, and Dess isn't your enemy."

Hope found herself sighing along with her mother's long yoga breath. Realizing her arms were crossed, she uncrossed them, consciously mirroring her mother's body language. Psychology could work both ways, right? There had to be some way to salvage this. "So, Mom," she began carefully, "it said that Dess's mother is in segregation? Is that protective custody, or—"

But Hope had miscalculated. Her mother stiffened, angry again. "Do you honestly think we're going to discuss this? You have enough information that doesn't belong to you. It is *confidential,* Hope." She lifted Hope's chin with a finger and looked down into her eyes. "There will be consequences for your actions tonight, young lady."

Hope pulled her chin away and crossed her arms again. "*Whatever.* I'm sorry I snooped, but I need to know what I'm dealing with. She's already in my face, and it's the first *day.* Can't I at least know if she stabbed someone at her group home or something?"

Her mother sighed, her righteous stance deflating. She leaned against the desk. "Hope, listen. We talked about

63

this before—how hard change is for you and what a hard transition this might be for Dess. She's a challenge—and will be a challenge for all of us. I know it's not going to be easy to have her here, but one positive from this situation is a chance to make new friends. In spite of what you've read, will you try to keep an open mind? It's not going to be easy for Dess to adjust to us, and I feel she needs an ally."

Hope again rolled her eyes and made a skeptical noise in her throat.

"I know," her mother replied, answering her unspoken comment. "It might not seem like she needs anyone—or *wants* anyone, to be honest. But I just left a very insecure, worried girl upstairs. She's going to be with us for a while, Hope, possibly until after Christmas, or maybe for the whole school year. She's going to have a lot of adults in her space—her social worker, some folks from the state, people interviewing and assessing her. I just hope she can have some friends her own age to de-stress with—"

Hope sighed. "*Mom.* I *know.* She's a foster kid. I'm a foster sister. I'll be *nice.*"

"—someone who will eat lunch with her at school, chat with her before homeroom—that kind of thing. Just until she gets the hang of being here."

Hope's insides curdled. "Are we talking about the same person? She won't want me in her face like that."

"She doesn't know what she wants yet, Hope. Give her some time, all right?"

Hope shrugged. "If I was a boy, it wouldn't be a problem. Did you see how she looked at Aunt Henry?"

Her mother laughed. "Sweet, be fair. *Everybody* looks at Henry that way." She sobered a little. "Dess will probably treat Dad and me differently. She probably hasn't had many positive interactions with men in her life—and maybe none with African American men, much less a whole African American family. This is all new to her, Hope, which is why I asked you—"

"To give her time. I know, Mom. I *know*," Hope groused.

Her mother straightened and squeezed her shoulder. "I was proud of you tonight, sticking up for yourself but still being kind. I am disappointed that this happened, but I have faith in you, Hope. It was the right decision to bring Austin's sister into our family. It's the right decision to keep kindness as our guide as we interact with her. We want to *share* our home with those in need, not be run over by them. We can handle this, right?"

Right, Hope thought the following morning as she heard a crash in the bathroom. The shower had gone on at five a.m., and noises—music, hisses, slams, creaks, bashes, crashes, with not even an *attempt* to be quiet—had been going on ever since.

Hope pulled the pillow over her head and moaned. What the hell was Dess *doing*? Who needed to get up *that* early to get to school at a quarter after eight? Usually Hope smacked her alarm for ten minutes, dragged herself through the shower-and-outfit routine, and got down to breakfast by seven forty-five. Fifteen minutes later she dragged herself and her backpack to the bus and was ready to sleepwalk through a new day. Five freaking *a.m.* was too early for anything. But now she had to get up—and not just because she was awake. One of the "consequences" she had received the night before was that she had to stick to Dess Matthews like glue—to be where she was and be "present" and helpful to her for her first week.

Thud. Thump.

Hope rolled her eyes at the sound of a blow dryer. Why couldn't Dess dry her hair in her room? Was she already using every outlet in there? Hope fought her way out of the covers. She'd better start off by letting Dess know it was her bathroom, too. She stood by the bathroom door and knocked. "Um, Dess? Dessa?" She tapped again. "Dess?"

Nothing.

Huffing, Hope shoved her feet into her slippers and stumbled out the door, heading to the upstairs bathroom. Dumb, secretive Odessa LeAnn, making so much noise before the alarm went off. Stupid, mean, name-calling stick, who was probably even now thinking up worse names than "heifer." And Mom said *she* had to be nice?

Being a foster sister sometimes sucked.

. . . .

Gone to the Downward-Facing Dogs

You can't hear nothing in this house—no wind, no trees, no dogs, no cars, nothing. The group home was in a decent neighborhood, but these rich folks are quiet like the dead. I didn't even hear the baby crying last night, and I know they do, all night long.

I'm not trying to be talking to Hopeless first thing, so I don't even push on her door very much to see if it's locked. It figures she sleeps right till the last minute. For sure she doesn't put any kind of *time* into her look, like I do. Whatever. It's time to find something more than the granola bars I boosted from the snack cabinet last night. I need food. Now.

But it's quiet in the hall—way quiet—and I don't smell anything coming from the kitchen. I strain my ears. Where the hell are these people? Finally I hear a soft thud upstairs. I follow the sound to the open doors of the family room—and just about choke.

"Oh, *nuh*-uh."

Foster Lady has her big backside shoved into a pair of thin cotton pants that hug her thick thighs. She's standing on a little purple mat, arms stretched high, right foot placed on her thigh, balanced only on her left leg. When she hears me, she doesn't even twitch. Her chin is pointed up, her eyes on the ceiling, and she's breathing slowly, in . . . out . . . in . . . out . . .

"Um . . . Mrs. . . . um . . . Robin?"

Foster Lady drops her arms and exhales a long *whoosh* of sound, smiles at me, and then reaches for her left leg. She places it high on her inner thigh, balances there for a moment, lifts her arms, and tilts her head again . . . in . . . out . . . in . . . out.

So can she not talk today or what? I raise my eyebrows, hands on my hips.

"Good morning, Dess," Foster Lady says finally, and keeps breathing.

"I didn't think black people really did yoga."

Foster Lady inhales slowly and then breathes out. "Black people are just people, Dess. People of all kinds do whatever they feel like doing." She exhales and smiles, bringing her arms and leg down again, standing still. "I feel like doing yoga."

"Yeah? So what are you . . . doing?" I move closer, curious. Foster Lady stands with her legs all wide, practically doing the splits, and then she stretches out her arms.

"I was just in what's called Tree Pose, followed by the Mountain Pose. Now I'm doing an Extended Triangle Pose, which is going to take me, next, to a Lunge. . . ." Foster Lady goes over sideways, slowly but smoothly, her arms still outstretched. She breathes a moment, then asks, "Did you want to try it with me?"

I hold up a hand. "*Please.* I am not into that hippie crap." Foster Lady's legs seem bigger than ever, bulging, as she uses her muscles to stay steady. It must be harder than it looks; a little sweat shines on her face and arms.

She laughs. "That's Hope, too. Yoga is too slow for her."

Riiight. Hopeless is nothing *but* slow. Foster Lady surprises me with her muscles and all, but I'm solid *certain* that Hope couldn't stand on just one of her fat tree-trunk legs if you paid her. Where is she, anyway? You'd think her own mother would make her lazy butt get up.

"You going to do this all day?"

Foster Lady grins and doesn't answer for a moment. "Breakfast will be on the table at seven, Dess. It's written on the schedule I gave you last night. Remember?"

"I'm not hungry, I just asked," I say, feeling stupid. She *did* give me some little green piece of paper to put on my bulletin board. I'm supposed to meet a counselor today, and then she's making me go for a doctor's appointment. I swear she's worse than Rena. I just *went* to the doctor with the group home, before school started. I keep telling these people there's never nothing wrong with me.

The sliding glass door rumbles in its track, and Hope comes in. She's wearing a pair of black sweats and a

T-shirt. She's holding a laptop under one arm and a pair of little balls in her hands. She tucks the little balls behind the recliner closest to the door.

"Hey, Dess. You got up early. You look nice."

What the hell does that mean? I give her the eye for a long moment, taking in her frizzy hair, T-shirt, and sweats. I wait for the clue that she's messing with me—an eye roll, the curl of a lip. Instead, she just keeps staring. Weirded out, I mutter, "I didn't think you were awake."

Hope shrugs. "I had to use the bathroom."

Oh, *now* she's trying to start. I glance at Foster Lady. "She could've knocked."

Foster Lady just looks at Hope.

Hope shrugs, her eyes widened. "I did. It's okay. There are lots of bathrooms in this house. I used the other upstairs bath, then went outside and messed around with the weights while I went online."

I blink at her arms. She doesn't look buffed to me. "Weights? You?"

Hopeless looks embarrassed. She tries to roll one of the little balls across the floor toward me, but it stops before it gets more than a foot.

I pick it up. It's soft and small, but the side of the ball has "2.2 lbs." written on it.

"Huh." I squeeze the ball in my hand and check out Hope's long-sleeve T-shirt. The letters *H* and *W* wind together above a little white mountain range. A tree-looking blue squiggle below it is supposed to be water, I guess. "What's that on your shirt supposed to be?"

"It's just the school symbol. This is the PE uniform from last year."

I give Foster Lady a look. "I have to wear a uniform—even at PE? Are you *kidding* me?"

"The upper school at Headwaters has free-dress Fridays," Hope interrupts. "Anyway, you're new, so nobody's going to care if you're not in uniform the first day. It's not that bad, I swear."

I shoot her a look, feeling panic thrum through my veins. "I am *not* wearing whatever crap outfit you're wearing," I blurt out. "Uh-uh. That's not even legal. We *have* freedom of expression."

Hope gives a twisted little grin. "I want to hear you tell that to our principal."

"You think I'm playing? I *will*. How can you stand it, looking like everybody else?" It's probably not that deep, but . . . uniforms? Seriously?

Foster Lady interrupts. "Girls, we haven't got time for a uniform debate. Hope, get a move on to that shower. We don't want to be late today. Dess, since you're ready, go in the kitchen and check the oven. The timer is—"

"Oven?" Foster Lady is bent at the waist with her palms on the floor, her butt in the air, and her head down. "What's wrong with the oven?"

A deep breath. "Would you go into the kitchen and check on the frittata? The timer should be going off pretty soon."

Frittata? I decide not to ask. "Fine."

"You don't need to take it out. Just look and see if it's browned and turn the oven off."

"Got it."

"You don't even need to open the oven. If it's browned, Russell will take it out."

I turn away, scoffing. "Lady, I can get a pan out of the oven." *Jeez.*

"Dess, don't try lifting that hot skillet," Foster Lady warns, her voice rising. "It's cast iron, and it's heavy."

I walk faster. "Whatever." Not that I signed on to do nobody's cooking, but she must think I can't do *anything*.

As I near the kitchen, I can smell something tasty. I hear music, too, little beeps and blips that sound like a video game. On the floor in the middle of the hallway, Baby is playing with something that looks like a little TV.

"Hey, Baby!" I stand over him a moment, waiting for him to look up and throw his arms around me. He's pushing buttons and arrows and making something—a little airplane? a car?—spin around and shoot little balls at a line of other little balls with numbers on them. "Tip-top!" a little voice exclaims as he shoots the red ball on his plane at another red ball.

"Tip-top!" Baby repeats.

I reach for him, then stop. Even little guys get pissed if you interrupt their games. Sighing, I glance up and realize Mr. Carter is sitting in a chair, smiling at me.

"Morning, Dessa. Ready for your odyssey in education this morning?"

"Hey." I give him a half smile. He's wearing dress pants and slippers. I can't see his shirt. Up top, he's all baby, wrapped up in some kind of blue cloth sling thing. In front of him, he has a mug and the newspaper open.

I nod at the lump. "Don't you people ever put that kid down?"

Mr. Carter chuckles. "We do. It's just that Jamaira has so many awful things in her life and so few good things that we indulge her. She likes to be held, so we hold her."

I click my tongue like Granny Doris, sharp and critical. "You're spoiling her."

"Nah." Mr. Carter grins, cheerful. "You can't spoil a good baby like Jamaira." He stands carefully, adjusting for her weight, and picks up his coffee cup. "You ready for breakfast, madam?"

"Uh . . . sure. Foster Lady said I was supposed to get something out of the oven—" I sneak a quick look up the hall. I saw Mr. Carter and forgot what I was doing. I thought she'd come running in here to make sure I didn't take out that stupid pan.

"Oh, I got the frittata out already. Do you like broccoli?"

"It's . . . all right." There had better not be broccoli for breakfast.

"If you don't like it, Robin boiled some eggs. There's also cold cereal, toast, juice, peanut butter, fruit—the usual stuff. During the school year, it's a good idea to eat a hot breakfast, though."

I follow him to the kitchen, noting that I don't smell broccoli at all but something much, much better. The skillet is on the stovetop, resting on the burner to cool. It's huge, and I'm glad I didn't have to take it out myself. "That's a frittata? I thought that was a quiche."

For some reason, I don't mind asking Mr. Carter stuff.

"A quiche is a tart with a crust," he says, and I nod.

I *knew* he'd know.

"Quiches are French, while the frittata here is an Italian dish," he goes on, carefully reaching above the counter to bring out a stack of white ceramic plates. "You want to get the forks and napkins out of that drawer to your right?"

I grab a pair of forks and a couple of cloth napkins and follow him to the table. He puts down the plates. "Now, a strata is close to that, but it uses pieces of stale bread and milk in the layers with the eggs and the vegetables and cheese."

I make a face. "What?"

"Stale garlic bread is delicious the next day in a strata. This I promise you," Mr. Carter says. "You want some of this? There's juice in the fridge, too, if you'd like."

"I'll try some frittata," I say. What the hell. I've had broccoli and eggs separately. I guess it can't kill me to eat them together . . . first thing in the morning. Ugh. "Is there coffee?" I ask hopefully.

"Oh, good, another one for my team," Mr. Carter says. The baby makes a noise like a kitten, a tiny mewing, and he pats her on the back. "Hope and Robin drink tea. I like my coffee, and the French press is in the cabinet there." He gestures with his chin. "But I'm going to have to leave you a moment and do some diaper duty."

"Eww, go—please. I'll make my own coffee," I say, stepping way back. There are some things I just don't need to think about in the kitchen first thing in the morning.

"Hey, Daddy."

Mr. Carter kisses Hope as they pass in the kitchen doorway. She's wearing a braided headband pushing back her wild frizz of hair, black skinny jeans, a long-sleeve denim top, and black lace-up canvas tennis shoes. The denim shirt has that little HW mountain range and water-tree logo on the pocket. I look it over and shrug. The uniform shirt's not that embarrassing, but Hopeless's outfit is all her: hopelessly boring.

"You're making Dad coffee?" Hope asks, and I shrug again.

"I don't know how to do it French."

"I'll show you," Hope says. "Do you drink coffee all the time? If you do, Dad's going to have to use an actual coffeemaker, because this only makes, like, four cups."

I give her a look. "I only need *one*."

Hope rolls her eyes in explanation. "Dad. He'll drink all four, trust me. Haven't you noticed he's hyper?"

I sit down at the table, reluctant to be the one to cut the frittata but not sure what else to do. It's almost seven, and no one seems to be in any hurry to get to the charter school. It's so different from the group home. At this hour, there'd be bacon smoking on the stove and eggs sputtering and popping in the fat, and the cook, Carol, yelling, "Order up!" like we were in a diner. People would be grabbing plates and grabbing jackets, social workers would be coming in the door, and Rena would be yelling at people to hurry and not miss the bus.

It feels too weird to be two girls in a kitchen, just . . . quiet.

I don't like it. I know I won't like this new school. Too much quiet, with too many rich people. And they're crazy, all of them. Skinny little Mr. Carter. Big old Amazon lady. Hopeless and that dying kid. Everything's messed up. Farris just had to move me in with Baby, didn't she? My life was getting too good.

"My tummy's rumbling," Baby announces, barreling into the kitchen. "Hi, Dessa!" he adds, like he hasn't already seen me this morning.

"Austin, what do you do if—" Hope breaks off, pausing as she dumps coffee from the grinder into the small glass pitcher. She glances at me and licks her lips. "Ask Dessa what to do if your tummy's rumbling," she says, and for a moment I panic. Why the hell does she want Baby asking me? And then I remember. I'm the sister. This is what I do.

"Um . . . no toys at the table, wash your hands, and sit down," I say, trying to sound like Foster Lady. It must work for her. Baby looks at me like I'm crazy, his little forehead all wrinkled up and cranky.

"I washed my hands yesterday," he complains, and stomps out of the kitchen.

I don't even know I'm smiling until I see Hope grinning back at me.

. . . .

Chameleon

On the front steps of the admin building, the vice principal was waiting in a bright fuchsia suit with a ruffled collar. "Hello, hello!" Ms. Aiello warbled, waving. Her lipstick, kind of a deep pinkish color, had come off on her top teeth. Hope thought this made her look like an aging vampire.

"Good morning, Mrs. Carter," the vice principal said, even though the two of them normally called each other "Robin" and "Barbara." "Is this our girl?"

Our. Hope winced. It was too early for this.

"Good morning. Yes, this is Dessa Matthews," Mom said, and gently set her hand on Dess's shoulder to bring her forward. Dess shrugged it off and stepped to the side, looking, as far as Hope could tell, at the fabric in Ms. Aiello's skirt.

"Nice suit," Dess said, unsmiling. "That's a great color."

"Why, thank you," Ms. Aiello said, and beamed with pink teeth.

Was she even *serious?* Dess had to be playing suck-up, because that suit was *seriously* hideous. Hope decided she didn't want to know—and standing around through introductions was pointless. With a wave to Austin, who ignored her in favor of watching the big kids in the hall, wide-eyed, Hope edged around to the side of the group, hoping to escape.

"Don't run away yet, Hope Carter," Ms. Aiello caroled. "You're Dessa's tour guide for the morning. After homeroom, please report to my office."

Hope grimaced. She was stuck with Dess at school, too? Mom must've told Aiello about her "consequence." Then Hope saw the look on Dess's face and felt a fresh wave of humiliation—Dess looked as if she'd swallowed something that wasn't going down.

It was obvious Dess didn't want to hang out with her. Well, Hope didn't want to hang out with Dess, either. She lifted her chin. "Um, Ms. Aiello? Can't somebody else do it?"

Her mother's eyes widened. Ms. Aiello's pursed lips looked like a pair of bumpy raspberries as she said disapprovingly, "I beg your pardon?"

"I don't mean anything negative or disrespectful," Hope said carefully, avoiding her mother's eyes. "It's just that we've already met, and we live in the same house. It would make more sense if Dess got a chance to—"

"I need to meet new people," Dess agreed before Hope

could finish. She met Ms. Aiello's frown with an un-Dess-like smile. "Totally fine with me. Thanks, Ms. Aiello."

"If that's okay," Hope said awkwardly, aware from her mother's sharp silence that not everyone agreed this was the best plan.

The vice principal gave a little shrug. "All right, then, if you girls have it figured out. Come on into the office and let's get to know you . . . Dessa? Or is it Dess?"

Hope exhaled in relief as Ms. Aiello herded Dess away, but her mother gave a disgusted *tch* and turned away.

"Mom," Hope began, but her mother shook her head.

"Not now," she said, hefting the baby seat in one hand and leading Austin toward Ms. Aiello's office with the other.

Hope waved again to Austin and shrugged off her mother's disappointment. It wasn't that doing one little campus tour would have been that bad, but Hope knew it was a gateway job for what Ms. Aiello really wanted. Just like her mother, Ms. Aiello no doubt wanted Hope to walk around campus and hold Dess's hand until she made a friend. But seriously, there was *no way*. Hope couldn't work miracles. Someone as mean and snarly as Dess wasn't going to *make* friends.

Like, this morning. Dess had been okay for five minutes in the kitchen, kind of relaxed and nice, and then, boom, she'd asked Hope what the "deal" was with her "bushy hair." Okay, so she'd smiled like she was joking, but *still*. What kind of question was that? Some African Americans wore their hair in really big crinkly curls, and so what? So what if Hope's hair wasn't bleached blond and smooth and straight? It wasn't *bushy*. She'd just combed it. Or she'd been going to before she'd heard her dad talking to Dess.... Anyway, the point was Hope couldn't *make* people be friends with Dess, no matter what Mom or Ms. Aiello thought.

Also, all Mom's talk about how Hope needed to "open up" and "make new friends" was kind of stupid. She didn't really need more friends—she had Natalie and Liesl Stockton and Jas Singh, when he wasn't being a total goof, and lots of other kids in her class. Yeah, so her closest friend had left the country. And? Hope had been on her own all summer. Missing Savannah didn't make her so lonely and desperate that she had to hang out with someone who sniped about her appearance.

She stalked down the hall, barely acknowledging the many clusters of students. Headwaters Academy was a charter school and catered to kids from all kinds of families: African American, East Asian, Haitian, South Asian, Latino, and Caucasian. Emphasis on math, science, and technology made it a California Distinguished School, but Hope thought of it as just plain school. She tried to see it from Dess's point of view, wondering what her foster sister would think of it.

In Mr. Workman's room, Hope dropped her bag on a desk three rows back, where she usually sat. Fortunately, today that was on the other side of the room from Rob Anguiano, who smelled as if he'd drowned himself in cologne that morning. An empty desk sat next to her, and

Hope put her bag on the seat, as if someone was coming back. She didn't want Dess coming in later and getting the wrong idea, and claiming space right next to her.

Maybe Dess would be on a totally different track. Maybe they wouldn't have classes together at all. But at a school this small, no classes together at all was probably asking a little much.

Hope frowned as she thought of Dess. She wished her mother hadn't come into the office last night. She needed to have found out more. It was so weird to think of Dess as a secret foster child, with her mom practically in protective custody. Did that mean somebody was protecting Dess— like she'd have a bodyguard, or "witness protection" people? Hope wished there was someone she could ask about Dess's father. What had he done to be put into jail? She wondered if Miss Odessa LeAnn knew the whole story, and felt a smug warmth building. She would bet anything that Dess didn't know as much as she did.

The bell rang. Mr. Workman quickly took attendance and then sat on the corner of his desk, reading out loud his "weird news item of the day."

During announcements, Ms. Aiello's voice sounded scratchy and tinny over the loudspeaker. "Good morning, Headwaters Academy! Donation boxes will be going up today in the cafeteria for our gift-card drive. We're collecting for the Embrace Kids Foundation. . . . Freshmen, please be sure to have your permission slips to Mrs. Stevenson by Thursday if you'd like to be included in the symphony trip on Monday. . . . Don't forget that the lost-and-found . . ."

As Ms. Aiello droned on, Hope felt a folded paper being shoved under her arm. She slid her hand around and picked it up and opened it.

doing hdwters tour for new girl. not 2b nosy, but is she staying with you?

Hope frowned and twisted in her seat. Two seats behind her, Kalista wiggled her fingers.

Hope scribbled back, *Yes, staying idk how long.* She hesitated. She didn't want to be unkind, but Kalista needed to be warned about Dess. . . . *tty after?* She folded the note and shoved it back under her arm toward Carey, sitting behind her, to wait until he noticed it and passed it back.

Ms. Aiello got through the Headwaters pledge— "Capable of meeting any challenge, we learners will be leaders. Headwaters Academy, it all starts today!"—just before the bell rang. Hope ignored whatever Mr. Workman was shouting over the bustle of movement and hurried toward Kalista, who was making a beeline for the door.

"Kalista—wait," she called, trying to hurry up the sea of students going the opposite direction.

Kalista was already in the hallway, waving an arm clattering with bracelets. "Ms. Aiello? I'm here!" Heads turned, and she bounded down the hall toward Dess, who stood, shoulders hunched, outside Ms. Aiello's office. The vice principal was beaming as Kalista came toward them.

Dess was looking over Kalista's outfit—skinny jeans and a tan Headwaters T-shirt under a blazer—and Hope was suddenly worried. Dess was giving her the same narrow-eyed once-over she'd given Hope, and she was going to say something—no doubt, about Kalista's wildly curly brown hair, her wide mouth, or her long, sharp nose. Hope pinched her bottom lip between her teeth unhappily. Even though Kalista drove her nuts, she wouldn't wish Dess on her worst enemy.

"So, Kalista, right?" Dess said, and then glanced up at Ms. Aiello with a shrug. "Okay. I'm ready. Thanks, Ms. A."

Ms. A? Hope blinked at Dess as she walked past, then looked again, more closely. Since Mom had dropped them off, Dess's messy ponytail had been changed to two braids that just brushed her shoulders. Over her gray tank she wore one of last year's pink button-down uniform shirts, tied at her waist, emphasizing her cleavage, which Hope was now positive was helped along with a bit of padding. Her jeans were cuffed into capris, and her black skater shoes had been replaced by the white ballerina flats she must have had stuffed into her backpack. Even her makeup looked lighter, less Goth stark and more smudged and smoky. The tiny, subtle changes made Dess look like a whole different person.

"Thanks for showing me around," Hope heard Dess say as Kalista walked her down the hall.

"No problem!" Kalista gushed. "I love meeting new people."

Hope shook her head as Dess smiled and gave a little wave at a group of students who were all staring at the new girl.

Okay, *that* was weird.

And things only got weirder.

By lunch, Kalista's table was full of girls from the drama club. The new girl had been to New York and had seen *Wicked* and *The Lion King* and had been in the drama club at her old school.

She also was rumored to be trying out for Headwaters cheer squad with Ronica Jones, since she had an Auntie Doris who had been a Dallas Cowboys cheerleader.

Fat chance, Hope thought darkly.

Hope *expected* players like Rob Anguiano, Micah Sherman, and James Gilberto to be all over a new girl, lined up three deep to be the first to get her number and then tell lies about how they'd hooked up with her. But even smart boys, like Clayton Stone and Jas Singh, who were on the Headwaters TAG team (for talented and gifted students), were talking to her in the hallway before study hall.

"What's going on?" Hope asked Rob, who was lurking in the vicinity.

"The new girl wants to try out for the chess team," Rob said, looking impressed.

Hope rolled her eyes so hard, she gave herself a headache. Blah, blah, blah, new girl, new girl, new girl. Who cared? Savannah's dad had tried to teach Hope to play chess last summer. Except for the queen, which moved anywhere it wanted, all across the board, she couldn't keep track of what any of the pieces did. And Dess knew how to play chess *and* was good enough to be in the chess club?

She was such a *liar*. Hope shook her head. People were such sheep. Obviously, *no one* was that amazing about everything. Dess was a total fake, and everyone would soon know it.

Hope was feeling frumpy, grumpy, and envious, and had concealer slathered on the zit beside her nose. But she pepped up at the second-to-last period of the day. The mixed concert choir had rehearsal on Tuesdays and Thursdays with Mr. Mueller, who was Hope's absolutely favorite teacher in the whole world. While everybody had to take an elective, not everyone loved their choice the way Hope did. Mr. Mueller always said he liked freshmen and sophomores best, because they still pretended to laugh at his (very bad) jokes.

Chorus was almost always fun. It helped that Mr. Mueller was insane and made them sing Broadway-style warm-ups and parodies of pop songs. There was only one thing Hope didn't like about chorus, and that was the very first day of the term . . . when Mr. Mueller heard auditions.

This year it would be even worse. Students would be auditioning twice first semester—once to make the cut for the winter musical and once for Stillwaters, the advanced show choir Mr. Mueller worked with all semester. Stillwaters didn't accept freshmen, but sophomores, juniors, and seniors could audition and sing for graduation at the end of the year. This year sixteen students from Stillwaters would get to compete at the Sunbelt Festival and, if they placed, perform at Disneyland. Mr. Mueller only took four of each part—sopranos, altos, tenors, and basses. Stillwaters members had to keep their grades high and their citizenship record perfect. Hope had always thought she'd get in if she auditioned. Mr. Mueller liked her, and she'd been taking voice lessons for three years. Mr. Mueller called her voice an "anchor" voice. It was pleasant and dependable, not too breathy and not too loud. She could sight-read a part and not get lost. Hope and Savannah had planned to audition as sophomores, the first year they were eligible. . . . Hope sighed. She didn't want to change the plan now. She was on her own.

She dropped her backpack on the floor and stood self-consciously at the edge of the room with her classmates as Mr. Mueller tried to make a circle of singers out of thirty-five dorks who were talking and laughing. He strode around, calming people into order and then starting them singing a warm-up. Today's was a baroque tune with the words "Seven silver swans swam silently seaward, swiftly sideways," which was ridiculous. But even worse, he made them sing it in a round. Half the kids were singing "silently seaward," while the other half were singing that those same swans swam "swiftly sideways." Even though everyone was singing together, it was hard for Hope not to feel as if she was singing a solo when Mr. Mueller abandoned the piano and walked slowly through the circle of students, listening.

When Liesl lost her place, Mr. Mueller mouthed the words until she jumped back in. He tilted his head and listened, nodding and smiling, commenting and singing along, until he passed in front of Dess, who was standing with her hands in her pockets. He took one giant step backward. And stopped.

Hope drew in a breath, straining her ears.

"Ah! Lovely! Like a young Sarah Vaughan," Mr. Mueller said, and smiled.

Who? Dess's wide-eyed gaze followed Mr. Mueller's return to the piano. When she saw Hope watching, Dess looked away and started singing again.

Hope felt a tiny spear of jealousy strike her in the heart. She looked down at the floor, her throat feeling full of rocks. Mr. Mueller had smiled at Hope when he walked by, but he hadn't said anything. It shouldn't matter that Mr. Mueller had said something nice to Dess. It shouldn't make any difference at all . . . but it did.

Okay, Dess probably couldn't play chess. She probably hadn't seen *The Lion King,* probably didn't have a cheerleader aunt. Dess lied about *everything*—anything and everything. But Dess couldn't make Mr. Mueller lie. And Mr. Mueller—the god of choir nerds—would never lie about a voice.

DESS

. . . .

Lost Girls

It's the end of the day, but the inside of my locker is still neat and clean. Which is just as well, since I feel like putting my whole head in there. Jeez, this *place* . . . At public school, I'm just a piece of sand in the sea. Here, at this charter place, I'm a rock in a puddle, all obvious and stuff. I hate it.

At first, my outfit was wrong. I *thought* all I needed was to look as little like Hopeless as I could—but that idea blew. Even with sixty kids in the entire sophomore class, this school's still too small for me to stand out like that, so while Foster Lady was yapping at Aiello, I ducked into the bathroom and pulled my act together.

In a bathroom stall I untied the hoodie around my waist, wriggled out of the padded bra, and toed off my shoes. Five minutes later, with a paper towel to lighten my eye makeup, I was more classic than punk, my edges blending in to the prep school vibe around me.

Rena calls me a chameleon because I've got the skills to blend in anywhere. After homeroom, I saw Hopeless staring, with her freak face sagging, and I almost laughed. She thought she had me down, like she knew me. Nobody does.

I'm the new girl. I can be anyone I want—right?

There're all kinds at this school. Besides regular—I mean, white—students, there are black students, a lot of Asians, some Indians and Mexicans and stuff. At lunch at Stanton, they'd all sit at their own tables, but here they mix it up a little. Maybe it's a rule or something.

And teachers are all over the place. During the passing bell, they just hang out in the hall, smiling and talking to people like they've got nothing else to do. And all day long, that vice principal lady kept showing up, in the hall, in my classes, just smiling with her big horsey teeth, all up in my face. I know her gig—she's just waiting for me to start something, like all foster kids are some kind of trouble. I hate her.

Some things about this school are lame. Between the uniform shirts and their blue and khaki dress-up day "slacks" and "earning" the right to non-uniform days and the little school pledge and all—"learners will be leaders," seriously?—it's completely weak. But it's superclean—cleaner than any school I've ever been to. They have breakfast, if you want it, and Kalista said they have a full-on lab for biology, with equipment and stations for every student. At my old school, there wasn't even a separate lab.

There's a computer lab, and the library is pretty good—reference computers, periodicals, squishy cube-shaped couches, and lots of new fiction to check out. I wanted to stay all day. I've never been to a school like this. I wish I could stay here for a whole year. If it wasn't for stupid Trish, I'd ask Farris—or Bradbrook or whoever my stupid social worker is now—if I could.

And I could make everybody like me—even Aiello, if I had to. I could at least try.

I mean, if I wanted to. But I don't. So what if it's a rich school district? That's got nothing to do with me. I only came to check on Baby, and once Trish is done with her stupid court case, I'm out.

I wonder if they'll take me back to North Highlands. Rena says I could come back.

I shove books into my bag—English and science—and the Algebra I take-home test we were given. I have way too much reading, and I'm already wiped. That Kalista dragged me to meet everyone in the whole school, just about, and now I'm in all the clubs and trying out for some musical thing I'm not even going to be here for, and I'm stuck with her blah, blah, blah-ing at me all day. I should've stayed with Hopeless. At least she knows when to shut the hell up. She doesn't even want me at her school.

"Dessa!"

I blink and look around my locker door. Baby's running down the hall, ducking between bigger kids like he's indestructible.

I slam my locker and shoulder my bag, a weird, loose feeling working its way up from inside my chest. "Baby! Hey! You're too little to be at my school."

Foster Lady's right behind him, of course, walking with Aiello. Well, the vice principal has nothing to complain about. Farris gave them my school records. I make good grades, and I stay out of trouble. Period. I ran away from foster care when I was eleven, yeah, but I'm not stupid.

"I already goed to school. You have to go to the doctor," Baby announces in his baby chipmunk voice, and several kids around me go "Aw," like everybody does. In his little jeans and red T-shirt, Baby's cute, no question. Shorty's got a big mouth, though, putting my business all over the street.

"I know. What else did you do all day?"

"Maira and me went shopping with Mama. And we looked at the leaves and got damatoes."

"Yeah?" He needs to stop calling her that. *Mama.* I start walking toward Foster Lady, mostly to keep Baby from investigating the contents of some kid's backpack that's sitting practically in the middle of the hall. Baby's nosy, but I've figured out if he thinks I'm listening to him, he'll follow me pretty much anywhere.

"Yeah, and Teacher Mavis let me ring the bell."

"Wow. Is that fun?"

"It's loud," Baby explained. "Mama, can we go now?"

"Bye, Dess." Some guy—Marcus? Rob? waves as he goes by.

"Um, bye," I say, wondering if he's someone important.

Foster Lady is beaming like I discovered a cure for cancer. "Hey, Dess, looks like you made lots of friends. Did you have a good day?"

I've made "lots of friends"? What, am I Baby now? "Yeah, school was amazing. Everybody loves me. Can we go now?"

"Hey, Mrs. Carter!"

Foster Lady and I turn around at the same time, and my neck tightens. Kalista. She's looking from me to Foster Lady and back, curiosity in her big green eyes. I don't need Kalista's fat mouth in my business. She told me everything she knew about everyone in the whole school. I know her type.

"Hey, Kalista, what's up?"

"Nothing much. . . . Hi, cutie!" Kalista's voice goes squeaky as she reaches for Baby's head. He scowls at her and hides behind Foster Lady's leg, and I give him a mental high five. Smart kid. Definitely related to me.

Since she can't bother Baby, Kalista looks over at me. "I didn't know you knew Mrs. Carter, Dessa," she says, and then waits, like I'm going to jump in and tell her everything I know. I stare at her and shrug a shoulder.

"I'm a friend of the family," Foster Lady says, smiling so big that Kalista smiles back. "We've got an appointment, though, so Dess will have to see you tomorrow or we'll be late."

Friend of the family, huh? Right. Foster Lady's as big a liar as I am.

But Kalista swallows it, and just like that, we're out. Kalista's waving, Foster Lady's got her hand on Baby's head, and I'm free to escape into the warm September afternoon.

Well, mostly free. Aiello appears and goes on and on about new uniform orders, and assessment tests, and blah, blah, blah. I walk faster when I see the van, and before I get there, the side door slides open. I love automatic doors.

I shrug off my bag and pause. Hope's already riding shotgun. I'm either going to have to crawl into the bench seat in the very back, which is half filled with a foldable playpen or something and bags of groceries, or sit between Jamaira and Baby in their car seats. I look at Jamaira from the corner of my eye. Right now she's still—probably asleep, but all I can think is, If she wakes up: uh-oh.

"Hey. Trade seats."

Hope pulls an earbud out of her ear and twists to face me. "What?"

I lick my lips. "I need to trade seats. Please."

Hope narrows her eyes. "Why?"

Stupid freak. I scowl. "Never mind."

Hope glances at the baby, then abruptly undoes her seat belt. I can't figure out the expression on her face. "Fine."

Everybody's out of the van when Baby climbs up to his seat, and it takes a minute to get going. Hope works him through snapping into his car seat, counting out loud, "One, two, three!" for the buckles, and Foster Lady throws her hippie bag—a small denim backpack with flowers on it—down between the seats.

"Everybody in? Hope, I don't have time to drop you off.

We're going to have to go straight to Dr. Perlman's office," she says, sliding a pair of oversized glasses down from the top of her head. "You can stay in the van with Maira, or you can come in with Austin and me. It shouldn't be more than about a half hour."

"I'll stay in the van and read," Hope mumbles, and yawns.

"I'll stay in the van and read," Baby parrots, and Hope snorts.

"No, you won't. Austin, you'd be bored and crying for Mom in five minutes. All I'm going to do is read big, long books with no pictures."

"Mommy, do you have my truck book?" Baby leans forward and digs in the pocket behind the driver's seat.

"Nope. It's at home. Sorry, Charlie."

Baby sighs. "I want a Popsicle."

Foster Lady rolls her eyes and glances at me. "Dr. Perlman gave him one of those pediatric pops once when I brought him in with a stomach bug, and he's been trying for another one ever since. Do you remember if you had a lot of fevers or ear infections when you were his age?"

Oh, right. Like I remember how often I had a runny nose or something. "How should I know?"

Foster Lady's smile is brief. "Hope remembers sitting on Henry's motorcycle when she was just two years old."

Hope laughs. "Only because you had a meltdown about it."

Foster Lady grins. "I did not. Henry shouldn't have put you on that bike. Ever!"

"Mom . . ."

While they go back and forth like people do, over an old argument, the rattle of the wheels over a rough patch of road turns into the rattle and roar of an engine, like fast axes spinning around and around, and chopping up sound.

My father, the Felon, would roar up to the house, strip off his gloves and his glasses, and throw them in his black bucket helmet. The helmet would sit on the floor by the door . . . somewhere that was home. I remember that helmet, dangling from a hand with thick blue ink on the fingers, those fingers that were choking strong.

I shiver and rub my arms, hard. Eddie Griffiths is in for twenty-five to life for drug and arms trafficking. I am never going to see him again. I need to stop obsessing.

"You cold, Dess?" Foster Lady stabs the temperature controls and turns down the AC. "You're not getting sick, are you?"

My neck is tight, my jaw tense, as I force out the words. "I'm fine."

And I *am* fine, like I told her. The doctor takes a quick listen to my heart and lungs, and we have a chat about birth control—I'm already on the Pill, not about to wreck my life like Trish—and it's over. It was a total waste of time, but the law requires me to have a doctor appointment within two days of being placed in a new home. It's stupid.

It's also stupid that, after everything else, there's still Bradbrook, the new social worker, to get through.

"Odessa LeAnn Matthews," he says, looking down at my file. He shifts his feet on the thick white living room carpet. "Pretty name."

Please. I shrug and wait. Bradbrook has a wide, crooked mouth, and I can see where the new hair on his pale chin is growing in after his shave. He should grow some on his face and shave his head. With his long legs and his knobby wrists poking out of his jacket, the tufts of yellow hair left around his ears just make him look like a scarecrow.

He closes my file and catches me staring. He clears his throat. "Are you comfortable here, Ms. Matthews? Are you and the Carters getting along all right?"

I shrug.

He keeps his steady brown eyes on me. "We don't want this to be harder than necessary, Ms. Matthews. We wouldn't normally settle a Caucasian girl with an African American family who has a child the same age, but Mrs. Farris felt you'd be happiest here, with your brother."

I shrug again. Down the hall, I can hear Baby singing along with his video.

"Misunderstandings happen, even in birth families. The way to prevent misunderstandings is to communicate," Bradbrook drones on, leaning forward to meet my eyes. "If you don't want to talk to me, you can call the office and leave me a message. I want to help you make this place-ment work."

I shrug a third time. "When do I see Trish?" I don't like him making me ask, but I guess only Farris knew she was just supposed to *tell me* what I needed to know. I'm gonna have to train Bradbrook.

He shifts, frowns, and reaches up to rub his neck. "I thought Mrs. Farris already went over this with you. Your mother has cut a deal with the district attorney's office in exchange for a shortened sentence. Because of threats made against her, she's in administrative segregation right now at Ironwood Vocational Center, and—"

"I know *that*. I just asked—"

"Ms. Matthews, do you understand why your placement was changed?"

I press my hands on my knee, to still my bouncing leg. I don't like him calling me "Ms. Matthews." He sounds like the child services lady when she talked to Trish.

"Ms. Matthews?"

I push aside the roaring in my ears. "Rena said . . . some stuff about family." I wave my hand. Trish had threats from my psycho father's friends, and she asked that Farris move me. So? I don't want to think about the Felon ordering a hit on Trish for testifying. Or ordering them to come after me . . . I slide down in my seat and rub my neck, feeling the smooth couch fabric against my jeans, knowing that I don't feel hard, tattooed fingers at my throat. I croak, "She's okay, right?"

Bradbrook licks his bottom lip and studies me. "Ms. Matthews—"

That wakes me up. "My name is *Dess*. You can call me Dessa if you want, but quit it with the 'Ms. Matthews' crap."

"Dessa," Bradbrook continues, "as I said, your mother is being housed in segregation. That means she's not being held with the general population—she's by herself. She's safe and well, and waiting to testify. I'll be happy to forward any letters you send to her and will make sure you get any mail from her, but it won't be possible to resume family visits until after the trial."

"I know."

Baby's gone quiet. Everyone seems far away, and the silence prickles against my skin.

Bradbrook lowers his voice. "Dessa, I know this is hard. I know it has got to be stressful to be put in a new placement with strangers in a whole new county, and get a new school and a social worker in the package. But you can handle this, Dess. We're all here to help."

Yeah, I'm sure. "We done yet?"

"No, we're not." Bradbrook digs in his file and comes up with a familiar blue envelope addressed in a familiar loopy handwriting. "Your maternal grandmother, Doris Matthews, has asked that I forward these—"

I make a buzzing noise. "Next. I don't talk to that bee-yatch, and she don't need to talk to me. Any letter for me you get from her, shred it."

Farris, who knows my history with Granny Doris, would never have let me get away with even pretending to call her anything, but Bradbrook's eyebrow only twitches. He clears his throat, and goes on like I haven't interrupted. "Now, I've talked with Mrs. Carter about your allowance—

you'll need to tell her if you'd prefer it every week or in a lump sum once a month. The amount hasn't changed."

Please. I get eight bucks a week from the state. A monthly lump sum is at least halfway to being real money.

Bradbrook continues, "And we'll see if we need to adjust your clothing allowance. Headwaters has supplied your basic uniform from some overstock, which is one logo golf shirt and one phys ed uniform. But any extra sports shirts, hoodies, tracksuits, or button-downs sporting the school logo you'll need to purchase on your own."

"Fine."

"Laura Molloy is still your lawyer. Her number hasn't changed, and anything you need from her, you just pick up the phone, okay? You know your rights, and you have all the contact information you need?"

"Got it." Farris asked me that, too, every single time. "Anything else?"

Bradbrook takes a deep breath and fixes me with his eyes again. "Dess, Doris Matthews—"

I bristle. "Look, Bradbrook, I *said*—"

"Ms. Matthews, lower your voice, please, and hear me out." He raises his own voice just a little, but it's sharp enough to shut me down.

I clench my jaw and glare. He's as bad as Farris after all.

Granny Doris taught me to sew and to look after myself, yeah, but she is an evil racist crone. She wouldn't take Baby and me last time Trish got popped. She told Farris no, Farris said, but I didn't believe her. I was *sure* she would take me, sure Farris just didn't let her know how much I needed her. I ran away from that nice foster lady they put me with, sneaked on a city bus with another family, walked, ran, and ran some more. I got all the way to Rosedale before I knew there wasn't anywhere for me to go.

She wasn't too old to take us. She just didn't want Baby. She said she told Farris that *I* could stay but not him. I shouted a lot, broke dishes and stuff, and bailed out of there that night, after she called the cops on me.

I haven't talked to that evil old lady since.

Bradbrook is still going. ". . . she told me that Mrs. Matthews has sent a letter care of the Department of Children and Families and Children's Services every month for the past four *years*. It seems to me that she is determined to reach you, Ms. Matthews—Dess. Now, it's our job to look out for your best interests—"

I snort.

"—and we *are* the Department of Children and Families. Family is important, Dess. The state will *not* relinquish you to her care, and you don't have to see Mrs. Matthews in person at any time. However, refusing to speak with her or accept her letters—"

"Shred them," I repeat, arms crossed. "I don't have to talk to her, and Ms. Molloy said nobody can make me."

Bradbrook, brow furrowed, drags his teeth over his lip. "Ms. Matthews—"

"I've got rights," I remind him, my voice rising. "You can't make me."

"No one can make you," he confirms, but he looks tired.

I don't bother walking him to the door. Instead, I stay in the front room, on the fancy couch, alone except for a patch of sun that slides down the wall to the carpet.

A letter—every month? Still? When Farris told me I was getting mail, I told her to shred it ages ago. Granny Doris kept writing? Curiosity pulses through my thoughts, and I give my head a quick shake. *No.* So what, the hag can write. She may have been okay once, but Baby and me don't need no racists in our family. We're fine without all of that.

"Shred it," I mutter again, and hug my arms around myself.

She didn't want us then, and it's too late now. *Too late.*

. . . .

Thief of Hearts

Two weeks later, in her second-period class, Hope took the sheet of paper Mr. Cochrane handed her and grimaced. She hated pop quizzes, and one of Cochrane's one-minute "multiple-guess" quizzes at the start of a new unit was the *worst*.

"No talking, please. Leave your quiz facedown until I say go," Mr. Cochrane said, dropping another sheet of paper on the desk to her left.

Hope fidgeted in her front-row seat as Mr. Cochrane, in his usual suspender-and-bow-tie combo, continued around the room. Surreptitiously she peeked out of the corner of her eye at Dess, who sat at the other end of the front row, five seats to the right. Usually Dess made sure to sit anywhere but in Hope's row. Her presence today itched along Hope's nerves like a rash. She couldn't stop looking at her.

Ms. Aiello had moved Dess around a couple of times as teachers had given her various tests. She had settled into three classes with Hope—chorus on Tuesdays and Thursdays, biology fourth period—and now it looked as if she'd be in Hope's American history and governance class, too, which sucked.

Mr. Cochrane had circled back to the front. He reached into his desk drawer and took out a miniature timer. Its red sand sparkled in its tiny base. "All right, folks, you have sixty seconds. Go."

Blocking out the automatic squeals of *One minute?*, she flipped the paper over and skimmed it rapidly, her heart pumping competitively. There was only one question, with a list of possible answers. *What are the Five Freedoms of the First Amendment to the United States Constitution?*

Oh . . . crap. This was fourth-grade stuff, but she couldn't remember it. *Crap.*

She gnawed on her bottom lip. Okay. She could do this. Those four paintings by Norman Rockwell were called *Four Freedoms.* Unfortunately, all she could remember was that one of them showed people eating Thanksgiving dinner.

Crap, crap, crap.

Around the room tense silence flowed, and pencils checked boxes. Hope's head turned slightly. Dess had just flipped her paper over and set down her pencil.

Hope straightened indignantly. No way—she couldn't be done. She was just—

"About thirty seconds left," Mr. Cochrane said.

Head down, Hope started checking boxes. Freedom of Speech? That sounded right. Freedom of . . . Listening? Um . . . Freedom of the Press? Oh, she knew that one for sure. Freedom of Education? Freedom of Petition?

"Sand's gone," Mr. Cochrane announced. "Pencils down."

With a spurt of frustration, Hope checked one last box and flipped her paper over.

"Give your paper to the person on your left," Mr. Cochrane instructed, adding, "and those of you on the left, take your papers all the way down to the end. You know the drill."

With a sick feeling in her stomach, Hope accepted the paper from Wynn Reiber, the girl next to her. Wishing she'd had time to change the last answer on her own sheet, she reluctantly dragged herself from her seat and slowly moved across the front of the room to hand her paper to . . . Dess.

Dess looked at Hope as she dropped the quiz on her desk. She pulled out her red pencil, and Hope looked away.

Crap. Hope knew she hadn't done well—and now Dess would know, too.

It doesn't matter, Hope thought as she slumped back into her seat. Dess thought she was dumb already. Last night after dinner, they had been watching *Jeopardy!* with Dad in the family room, and when the clue was *They're not onion rings, but THIS seafood appetizer,* she'd shouted, "What are shrimp?"

"What are calamari?" Dad and Dess had answered in unison.

"The clue is 'rings,'" Dess explained superciliously. "Calamari is in rings—get it?"

Hope, who wouldn't eat anything that even smelled as if it might have been *near* fish, just shrugged sullenly. Her uncle Peter liked popcorn shrimp, which is why she'd thought of it—popcorn was a snack, like an onion ring, right? Hope knew zip about fancy seafood, and right now she knew zip about the Five Freedoms, too. That same tide of prickling self-consciousness she'd felt last night washed over her whole body and threatened to drown her.

"Freedom of Religion—raise your hand if you've got a check mark."

Most of the class dutifully raised their hands, and Mr. Cochrane counted aloud the number who agreed and wrote it on the board. "Freedom of Listening," he continued, and counted the students again. He worked his way through the list, down to Freedom of Assembly and Freedom of Shopping, which obviously wasn't a real freedom, because if it was, you'd have to have Freedom of Money— and when they'd deconstructed the Declaration of Independence two weeks ago, Mr. Cochrane had pointed out how only the *pursuit* of happiness was considered a human right, not actually *being* happy.

As it turned out, Freedom of Listening was an *implied* freedom, tagged on to Freedom of Speech. Freedom of Education wasn't even *in* the Bill of Rights but something from the Convention on Human Rights, which didn't have anything to do with the First Amendment, either. Kalista argued that *technically* Freedom of Shopping could be about all people being free to shop anywhere they wanted. Mr. Cochrane said that *technically* the question had been about the First Amendment, and since the quiz wasn't about amending the First Amendment, Kalista was going to have to accept that she was wrong.

At least Mr. Cochrane always asked them to mark only the answers that were correct. It wasn't nearly as bad as checking off all the ones that were wrong.

When it was time to return the quizzes, instead of getting up to give Hope her paper, Dess passed it across the row. Kalista, sitting next to Dess, looked at Hope's paper and laughed. Kalista passed it to Marcel Thomas, who didn't even glance at it. Marcel passed it to Grayson Cho, who snickered, looked down the row at Hope, and laughed again. Grayson passed it to Wynn, and Hope cringed as Wynn fiddled nervously with her hearing aid, barely meeting Hope's eyes. Dess had put big red frowning dog faces and *No!* and *Bad Girl!* next to the two answers that were wrong.

That little troll-faced bimbette! Hope leaned forward so Dess could see her face and *glared.*

Down the row, Wynn, Grayson, Marcel, and Kalista all leaned forward and looked over at Dess . . . who wasn't even paying any attention. Finally, the feeling of so many curious eyes made her lift her head. Instead of looking embarrassed or apologetic, as Hope thought she should, Dess raised her eyebrows and jutted out her chin aggressively. "What?" she said out loud.

Mr. Cochrane, who had just told them to open their social studies textbooks, looked up. "Miss Matthews? Did you have a question?" he asked.

"Nope," Dess replied, smirking.

Hope muttered under her breath. When Mr. Cochrane glanced her way, she simply held up her paper. Mr. Cochrane frowned first at Wynn. Then, realizing who had marked Hope's paper, he looked to the right. "Miss Matthews, next time, please follow directions for the marking," he said, calm as always, but Hope felt a zing of self-righteous satisfaction.

So there, you skinny little heifer, Hope thought. As much as she had hated Dess using the word, Hope found that she liked it. "Heifer" wasn't as nasty as "whore" or "bitch," so she was only slightly insulting Dess, not tearing down a fellow sister in the feminist point of view. The word spoke to Hope. It was specific and said "young" as well as "female." Plus, it sounded so much *worse* than plain old "cow."

Dess just shrugged at Mr. Cochrane, as if she didn't understand what she'd done. Of course, the minute he'd turned back to the board, Dess rolled her eyes and sighed, making a big show of facing away from Hope's side of the room.

Grayson, seemingly disappointed that nothing else was going to happen, turned to Hope and shook his head. "Don't be such a baby," he muttered. "It was just a joke."

Mr. Cochrane cleared his throat. "Mr. Cho, since you're already chatting, I'll start with you. We have a student in our class here, Jas Singh, who wears a *patka*. Why does he wear this head covering?"

"Uh . . . because he feels like it?" Grayson cracked.

Grayson's stupid friends snickered. To Hope's disgust, a couple of them slapped hands. Mr. Cochrane gave them all a narrow-eyed look. "And now Miss Carter will give the class an *intelligent* answer. Pay attention, Mr. Cho. Miss Carter?"

Hope felt her face get even hotter. Of all the students in the whole room, Mr. Cochrane would have to ask *her* about Jas. She cleared her throat. "Jaswinder follows the Sikh religion. He wears his *patka* because it's part of his religion, and part of the First Amendment is that you can wear what your religion, uh, tells you to, so . . . ?"

"Is that your answer, or is it a question?" Mr. Cochrane asked, brows raised.

Hope blurted out, "Well, it's my answer, but I don't see why. It doesn't seem like a religion should tell you how to dress. Sorry, Jas." Hope turned in her seat and gave her classmate a mortified look.

"No, I don't have to wear a *patka*," Jas explained. "I do it because I want to—"

"Ha! I was right!" Grayson crowed.

"—show respect to my faith." Jas ignored Grayson. "That's why I do it."

Hope nodded. "Basically what I said." Though it sounded better coming from Jas.

"Thank you, Miss Carter, Mr. Singh," Mr. Cochrane said. "So, back to the topic . . ."

The rest of the class was actually interesting. Mr. Cochrane talked about the historical importance of religion in Western Europe and in the brand-new colonies of the United States. Hope listened, but she was distracted, wondering what Jas thought of her answer. Should she apologize again after class? Jas had beautiful eyes, with these amazingly long, distracting lashes. Could Hope even get through an apology with that much lash going on?

"Three delegates to the Philadelphia Convention at Independence Hall in 1787 were so upset that nobody would agree to a bill of rights, they refused to sign the Constitution," Mr. Cochrane added. "Because they were so sure that one was needed, they inspired James Madison to start work on a bill of rights when the session was over."

1787, Hope wrote, as if she'd been taking careful notes. She only sighed a little when Mr. Cochrane wrote a short-essay homework question on the board. He'd already given out a reading assignment at the beginning of class, and he said the short-answer essay was extra credit. The question he asked—*Would a family whose religion doesn't permit them to go to the hospital have the right to keep their sick baby at home?*—got her thinking. Hope, who knew more about sick babies than most of her classmates, thanks to Jamaira, scribbled the question on a notebook page and nodded to herself. She could use the extra credit to make up for the First Amendment quiz she'd screwed up. Perfect. She glanced over her shoulder. Now, if she could just make sure she hadn't screwed up with Jas—

"Essays should be in complete sentences. Note your

sources, and, of course, spelling and grammar always count." Mr. Cochrane raised his voice as the electronic chime that signaled the end of class rang. "Good class today, people."

Hope shoved her books into her bag as the rush of students moved toward the front of the room. She'd just swung her bag onto her shoulder and was walking to the door when Jas, his backpack casually slung over one shoulder, fell into step next to her. Hope beamed, then looked away. Every time Jas got anywhere near her lately, she got this huge, dorky smile on her face.

"So you don't think the Sikhs should have to wear turbans?" Jas asked, turning sideways to shoulder around a girl who had stopped smack in the middle of the hallway.

Hope flinched. "Uh, I—" she began, then scowled. Jas was grinning. "Shut up," she said, relieved. "You know I didn't mean that like it sounded."

Jas elbowed her. "Naw, I know. At least you never thought I was Taliban. Remember when Grayson asked me that in seventh grade?"

"Jeez." Hope shook her head as she reached her locker. "He hasn't gotten any smarter, either."

"So, um, Jas? Hi." Suddenly Dess was there, wedging herself into the space between Jas and Hope.

Hope sucked in a breath of irritation.

"Hi, Dessa." Jas gave her his usual friendly smile. "What's up?"

"So, Jaswinder? Am I saying it right? Does it mean any-

110

thing?" Dess questioned Jas as if she had handcuffs and an interrogation room.

Hope hesitated, then turned away to open her locker. She didn't *own* Jas or anything. He was friends with everyone in the whole school, and he'd talk to anyone . . . even someone like Dess. Unfortunately.

Hope slapped her history textbook on her locker shelf and grabbed her geometry book, ignoring the conversation going on next to her. Dess, looking up at tall, lanky Jas, had an intent expression on her face that almost made Hope believe she really cared about his answer. Jas was taking her seriously, treating her as he treated everyone. It bothered Hope that Jas was so nice to Dess. Didn't he see what she was really like? Of course not. Nobody did.

Hope sighed and resisted the urge to stab Dess with her own red pencil.

"It's called a pat-wha? How do you spell that?"

Oh, for— Hope rolled her eyes. Dess had found any guy's favorite topic—himself. Jas would keep answering Dess's questions about his *patka,* his hair, and where he'd gotten the cool steel bracelet he wore on his left arm—forever. And it wasn't as if he wasn't supposed to. It wasn't as if Jas owed Hope his time or anything. She swiped on some lip gloss, glaring at herself in her locker mirror. She was being stupid and selfish, two things she hated. To make matters worse, she couldn't stop herself.

She slammed her locker in disgust and brushed past with a terse "Excuse me."

Dess's smile was serrated. "Oh, sorry. Are Jas and I in your way?"

Jas and I, as if they were already a thing. "Don't you guys have class?"

Jas jumped as if pinched. "Oh. Yeah. Geometry. I'm coming." He smiled at Dess. "See ya."

Dess beamed. "See you at lunch," she said, sounding perky and cheerful.

Hiding out with a book and her lunch in the library suddenly sounded to Hope like the best idea ever.

· ·

Curiosity and Doubts

A caseworker at the group home when I was thirteen had a red dot on her forehead. She was Hindu. I remember, because I'd never met anyone before with a dot on her forehead on purpose. It reminded me of when I was really little and Granny Doris picked me up from school with a black smear on her forehead. I bugged her about it all afternoon and just about drove her crazy. She finally told me she got it at Mass and to leave it alone—and *no*, she wasn't going to wipe it off and *no*, I couldn't have one. I remember I made a streak with a smelly black marker instead and got a smack for drawing on myself in permanent ink. Granny Doris just about scrubbed all the skin off my face trying to get it off. She always said I had more curiosity than was good for anybody.

Maybe it's true—I've wanted to ask for weeks about Jas

Singh's *patka* and that little bracelet with the curly writing, that *kara* bracelet. I looked it up on the Internet, but there was so much it didn't say. Do guys *like* keeping their hair that long? And is it the same thing like that guy Samson from Sunday school with the long hair or what I saw on the Internet—those guys with fingernails so long they curl? Why would a religion care how long hair gets? I want Jas to stand and tell me stuff until I can't think of anything else to ask him, but I see how Hopeless looks—like I'm stealing her lunch.

Weak. If I'd gotten too cozy with some girl's boy at Stanton High, she would have stomped down hard and made sure I knew. Instead, Hope's acting all hurt, like Jas is going to notice and do something. *Sucker.* Boys never notice *anything.* Girls do. Hopeless is stupid. She takes boys—and everything—way too seriously. I wouldn't have bothered flirting with Jas if I hadn't seen how badly it pissed her off. She won't come at me and just *say* something. She's all polite and pretending. I hate that.

I open the door to my classroom just as the bell rings. It's language arts, which three days a week is English and two days a week is Spanish. Spanish is pretty cool. Señor Jacobo is writing our homework assignment on the board. He has the fanciest handwriting I've ever seen. The first day of class, he made a swan out of the *J* in his name, and he teaches us a new piece of letter art at the end of every class, which is cool. He even makes vocabulary fun.

I scribble down the assignment as Señor Jacobo takes

out two goofy cardboard dolls with button eyes and black yarn hair glued to their heads. *"¡Buenos días, clase!"*

"Buenos días, Señor Jacobo," the class mumbles. Behind me, James Gilberto says loudly, "Whassup, Mr. J?" His friends laugh. Señor Jacobo ignores him.

"Estos son mis amigos Larry y Roy."

"Hola, Larry y Roy." Last week his puppets were named Peter and Paul.

"Les gusta . . . ¿Señorita?" Señor Jacobo points to me. Crap. They like to what? "Um . . . *¿Les gusta bailar?"*

"Ah, sí!" Señor Jacobo makes his puppets dance. *"¿Señor Jaime?"*

Señor Jacobo's puppets move around the room with our teacher as they go to *el baño* (James's disgusting contribution, but Señor Jacobo only has them wash their hands), play ball, eat, run, and do whatever else as the class uses up as many verbs as they know from our Spanish I book.

Even though the puppets and the costumes Señor Jacobo has are dumb, I love Spanish. When I was eleven and on the street, this one Mexican grandma gave me a couple of apples when I was hiding from the rain at a bus stop. All I knew how to say then was *"Gracias,"* but now Spanish is one of my best classes—which is why I am pissed when the door opens behind me and I hear my name.

Señor Jacobo glances up and smiles, then gives me a nod. *"Adelante,"* he says, making a little shooing motion with his hands. Then he turns to the rest of the class. *"Grupos de tres, por favor, señores,"* he instructs them. "Groups of three."

Resentment scratches like a tight wool sweater as I shove my book in my bag and slouch into the hallway, ignoring the small Asian woman who's waiting for me. I cram my bag in my locker for safekeeping, slam the door, and head outside.

I tried to skip this therapy before—like that made any difference. When I didn't show up the first time, Ms. Wang—Stella—came and sat in the back of the classroom. I ignored her, so she followed me to lunch and sat at the table behind me the whole time. And then she followed me to the class after that one. Ms. Aiello came, too.

"It's thirty minutes, twice a month," Ms. Aiello said, sounding out of patience. "I wish someone wanted to listen to anything I said for that long."

Ha. Nobody wants to listen to anything Ms. Aiello says, *ever*.

Stella said it was either do therapy or have her following me to every class all day so she could tell Bradbrook how I was doing. So I sat down on a bench in the hall and said, "Fine. Right here. Go." And we did therapy, which was Stella asking me little questions and me either pretending to answer them, totally lying, or, mostly, ignoring her.

Whether we've sat on a bench or outside on the lawn, it's been a total waste every time.

The Loop runs in front of the admin building, around the upper field, and behind the cafeteria. Aiello has a fancy name for it, the Headwaters Memorial Path, but everybody just calls it the Loop. The wind ruffles Stella's razor-cut hair as she falls into step next to me. At least I don't have to sit at a desk or anything with this therapist. Stella says it's therapeutic to walk.

The cement under our feet is mixed with blue and green glass and pieces of shell. Every few feet there are "waves" of fancy mosaic tiles in all shades of bluey green and white, which just shows you how rich this school is, because anywhere else they'd have to have somebody scrub off all the paint and put the tiles back right every single day.

Stella walks so quietly I can barely hear her, even though she's wearing stomper boots with platform soles. Her voice is just loud enough. "How are you, Dess?"

I shrug. "Okay."

"Classes going all right?"

It almost seems like my shoulders hear before my brain does. "Fine."

"Things going all right at home?"

A third shrug.

"I'm hearing positives," Stella says. "Ms. Aiello's really proud of you."

Yeah, yeah. Ms. Aiello expected me to be some kind of lowlife thug just because Trish is in jail and I'm in foster care. Whatever. School is fine. It's always the same—no big changes, no big surprises, the bell rings and everybody knows where they're supposed to be. No matter what Aiello thinks, I know it's good for me, and I'm not going to jack it up.

Stella zips her black corduroy jacket as we walk on, facing the wind. "What's your check-in number, Dess?"

I make a little *Hmm* noise while I think. Stella does this

117

thing where I give her a number from one to ten to check in with, one being evil bad and ten being exceptionally good. I give a halfhearted shrug. "Five, I guess."

"Five. Okay. Not affected by your grandmother's letters?"

I frown. I forgot I told her about those. "No. Bradbrook just keeps telling me every time he gets one, but I don't really care. He's supposed to shred them."

Stella just makes a little noise in the back of her throat that might mean "Supposed to?" or "How does that make you feel?" Or maybe she was just clearing her throat. I can hear shouting from the soccer field at the end of the track. Kids are running drills and kicking balls back and forth with their socks pulled up to their knees. Soccer outfits are straight *stupid*.

Stella's voice focuses me. "Anything you're dreading in the next little while?"

A pause. "Nope."

"Anything you're looking forward to?"

I snort. *Please.* How am I supposed to know what to look forward to? "Nope."

Stella glances over at me. "Anything you wish you could tell me, or anyone else? Are there any messages you'd like me to pass along to the people in your life?"

"Nope."

Stella never bothers getting mad that I don't answer. She always asks, "You're still feeling stubborn about our meetings, hmm?"

"Yep." That answer always stays the same.

"Stubborn isn't always smart, Dess."

Stella hasn't said that before. I scowl. "I *know* that."

"I'm available to talk to you, whether it's just on our walks or anytime, Dess. Anytime you start to feel stressed in a classroom situation or angry or frightened, you can ask for a pass and come and see me in my office."

I stop in the middle of a tile wave, a shudder fingering my spine. "Why?"

Stella stops, too, eyebrows raised. "Why?"

"Yeah. Why would you say that now? Is something happening? Did you . . . did my social worker call you or something?" I wrap my arms around my torso, feeling my pulse in my throat.

Stella leans away from me, studying me closely. "No, Dess, no one called me. No one from the school has spoken to me, except in positive reference to your grades. I tell you every time that you can always come and talk to me."

I shake my head, rubbing my arms. "No, you don't. You don't say it like that."

Stella watches me a moment, then cocks her head. "Like what, Dess?" she asks, her voice patient and slow. "How did I say it?"

I back away. I don't like how she looks at me, and I don't want to talk anymore. "Forget it. Are we done?"

Stella doesn't even glance at her watch. She's still studying me, looking at my face like she can see through my skin into my head. "Do you feel like we're done, Dess?"

I manage a nod, arms still tight around myself.

A long pause, her dark eyes steady on mine. An abrupt nod. "Okay, then."

She takes the lead, cutting across the corner of the science building and behind the admin building. We walk until we see the plate-glass windows of the cafeteria.

This is the back side, and mostly students don't come in from this side. Freshmen from first lunch are still there, but most of them are getting up and putting their trays away and going out the exit.

I expect Stella to break off and disappear into her office in the basement, but she keeps pace with me all the way to the cafeteria. "I think I'll get a cup of coffee before I go back," she says, her voice even and calm, as always. She holds the door open with a smile. "Enjoy your lunch."

When she's gone, I rub my arms, trying to figure out what she just said. Does she think I'm going to be "angry" and "frightened" and have to call her? Screw that.

I told Aiello and them, I don't need help. These people need to recognize I'm just here to see about Baby while Trish is messing around testifying, and then I'm out, I'm done. They'll take me back at the group home. I can keep my head down and go to school and get out of the system. I don't need this therapy shit and everybody getting in my face.

I told Stella and Aiello, and Foster Lady, and everybody: Just leave me *alone*.

Coffee Clash

"Dessa, come on!" bellowed Austin, standing in the kitchen doorway.

"She might not want to come, little man," Hope reminded him, and tried to herd him toward the van. "C'mon, let's get you into your seat and go to Saturday school."

"But I want her to *come,*" Austin insisted, sounding exasperated.

"Nobody gets everything they want, Austin," Hope said for the *n*th time.

Although plenty of people *did* seem to get what they wanted from Dess Matthews. For the past three weeks, Ms. Aiello had gotten the perfect student. Hope had heard Dess doing a humble-brag about a 3.7 GPA from whatever school she'd last attended. For three weeks, Natalie

121

Chenowith had gotten a super partner in biology lab. Liesl Stockton had gotten the perfect co-chair for Couture Club. Micah and Rob had gotten someone new to flirt with.

At home, Dad had gotten his *Jeopardy!*-watching partner—and he and Dess had actually played a few games online. And whether Aunt Henry wanted one or not, he had gotten a lifelong fan-slash-stalker, especially after he started calling Dess "Texas."

Dess was equally good at dishing out the unwanted, however. Despite her being a halfway decent housemate—her "germophobic" tendencies meant she cleaned the bathroom twice as much as Hope did—she was snarky, sneaky, and sullen to the female members of the Carter household. She turned up her nose at Mom's cooking, rolled her eyes at attempts at conversation, and made fun of Hope's appearance, hurling a constant barrage of insults every time they were alone. It was actually a relief that at school, and on the bus to and from school, Dess pretended Hope was invisible. Hope felt battered and resentful after five minutes in her company and was glad each night for her after-dinner escape.

But Dess's attitude didn't seem to bother Mom, who kept reminding Hope that not everyone on earth liked everyone else and that, after only three weeks, Dess was still settling in and it would all take time. But while Mom was busy being Zen, Hope was counting the days till Thanksgiving. October had barely started, and she wasn't sure she could get through the next forty-five days until Dess's social worker finally put her back where she came from.

Hope felt twisted inside. She *hated* this. Unlike Mom, who loved to meet new kids, Hope was usually unnerved by the revolving door of foster kids. Her impulse was to cling to each and every baby, every toddler and scared-of-the-dark seven-year-old, and keep them safe. She wanted them to stay forever. This time, though, with *this* foster sibling, Hope couldn't wait to get her out of the house.

"Just us this morning?" Mom asked, jogging out to the garage as Hope watched Austin buckle himself in. She was wearing a long gray hoodie over her teal yoga pants.

"Yep. It's just us," Hope chirped, feeling a real smile break free for the first time in days and her shoulders relax. "Hey, Mom, since we're by ourselves, on the way back can we—"

The door to the garage opened, and Dess stumbled through, her blond hair gathered in a messy ponytail, her sheet-creased face twisted in irritation.

"Defsa!" Austin cheered.

"It's De*ss*a, little man. Find your esses," Hope managed to say, though her throat was constricting with disappointment. She sighed, glaring at Dess's clear skin and sexy-shaggy bedhead. Even half-asleep, her eyes ringed with dark shadows, Dess looked somehow as if she'd just popped in from an all-night party, not as if she'd just rolled—without a shower—out of bed and into probably dirty clothes.

And speaking of clothes, what about that outfit? Hope glowered down at her own white leggings and navy hoodie. Dess was wearing almost the exact same thing but looked totally different. More . . . put together . . . better. How did she *do* that?

"Good morning," Mom said, smiling at Dess, who had shoved on sunglasses and pulled up her hood.

"God," Dess grumbled as she slammed her body into the backseat. "Why would anybody be up this early on a Saturday?"

"God. Good answer." Hope's mother chuckled and backed out of the garage.

Dess kept grousing. "Who goes to church on a Saturday?"

"Um, Jewish people go to temple," Hope blurted, then rolled her eyes. *Don't engage,* she warned herself.

"Not to mention Anabaptists and Adventists," Mom added, smiling.

"What, so now you're whatever-baptist and Jewish? I don't know any black people who are Jewish."

"Like you know the whole world," Hope muttered, then bit her lip. *Ignore her.*

Mom sighed and rubbed her forehead. "You may not know any, but there are many people of African descent who *are,* in fact, Jewish, Dess. We are not Jewish, however. We're going to my friend Geri's church, which meets on Saturdays, because Geri does songs and stories for the little guys, and Austin loves her. After that, I'm going to my yoga class, and Austin's going to his play group. You can join my class, or there's a coffee shop and a bookstore next door, or you can walk around the lake downtown—"

"Seriously?" Dess interrupted. "I got up this early on a *Saturday* for a *walk?*"

124

Hope opened her mouth to retort but closed it when Mom blew out an explosive breath and pinched the bridge of her nose. "Y'know, Dess, I'm not sure *why* you got up." There was a slight edge to her voice. "I assumed it was because your brother asked you to or because you felt like it. No one forced you out of your bed this morning. If it makes you happier, stay in the car and go back to sleep."

And suck it up. Hope flicked a glance behind them as Dess took this in.

"Whatever," she said sullenly.

Hope's mother exhaled again and said in a lighter tone, "Okay, then. How's your homework this weekend, ladies? Do you need anything from the mall? I'm going to look at booster seats, and I can drop you off by the Sears entrance this afternoon." She glanced into the rearview mirror to include Dess in her invitation. "You're welcome to join us for anything or nothing at all this weekend."

"Hey. Where's your dad?" Dess poked Hope in the shoulder, ignoring Mom.

Hope half turned. "Last I saw, he was in bed, reading and holding Maira. Why?"

Dess looked as if she'd bitten something rancid. "Why doesn't *he* have to go to church?"

"I repeat: *Nobody* in this family has to go to church, Dess!" Mom was practically yelling. "You're in this van because you chose to get in when I was ready to *go* to a church, and to yoga. Now I'm going to drop you and Hope off at Moschetti's, so you can maybe get some juice and a muffin to hold you until the coffee hour."

Hope recoiled. "Wait, Mom. I was going to the youth group—" she began.

"Hope." Her mother's voice carried a warning.

"Well, I was," Hope mumbled. This was so beyond not fair. The youth leader, Alex, was cute and funny and, like, ten years older than her, and Hope liked to hang out and wish they were together. She'd planned to maybe stick around after the meeting and help clean up—a total kiss-up move, but the more time she got to spend with Alex, the better.

"Do we need to talk about this?" Mom asked in a low voice, and Hope rolled her eyes. Her mother wouldn't remind her in front of Dess of her earlier snooping, but Hope knew if they "talked about it," it wouldn't change anything. No youth group. There was no getting away from the caustic presence that was Dess. For today, and for as long as Mom said so, where Dess went, Hope went. She was stuck, and it was her own fault.

"Fine," she said heavily, not looking forward to an un-interrupted forty minutes of Dess's company. She silently promised herself a mocha with extra chocolate.

When her mother dropped them at the corner, she leaned across the van and gave Hope's shoulder a firm squeeze. "Sweetheart, thank you," she said, shoving a twenty-dollar bill into Hope's hand.

"Sure," Hope said, stuffing the cash in her pocket in a daze. Mom wasn't usually big on handing out funds with-out effort, but Hope wasn't going to argue. "No problem."

Her mother gave her a serious look. "Buy Dess something tasty. And please, Hope—for Dess's sake—try to keep an open mind. Practice kindness?"

Kindness. Right. Could anybody really live by that rule, even the Dalai Lama? Hope grimaced and waved to Austin. As the van pulled away, she took a deep breath and turned, trying to find a friendlier expression. "Okay, so the coffee shop—it's got pretty good pastry. Savannah and I used to—"

Dess interrupted. "Don't be hanging on me like we're friends or something. You don't know me that well."

"*What?* I—I don't—" Hope stuttered.

"Look, your mommy's not here, all right? You don't like me, I don't like you, so let's drop the act. Okay?" Dess strode up the path to the shop, head high, sunglasses between her and the undesirable world that included foster sisters.

Hope ground her teeth and seethed. *Keep an open mind.* Ha! That snooty heifer could buy herself coffee and a muffin with her pocket lint, as far as Hope was concerned. The money Mom had given her had been for both of them, but not anymore. Hope was going to buy herself a muffin as big as her head . . . and she wasn't going to share *and* she wasn't going to feel bad.

Kindness? Please. You might as well try to make friends with a rabid dog.

The Gang's All Here

Sometimes when Rena took me to the doctor's, we'd go by the coffee shop while we waited for the pharmacy to get done. They played nice music and gave away broken cookies for free, and there was always some guy on a laptop, probably pretending to write a novel so he could pick up women. I loved it. I love coffee shops. Usually.

Hopeless is right behind me, practically breathing down my neck, even though I *told* that heifer to get off me. God, can't she take a hint? What, did Foster Lady say we had to buddy up and hold hands like in kindergarten? It is *too early for this*. Sighing, I adjust my earbuds and turn up my tunes. Never mind Hopeless. I'm gonna get my weekend on.

This is actually a cute little shop. The floors are black and white tiles, and all the specials are handwritten on a little chalkboard that is leaning against the glass pastry case. They have quiche and something called pierogi as well as scones and little fried doughnut-looking things, powdered with sugar. *That's* what I want—maybe two of those. Good thing I've got my pitiful little allowance for this month already.

When the scruffy dude in the tight burgundy pants in front of me is *finally* done making his order for a double nonfat half-caf whatever, I saunter up to the counter. The fried thingies are actually kind of small. I point at a muffin under a glass dome.

"What kind are those?"

"Rhubarb and apple, and the ones in the orange paper are pumpkin," the counter guy says. The stud in his nose winks as it catches the light.

"Uh, okay. I want an extra-tall hot chocolate, double cream, a chocolate-chip Danish, a mixed berry one, and a postcard." I point at the rack of cards illustrated with a line drawing of the coffee shop.

"Yep. Your name?"

"Mary Jane," I say. I don't even want to hear him try and mess up "Odessa," and every time I tell the people at Starbucks "Dess," I get "Jess" or "Lexi" or "Tessa" or something else stupid.

He writes "MJ" on a cup with his grease pencil. "Right. Need a stamp?"

I nod.

"Nine seventy-five, please."

I uncrumple a ten from my pocket and smooth it

between my hands before passing it over. It feels good to stand at the counter, getting back a quarter change and dropping it into the tip jar with a little clink. I take my postcard, adjust my hood, and put my earbuds back in, losing myself to the beat of the music, the amazing aroma of roasting coffee, and the press of the crowd. I feel like I can handle myself, live in the world and be there, without the group home hanging on me, without the whole social services thing. No housemother, no foster lady, no social workers. I could be anybody, giving money to the cashier and waiting my turn. I could be anybody.

Behind me, I hear Hope make her order. Two spinach-and-cheese pierogies and a tall cranberry cider. Ugh. What is with these people and vegetables first thing in the morning? Ignoring her, I move to scope out a table, making a beeline for someone's abandoned newspaper, and settle in, my back to the rest of the crowd. I scan the contents on the first page of each section until I find it, nestled at the end of the auto sales section. I ignore the word scramble, the crossword, and the sudoku puzzles to get to my favorite part.

The infant of the zodiac, the Aries is passionate and enthusiastic, but also confused and hasty. Today your jump to conclusions can land you in hot water! Your day may start in disaster, but you have the skills to tame it. It's a good day for lateral thinking and flexible actions, so get ready for almost anything. Keep your cell phone on and your battery charged. You have the power to solve your mysteries, so ask the questions in your heart.

Satisfaction hums through me. Okay, so maybe I don't exactly *believe* in my horoscope, but it doesn't hurt to look, and besides, I have the skills to tame my disasters and solve my mysteries. It's not like you know that kind of thing just automatically.

I tap my fingers on the table, watching scruffy tight-pants guy sprinkle crap on his half-caf. As much half-and-half, cinnamon, sugar, and chocolate sprinkles as he's putting in there, he should have just ordered what he actually wanted. He's pissing people off, too. There's a big guy behind him in a worn biker jacket and stained jeans trying to reach around him. Scruffy's totally clueless. It's not like guys like that, posers, ever pay any attention to anybody—

I duck behind my raised paper, my body half turned toward the door. God, my hands are shaking and I'm strangling for air.

It's the jacket that holds me first—the fat black spider with the red-tipped fangs against the worn black leather. My eyes flick next to the hands, with grease under the nails and that familiar cobweb tattooed on the web of his thumb. It's one of them—one of the men from the Felon's motorcycle club.

How is he here? He didn't even know we moved to North Highlands. Farris says my father, Eddie Griffiths, is in Eyman State Prison in Arizona—for at least the next twenty-five years. It's a common tattoo, that's all. A spider-web tattoo between your thumb and first finger is common, right? It's just some dude, probably picking up coffee for his old lady, nothing to do with me. Sucking in a deep breath, I close my eyes. God, I wish I could call Farris. Bradbrook doesn't know shit about me or my life. My left eyelid twitches to the beat of my heart. It's not him. It's not him. I know that. But I just want to get out of here—

"Mary *Jane?*" I jerk. The way he says it, I know he's said it, like, six times. The counter guy is leaning over the counter, waving my bag. "Mary Jane, right? What, you don't want it now?"

"Sorry," I say, my voice coming out in a dry croak. It takes everything I've got to get up from the table. My neck is so stiff I can't turn. Where is he? Where did he go? I force myself to reach for the paper sleeve around my hot chocolate, and my hand slips. It's shaking too much to hold the cup straight, and scalding liquid spatters over my hand. I swear and lick away the burn.

"*Day-um.* Looks like you need this," the counter guy says, and hands me my bag.

A nervous giggle erupts as I turn away. I've got to get out of here.

Outside, the cool air chills my face. I walk, stiff-legged, to the end of the parking lot, to the sidewalk, and keep going, faster and faster. At the corner I turn right, nearly running.

"Wrong way, *Mary Jane,*" snarls a voice behind me, and my whole body jerks. My feet tangle themselves in panic, and the paper bag in my nerveless fingers goes flying.

. . . .

The Meltdown

Oh, *crap*. Hope took a step backward, her pulse thudding in her throat. Nobody liked an audience when they tripped over their own feet and spilled chocolate down their arm, but this was worse. She'd only meant to mock Dess's use of a fake name, but the way Dess had cringed and held her arm over her head, as if she thought Hope was going to hit her—

Crap, crap, *crap*.

Hope took another big step back and rubbed her forehead. Dess was just standing there shaking. What were the chances that Hope could just walk around this . . . like, cross the street and pretend she didn't see?

Crap. This was like what soldiers got, after war, post-traumatic shock or whatever. She couldn't just walk away. She sighed, and shifted her weight. "Um, Dess?"

Nothing.

She tried again. "Your Danish didn't fall out of the bag, but if someone makes a right turn, they're totally going to run it over."

Dess brought down her arm and scrubbed it across her face.

Hope shifted her weight from foot to foot. Dad was the funny, friendly one, and Mom was the organized, patient, Zen one. But Hope was *useless* with stuff like this. Should she ask what was wrong? Should she give Dess a hug? No, Dess would probably bust her lip. Dess probably wanted that Danish, right? Hope should get it. And she'd gotten napkins when she'd gotten her pierogies; maybe Dess wanted to wipe her—

Dess stalked into the road, picked up her bag, and brushed past Hope, stomping down the sidewalk in the right direction this time. Torn between resignation and relief, Hope shrugged and followed.

At the next corner Dess stopped and waited. She glared straight ahead, not looking at Hope. "Where next?"

"Depends. If you want to go walk around the lake—"

"Where's the van?"

Hope sighed. "Two blocks to the left, and she probably parked in the back."

Dess grunted and started walking again at a fast clip. The top of her pastry bag was crumpled in her fist, and she swung it like a weapon. Every time a car came by, she stiffened and whipped her head around, her blond ponytail making a sharp arc.

Hope stayed a wary half step behind Dess on their march to the van. She didn't like drama and she didn't like confrontation, but something clearly—seriously—was wrong with the other girl. She hoped Dess would talk to Mom, because Hope wasn't asking, no way.

At a distant intersection, a motorcycle opened its throttle and roared toward them, barely pausing at the stop sign.

"Seriously, Dess, what's up?" Hope asked as Dess seemed to freeze. The motorcycle roared down the road, and in the quiet Hope could hear the hitch in Dess's breathing. Her shoulders were shaking.

"Are you okay? Dess—"

The foster girl's voice was ragged. "I spilled on my arm. No big."

The obvious lie squatted, bare, in the air between them. Hope hesitated, then dug into her own bag and pulled out a wad of napkins. "Here."

Dess was clumsy and dropped half the napkins, trying to sponge at her sleeve with shaking hands. Hope leaned to pick them up, narrowly missing knocking heads with Dess on her way back up. Around them the autumn morning went on. A woman walking her black schnauzer gave them a careful smile as she edged past them on the sidewalk. The schnauzer sniffed the pavement and gave the sidewalk a few experimental licks before the woman jerked on his leash and scolded him with a quiet "No."

Dess wiped her sleeve one last time, head down, then dropped the wet napkins on the sidewalk.

"Jeez, Dess!" Hope picked up the napkins in her finger-tips.

Dess ignored her and kept walking.

Hope's face heated. "I guess a 'Thank you' for the napkins is too much to expect. And you're not going to say what's wrong with you, either?"

"I'm fine." Dess clearly had gotten her equilibrium back.

Hope finally found a trash can on the corner next to the bus stop. She quickened her pace and passed Dess, dumping the sodden paper as she gave the other girl a narrow look. Dess was actually peering into her bag now, picking at her Danish with a reasonably calm expression on her face. It was as if nothing had happened.

What *had* happened?

"What scared you?" Hope asked before she could stop herself.

Dess's glare made Hope flinch. "I'm not scared of shit, freak. You got that?"

Stupid, Hope told herself, and shrugged tightly. If she hadn't seen Dess pale and trembling only minutes before, she might have been convinced. She held up defensive hands. "All right. I was just trying to help." *And that's the last time I'm going to,* she thought firmly. Dess was *Mom's* project. Hope was just the foster sister. Wasn't it enough that she'd done what Mom had said? She'd taken Dess to the stupid coffee shop. She'd been patient. She'd been "nice." And now she was *done.*

She picked up her pace, and soon the church was in sight. Cutting past the flowering bushes planted along the side-

136

walk, she headed into the steeply sloped parking lot. The Y-shaped building enclosed a sunny cobblestone courtyard, and its brick planters would make a great place to soak in the sunshine while she waited for Mom and Austin.

Hope made sure to keep an eye out for the van. Once she spotted it, she lifted an arm to point it out. "Van," she announced, and continued toward the courtyard. The van was probably locked, but that wasn't her problem. She'd done what Dess wanted.

"Hey."

Hope rolled her eyes and kept walking. "Silver van, right there. Can't miss it," she said, pointing again in the vague direction.

"Hey!"

At Dess's shout, Hope stopped, hands on her hips, eyes wide. "What?" she said through gritted teeth. In spite of her anger, she kept her voice down. Mom would have a *fit* if the church people got upset, and it would look horrible if anyone saw Hope shouting at a foster kid.

Dess was leaning against the van, her arms crossed. The crumpled pastry bag was still clutched in her fist. "I want to talk to you."

"So *talk*." Hope bit off the words. If Dess was just going to insult her some more, she was going to . . . "What?"

"Are there a lot of gangs around here?"

Hope blinked for a slow second. "Gangs? Seriously? That's what you want to talk about? Gangs?"

"Yes, *seriously*," Dess snapped. "Gangs. Like, who's in this area?"

"Gangs," Hope said flatly. "In Walnut Hills. No." She turned on her heel and stared toward the church again. Whatever game Dess was playing, Hope wasn't interested.

Dess caught up. "Um, excuse me, but *yes*. There are gangs everywhere in California."

"In cities, yeah." Hope shrugged. "Near big cities, like LA, yeah. But here? Dess, we're two hours from decent shopping and high-rises."

Dess shot her a sidelong glance. "Motorcycle gangs are *everywhere*."

"Not in Walnut Hills," Hope repeated. "In Walnut Hills, people drive fancy Japanese motorcycles to work, not chopped-out Harleys. In Walnut Hills, you might get run over by jogging strollers, not gangsters. Trust me, Dess." Hope shook her head. "This is boring old suburbia. There aren't gangs."

They had reached the courtyard. A few nicely dressed people stood in groups and chatted. Under an awning, an Asian woman was setting up plates of cookies and a coffee urn. An elderly man sat on the edge of a planter, his pale, wrinkled face tilted to the sun. Hope chose a spot close to the beginners' room, where Austin was, and sat, carefully placing her cup of cider on a flat patch of dirt between flowering bushes. She rummaged in her bag and took a bite of a pierogi, glancing over as Dess sat beside her.

Hope swallowed. "So what's with the gang thing?"

Dess leaned in, her voice low. "Did you see that guy at the coffee shop?"

"Which guy?" Hope asked, checking her teeth for spinach. She took another bite, savoring the flavor.

"The guy with the spider on his jacket and the tattoos all over his hands. He was right behind that guy with the stupid pants."

"Oh, him I saw. They were, like, red-and-black plaid? Fashion *don't*. Anyway, I didn't think he had any tattoos."

"No. I said, the guy *behind* him, stupid." Dess sounded impatient. "You couldn't miss him—he was huge."

Stupid? Hope felt a flare of hurt indignation. She gave Dess a cold look. "Sorry."

Dess made a sound of frustration and crumpled her bag. "I'm going to the van."

Hope closed her eyes and sighed. "Wait. Look, I'm not trying to be difficult, but you can't keep calling me stupid, okay? *What* guy? He was huge . . . ? Huge like fat? Huge like tall? Was he white? Black? Asian? Latino?"

Dess hesitated, then settled again. "He was . . . white. Big. He had on a leather jacket. His jeans were all stained. He had tattoos on his hands, between his fingers."

"Huh." Hope gnawed on her lip, trying to think back. "Between his fingers? A picture?"

"A spiderweb between his first finger and his thumb," Dess said in a low voice.

Spider tattoos? Hope frowned. "Well, I did see a kind of scruffy guy with stubble and a leather jacket, but I didn't look at his hands, really. I mean, I didn't see tattoos."

"Well, he had one. It matched the spider on his jacket."

"So?" Hope raised her eyebrows encouragingly.

"So he—he's in a gang. And whatever you think you know about your little town here, you're wrong. There are gangs here. There are gangs *everywhere*. Like I *said*."

Hope swallowed and wiped a smudge from the corner of her mouth. "*Okay*. So, is he from your old gang or something? Did you want to, um, contact him?"

Hope cringed back as Dess's face went from milky pale to blotchy red.

"You *are* kidding me? I came from a group home, so now I'm in a gang?" Dess threw up her hands. "Why do I bother talking to your idiot self? I'm going to the van." She stalked off, her passing noted by the people in the courtyard, who turned concerned looks on Hope. She bent her head over her cider with an embarrassed grimace.

No matter what Mom expected, Hope apparently couldn't do "kindness" with Dess, even when she tried her hardest. She couldn't get the words right or the patient voice the way Mom did it. She couldn't make Dess like her, no matter what.

Nice job, Carter, Hope thought. *You're the best foster sister ever.*

DESS

. . . .

Later That Same Afternoon

"The library doesn't hold police records." The librarian looks across the counter at me, her gray eyes flicking up from the computer screen in front of her. "Are you looking for a specific crime or a specific criminal or—"

"I . . . um . . . Just some information about gangs," I say, and back up from the counter. This library has three of those self-check machines, so the librarians must get bored. This one's way more interested than the one at Stanton High School.

"I have plenty of nonfiction books on the topic," the librarian says, moving from behind the counter. "If you'll follow me to the 300s . . ."

"That's okay. I just . . . wanted to know something."

"Well, you're in the right place, at least." She smiles, and

I look away. I don't want her looking me in the face, try-ing to recognize me. She said hello to Hopeless when we came in, but she doesn't know me. I'm surprised she didn't say something about "appropriate" reading topics, like that social worker at the group home. Rena said information is free and knowledge makes you powerful. Everyone has the right to find out things.

"There are plenty of books, statistical records, and that kind of thing on the shelves if you want to browse around by yourself," the librarian says. "You can also find this on the Internet. Crime statistics are listed by cities. If you re-search 'Walnut Hills city data,' you'll find police reports and the sorts of things they give to people who want to buy a house. There's a lot of information—"

"Thank you," I interrupt. "I'll look on the Internet."

I back away. The librarian's eyes follow me. I think she wishes I would let her help, but I can't. I don't even know what I'm looking for.

There's one computer left, and I head for it at the same time some guy does. He looks at me like I'm going to back off, but he's got another thought coming. Fortunately for him, a lady gets up from another computer and leaves. Good. I don't have the time to beat down some loser who's probably going to try to look at naked pictures on the Internet.

Using the search function, I leave the library system and find the Internet. If the Felon's motorcycle gang is here in Walnut Hills, they're selling drugs, probably. Maybe it will be in the local newspaper. That's what they did before, I think—drink beer, sit around, and get money from all the people who came to the house late at night. It's hard now to remember. When the Felon was there, he made Trish go out and get food, and he'd sit on our saggy couch—where was this?—and watch TV in the dark. Sometimes, Trish made food in a pan. Once there was a pan. And a kitchen. He hit her, and I remember a pan came off the stove and burned a black half circle on the rug. And I screamed. Then he hit me, and she screamed, "Don't, Eddie! No!"

I rub down the bumps on my arms. I hate thinking of this. I hate that, even locked up, he's still got power. He's like a big black spider, sitting in the middle of his web. I hate, hate, *hate* feeling that—

I don't care about Foster Lady or Hopeless or this stupid school. I only care about Baby. But I can't just up and run out of here with him. I can't take care of nobody who's only four years old. I couldn't take care of him when he was little enough to carry, and now I'd have to carry him and all his toys besides. And he'd holler. He thinks Foster Lady's his mama now.

What am I supposed to do?

Farris shouldn't have let me anywhere near Baby.

"Dess?"

I blink. Hopeless standing that close to me means she's said my name more than once. I didn't even see her.

"Dess?"

"What?"

She rocks back away from me like I knew she would. "Jeez, don't bite my head off. Mom's here."

Oh. I stomp out my frustration all the way through the library, stopping at the door to throw my postcard in the mail. I hope Rena appreciates hearing from me.

Hopeless trails after me, looking worried. "If you weren't ready to get off the computer, you can use the laptop at home. I just have reading to do, so I don't need it."

I shrug. It doesn't matter.

"Look . . . don't stress, okay? If you're working on a project or something, we have the encyclopedia online at home, too." She's walking too close to me, her hands balled up in her sweatshirt. "And, Dess, I didn't mean to— I didn't say I thought you were in a gang. I just . . . I don't know anything about gangs. I just . . . Did you think the guy in the coffee shop was someone who knows your, um"—her voice drops to a whisper—"your family?"

My foot lands on the rug in front of the automatic doors, and they open with a *swoosh.* I wince at the too-bright sunlight, then glare at my annoying companion. "You don't know shit about my family, Hopeless."

She recoils at the name, and her mouth twists like she's bitten into an orange peel. "I know enough," she mutters, and moves away from me.

"What's that supposed to mean?" I ask, but her fat butt has some hustle in it after all. Hopeless gets to the van first, and she takes shotgun, too.

Heifer.

"You girls have a good time?" Foster Lady asks as the van door slides open. From his seat by the window, Baby gives me a glassy-eyed look, half-asleep already.

"Fabulous," Hope says, yanking on her seat belt.

"Yeah, it was great," I say, climbing in to sit next to Baby. I touch his fat cheek without meaning to and pretend I don't care that it feels like peach skin. "Hope's helping me with a project."

"Oh, is she?" Foster Lady glances from me to Hope, her expression tentative. "That's . . . great. If you two want to keep working, I'll make lunch. Maybe we'll do a nacho bar?"

Hope gives me a slitty-eyed look. "We're done with our *project,* Mom. We did everything at—"

I interrupt, "You mean bar nachos? Like, with cheese sauce—like you get at the bowling alley?"

"A nacho bar is like a salad bar," Foster Lady says. "I make my own cheese sauce, and there are peppers and tomatoes and onions and olives and beans to put on top of the cheese and chips. It's *way* better than bowling alley nachos."

My taste buds ache. Right now I could *kill* for some nachos.

"You don't have to make us anything," Hope argues, but she sounds weak. "I'm not really hungry, and I'm *done* working with Dess."

"We're not done yet," I mutter, and Hope glares at me.

"We're *done,* I said."

Foster Lady keeps talking, navigating through the half-mile trip home like she doesn't notice. "Well, the sauce is in the freezer, so I'll just put it in the Crock-Pot." She glances over her shoulder. "Since it looks like the boy's having n-a-p time early today, your dad and I can manage the prep—you girls come make a plate when you're ready." Foster Lady pushes the button for the garage door. "If you're inspired now, by all means, keep working."

Hopeless gets bogged down with her library books—she checked out a stack of steampunk novels—so I'm right behind her when she slams her bedroom door in my face. I feel a little guilty for leaving Foster Lady with Baby, but I've got things to do. I go straight to my room, into the bathroom, and throw open the door on the other side.

"Now, where were we?" I ask as Hope freezes.

The Throwdown

"Stay out of my room," Hope warned, backing away until her legs hit the bed behind her. Her heart was pounding, but she refused to panic. She was a talker, not a fighter, yeah, but she had rights, too. If Dess stepped one foot into her room, laid a hand on her, just one—

"I'm not *in* your room. I'm in the bathroom."

Hope crossed her arms. In her baggy white sweats, she felt like a polar bear, but without the protection of vicious teeth and claws. "Well, close the door if you need the bathroom. I don't have to talk to you." *You rat-faced stick chick.*

"You do unless you want me to tell Foster Lady you're talking trash about my mother—"

"She wouldn't believe you." Hope lifted her chin. She hoped this was true.

"Think she won't?" Dess gave her an evil smile. "Your mom's dumb as a big fat box of bricks. She's dumb as *you*. All I have to do is tell her you aren't being *kind*—"

"Don't you talk about my mother, you, you—" Hope's fury ignited. Her brain felt packed with angry words, each jostling for their turn in her mouth. "You won't ever be half the person she is. My mother is good, and smart—a lot smarter than you," she managed. *You vicious yellow-haired harpy.*

Dess gave another smile that was mostly a sneer with uptilted lips. "Oh, sure, Foster Lady's totally onto me. That's why she's making me nachos."

Hope ignored this, fists clenched. She had to stop this now. She should just . . . walk away. Take a deep breath and walk away. That was unrealistic, though, with Dess standing there, sneering at her—

Hope sucked in a breath and tried for calm. "What's really wrong, Dess?" She moved aside her books and perched on the end of her bed, careful not to cross her arms. She tried a small smile, which she felt wavering. She dug her fingers into the bedpost. "Let's get this all out in the open. What do you want?"

"Nothing you've got, Hopeless," Dess said. "You run your big mouth, but you don't really know nothing about my family, do you?"

Hope threw up her hands as heat roared into her chest. "I know *your mom's in jail,* Dess. But you know what? I don't *care.* Seriously, *I don't give a rat's ass.* I've been nice to you, nice like you don't deserve, and all you can do is call me stupid, and talk crap to me about *my* mom? I'm done. I. Am. *Done.*" *Skinny little gutter-mouthed troglodyte.*

Dess recoiled, hands raised in mock terror. "Ooh, Nice Girl's *done.* I'm scared."

Hope talked louder. "The thing is, *you're* completely stupid. At first I thought, 'Okay, she's had a bad life, give her a break, so what if she doesn't want to hang with you? Maybe she has issues with black people. Maybe she might not want someone black to buy her coffee, which is *dumb,* because coffee's coffee, but what*ever.*' But then, Dess, you leave the coffee shop and freak out, and I didn't laugh at you. I just tried to be nice, and I've *kept* trying to be nice, and all you can say is—"

Dess interrupted, practically breathing fire, "My life is *fine.* And I'm *not* racist, so shut up! Just because I don't want to hang with some stupid heifer who—"

"*Stop calling me heifer, you skinny stick!*" Hope shrieked.

"Well, stop being such a stupid dumbass!" Dess roared back. "Why you trying to call me a racist? I don't have a problem with my own blood!"

Hope flung out her arms. "Oh, dear *Lord.* Did I call you a racist? Nooo! I said you *might have issues with black people!* What I'm *calling you,* Dess, is *evil.* You are rude and evil and mean. You're stupid and fake, and vicious and ungrateful and *evil.*" Hope's voice grew more shrill with each repetition.

"Oh, so I'm mean, *boo-hoo-hoo.* It's better than being a big, fat, ugly, *stupid* princess. You're such a princess, you don't even know!" Dess snarled.

"Princess?" Hope stared, disgusted. "You're crazy—you know that? Who's the one acting all high and mighty?" she sputtered. "You're such a *fake,* you don't even know what's real. How am I a princess? The only one acting like a royal *B* around here is *you!*"

Dess shrugged jerkily, then focused on picking at her nail polish, her jaw tight. "I know what's real, Hopeless," she managed. "You're stupid. You don't know anything."

"Don't you 'Hopeless' me, Odessa *Dessturbed!* Odessa *Desspicable!*" It was a lame comeback, but Hope hated being called Hopeless. "If I have to be *stuck* with you till your crazy mom decides she *wants* you, you better stop calling me—"

"*Shut up!* You don't know *shit* about Trish, so just *stop* talking!"

"Stop talking? *You're* the one who came into *my* room! *You* started it!"

"Well, it's *finished now!*" Dess bellowed, slamming the bathroom door.

Hope screamed at the closed door and kicked it several times. That troll-faced, raccoon-eyed, tone-deaf, gutter-mouthed, faking little *freak!* Hope stomped around the room, breathing heavily, kicking the wastepaper basket, the wall, and the bathroom door again. She wished it was Dess's *head* she was kicking. That girl *totally* had it coming. Totally.

From next door, Hope heard similar crashes and booms, and for every crash she heard, Hope made one louder. It was weirdly satisfying, like getting the last word for real. When she stubbed her toe on the corner of the bed, she swallowed a curse and limped to sit on the bed, sitting stiffly. *Ow.*

Then she heard a muffled voice shouting her name.

"Hope? Dessa? *Hope!*"

Crap.

Pretty much all of the rules for foster sisters had been completely broken. You weren't supposed to scream at your foster siblings. You weren't supposed to fight with them. You *definitely* weren't supposed to call them names, or kick their walls, or wish you could kick their heads.

A sharp knock on her door. *"Hope. Harmony. Carter!* Answer me!"

"Yes, Daddy." Hope opened her door and stood in the hallway, licking her lips. Her father was usually a soft touch—usually—but when he shouted her name like that . . . Hope knew she was in trouble. She cringed as he scowled at her.

Her father breathed noisily, his nostrils flaring. "What. Is. All. This. Shouting?"

"I— We're fine." Hope looked down in shame. Nothing was fine, of course, but she couldn't think of anything else to say.

"Fine? It doesn't sound fine." Her father appeared rumpled in his pajama shirt and jeans, and he was holding Jamaira tucked against his chest without her sling, which meant they'd gotten him out of bed. He scrutinized Hope's face, then looked over her shoulder as Dess's door clicked open. "There you are, Dess. What's going on here? Do you need arbitration?"

"What, like a lawyer?" Dess asked, sounding amused— cool and calm, even. "No, Mr. Carter. It was just a little argument."

Hope turned and glared at the other girl. A *little* argument? Oh, wasn't *she* just turning on the charm. Dess was so *two-faced,* so totally, ridiculously fake, just like the blond in her hair. Didn't Dad *see*?

"A little argument, huh? There's nothing 'little' about all the hollering I just heard. If you girls need a listener for both sides, I can do that. There's no need to shout when you can talk."

"Dad, I don't—"

"No!" Dess blurted. "I mean—um—"

There was a little silence. "We can work it out, Dad," Hope said finally. She felt her shoulders hunch under his frown.

"I expect you can. I expect you can also work it out *civilly.* Both of you know the rules. No more of this hollering and name-calling and carrying-on. *I will not have that in this house.*"

The last words were so hard and sharp-edged that Hope recoiled and deflated a little more. "Sorry, Dad," she said in a small voice. Her father hated shouting. He'd grown up with parents who shouted and threw things when they were angry. Hope knew better than to scream like that— that wasn't what they did at home. At school Mr. Workman had told Hope she had an *exceptional* vocabulary. Hope knew she could have told Dess where to go using four-syllable words and without raising her voice once—if she hadn't gotten so pissed that her brain had shut off. Hope wished she knew why it was so easy for Dess to get to her. She was the one with the advantages here—the family, the mom who was home, the father who was *not* in jail, who was staring at her just then with his mouth a thin, tight line.

"Sorry, Mr. Carter," Dess said, sounding subdued.

Hope gave Dess a narrow-eyed look. *Suck-up.* She used her most mature voice. "We'll work it out, Dad. I apologize for shouting."

Her father let out a long sigh. "All right. Both of you probably need to raise your blood sugar. Come and eat," he said, and waited as Dess preceded him up the hallway. Hope, taking a step to follow, slumped as her father barred her way. She sighed, anticipating his additional dressing-down. This *so* wasn't fair. Dess had *started* it.

"So you want to tell me what this was about, young lady?"

Hope shifted uncomfortably. "No, Dad."

He shifted impatiently. "Hope, I know you're struggling to adjust to the changes going on. I know it's tough sharing space with someone your age, but first you snoop in private papers and now you're screaming and carrying on. Your mother and I expect better of you."

Hope's eyes stung as she staggered beneath the weight of his disappointment. It wasn't *fair*. Dess had started everything, but only *she* was in trouble. Wasn't she allowed to be hurt? Wasn't she allowed to be mad? She said, a little bitterly, "I know what you and Mom expect, Dad."

Her father gathered Jamaira closer to his chest and stared at Hope a long moment. Eventually he sighed and looked away. "Go on and eat. Since you two obviously aren't working on any project anymore, you've got time to help get the groceries and wash the cars when you're done."

Hope sighed. She knew punishment detail when she heard it. "Yes, Dad."

Shopping with her father was an exercise in efficiency. Usually Hope, her father, and her mother each had their own list and their own area of the store. They split up, each with a cart, and then reconvened in the checkout area fifteen minutes later to consolidate their haul and go through the self-check. It worked: Hope didn't have to stand around sighing, bored stupid while Mom read *every single word* on ingredient labels; Dad could talk to strangers without embarrassing everyone; and an hour and a half's worth of shopping was usually crunched, all told, into a half hour, if Mom could help and Austin wasn't whiny or Maira didn't need a diaper change in the middle of everything. Since a few weeks ago, when they'd had to go *back* to the store to return a pack of gum that Austin had walked away with, Hope and her father had been doing the shopping by themselves, and Mom had been keeping Austin's sticky fingers at home.

"Okay," Dad was saying, whipping three small sheets of yellow paper from a sticky pad. "Dess, you're on 'baking' through 'cans.' Hope, you've got 'toiletries' through 'frozen.' I'll take 'dairy' through 'produce.' Okay—twenty minutes, ladies."

Hope headed for the carts and yanked one free. Dess, looking wary, grabbed a cart of her own and followed Hope into the store. When Dad took off toward the right, Dess started to follow, then halted as Hope headed left. She stood with her cart in front of a pyramid display of tangerines, looking confused.

Hope shrugged and looked down at her list. Dess looked lost, but Hope knew better than to try to tell her anything. Wasn't Dess always acting like she had it together? Fine— let her. Dess Matthews wasn't Hope's problem. Not anymore.

Hope raised her chin and pushed her cart away.

DESS

. . . .

Bonus Bargains

"Hopeless—Hope! Wait!"

"What?" Hope's voice is flat. At least she took off those big old sweats; in jeans and a T-shirt, she looks normal, the kind of normal other people in the store have, confidently pushing their carts. Hope looks more normal than I do, stuck on *stupid* here with a little piece of paper in my hand. And a cart. When was the last time I got groceries by myself? When was the last time I was *pushing* one of these things instead of riding in it? Oh, that's right, *never.*

"What, Dess?" Hope asks again, sounding impatient. "We've only got seventeen minutes before we're supposed to meet at the self-check."

"I—I don't know how," I tell her, frustration wrapping the words in barbed wire. I hear the nasty tone in my voice, but I can't stop it. "I don't do all this domestic shit. I didn't have to shop at my group home. They just fed us, like normal people."

"Normal?" Hope sneers, stiffening. "You know the only other places where people who aren't sick or old just get fed and don't have to shop? They're called *prisons*. That's not normal, Dess, that's an institution."

"You know what? *Shut the hell up.*" If she starts in on Trish being in jail, I swear I'll—

Hope raises her hands defensively. "Look, I'm just saying. The only people who don't shop are in hospitals, in jail, or so rich they don't have to bother. None of that's us, so suck it up and come on. Or don't. I don't care either way." Hope turns away, but I hear her mumble, "Dad probably wanted us to do this together anyway."

Oh. I get it. This is Mr. Carter's idea of punishment. But for who?

Leaving my empty cart behind, I trail after Hope, stuffing my hands in my pockets. She pretends she doesn't see me glaring at her.

"Okay—since my list covers the far end of the store, let's do mine first."

"Fine. Whatever."

Hope checks her paper. "TP's on the back wall," she says, and turns the cart.

"What kind?" I ask, jogging toward the neat stacks of plastic-covered rolls.

"Meh, whatever's on sale," she answers.

I frown and turn back, hands on my hips.

"On sale? Seriously? You guys are rich. Who cares what's on sale?"

"Jeez, Dess, we are *not* rich." Hope rolls her eyes. "We have enough money, but we have bills to pay, just like everybody else."

Bills. Ha. When you've got bills, you have something to show for them. People who live in motels and then get kicked out just have stuff in the back of the car. I shrug. "Whatever, fine. You're the richest people I've ever met."

Hope hunches her shoulders. "Well, we're still not rich. And the one with the little puppies on it is on sale, so get a nine-roll pack, okay?"

"Fine." I grab the package and shove it down under the cart. "What else?"

She reads aloud from the list. "Contact lens solution. Diapers. Toothpaste. Tampons. Pasta. Cheerios. I'll get the toiletries and stuff. Do you want to see what you can get of the rest?"

"Fine, I've got it." I can do this. Mr. Carter had just better be there when we're done, though. I'm not standing around in public next to someone with diapers *or* tampons.

When we go inside with the first bags, Baby's dancing around with a toy microphone, singing Elvis songs along with the tinny little voice coming from the speaker. Foster Lady comes out to help—but I notice Hopeless disappears after one bag. Figures. Lazy heifer. Not gonna lie, though.

I'm only going to unload till I find my chocolate pudding, and then I'm out.

By the time I think about her being gone, she's back—in her ratty white sweats.

"What are you doing?" I ask after her third trip into the house with a load of Baby's coloring pages, stray socks, toys, and plastic sippy cups. All that mess was in the van, but Baby's just going to put it back.

Hope gives me a hard look. "What's it look like?"

I almost laugh. She looks guilty almost as soon as she opens her mouth. Mr. Carter probably told her she has to be nice to me. *Sucker.* I trail outside after her, smacking on a piece of jerky I liberated from my snack cabinet stash. "You have to clean up after Baby, too?"

"Dad wants the cars cleaned," Hope says shortly, and drags a vacuum behind her to the vehicle. She unhooks the hose from its housing, plugs in the vacuum, and flips on the switch.

It's boring watching someone vacuum, but I really have nothing better to do, and from the expression on her face, I know it's annoying Hope that I'm just lolling around in front of the house, in the sun, watching. I finish my jerky and pull out some chocolate-covered almonds, which I toss in the air and catch in my mouth. I throw the ones I drop into the garage, trying to hit Hope. She ignores me.

Eventually she climbs out of the van and picks up a spray bottle and a rag. Within moments, I smell fake orange scent wafting out of the van as she wipes down the seats, the dashboard, and the steering wheel. She is seriously *cleaning.*

That girl's trying way too hard to make me look like a slacker. Ha. Like I care if she works harder than I do. "You know, you're *so* good at cleaning," I say when she stops to wipe her sweaty forehead. "You should go into business."

Hope grimaces. "Please. I am going to school so that I can*not* do this, thank you. I hate cleaning."

I roll my eyes. Granny Doris cleaned *houses,* toilets and stuff. Cars are nothing.

She says, "Last summer? We had *ants* in the van 'cause Austin dropped a cookie under the seat, and Mom left the windows open. We had ants for *weeks.*"

I shrug. "It could've been roaches."

Hope gives me a sour look. "Either way, no thank you, I am not opening a cleaning business. Austin's enough of a slob for me."

"Baby's not a slob—he's *learning,*" I say, pricked by her criticism.

Hope points her spray bottle at me. "Yeah? *You're* the one who looked like you were going to throw up the last time we had burritos and he licked out the refried beans. He's 'not a slob—he's learning,' though, right?"

The smears of brown on Baby's face did make my stomach turn. Foster Lady had told him if he didn't use better manners, he was going to eat by himself, in the yard. Baby just kept licking his limp, disgusting tortilla, caring exactly nothing about what anyone thought. I shudder. "Okay, you're right—that was nasty."

Hope tilts her head—like she always does when she's about to get nosy. "So why do you call him that?"

"Who, Baby? Because . . . that's what I always called him. I thought that was his name when I was little."

"Cute." Hope climbs in to do the backseats.

It isn't. It's what *He* always said. *"Trish! Shut up that damned baby!"*

"Shut up! Shut him up!" Hard hands, shaking me. Him shoving me against the wall. Trish screaming, "Eddie—" Damn. My hands are so sweaty, they skate across my thighs as I try to dry them. My heartbeat is too fast, and I rub my chest as I shove the bad thought away, away into the dark, and heave myself up from the sidewalk. I talk myself down, like Rena told me to. Count backward from a hundred. *Baby's not ever going to see him, they got him for twenty-five years, Trish will make sure it's life—all that's over, so let it go.*

I blow out a breath and cross my arms. "So . . . you need some help or something?"

"Oh, you're offering now, when I'm almost done? Excellent." Hope gives me a sour grin. "Thanks *so* much, Dess."

"Not my cars." I shrug. "Do you want help or what? I can put the vacuum away."

She gives a nasty smile. "Yes, I want help. Thank you. Start on Dad's car."

I glance over at the ice-blue muscle car tucked into the garage. "Seriously? You have to do his, too? Are you in trouble or something?" I ask, suddenly catching on.

Hope makes a rude noise. *"Ding, ding, ding!* The girl

wins a prize. *Duh.*" She rolls her eyes. "Do you seriously think my parents can't wash their own cars? I usually vacuum only if I want money for something and they think I should suffer first."

"Suffer." *Please.* This little princess doesn't know what the word means. I roll my eyes at her drama. "Okay, fine. I'll vacuum Mr. Carter's car."

Hope pauses. "Seriously? Thanks. That would help. Um . . . pick up the floor mats and make sure to vacuum in the cracks of the seats, okay?"

I give her a slitty-eyed look. "I *know* how to vacuum out a car, Hopeless."

"You may think so, but Dad will just make us do it again if you don't get under the floor mats and into the seats, so try to get it right the first time, *Dessturbed.*"

I make a face behind her back and drag the cleaner to Mr. Carter's car. I've never actually vacuumed a car before, but how hard could it be? Rena showed me how the vacuum at the home came apart, so I figure out how to take apart this one and get up under the seats with the hose. It's not a huge car—it's a classic car from the '70s with only two doors—and since Mr. Carter doesn't have half-chewed animal crackers glued to the floor, there's not much to do.

When he comes out to check on us a little later, he sees me winding the cord for the vacuum. "I've got two worker bees!" he says, including me in his smile. I glare at him, slightly offended. Yeah, the bucket seats in his car look clean enough to eat off of, but I'm nobody's worker bee.

He opens the door to the minivan and looks around the inside, bending to check under the seats, prying up the floor mats, and checking the mirrors. He even opens the back doors and looks where the tire sits. Hope was serious—he is inspecting. I expect him to drag out white gloves. He nods. "Fine," he says gruffly to Hope. Then he smiles at me. "So you know how to work, Dess. Good for you. Go ahead and leave my car. I'll drive it through the wash at the gas station in the morning."

"I've already got water in the bucket," I complain. And I got my shoes wet filling the stupid thing, too.

Mr. Carter beams. "Well, thank you very much." He digs in the front pockets of his jeans. "Wait a minute, now, let me look . . . I can probably find a couple of bucks for my worker bee. Or at least a piece of gum and some lint."

He's making bad jokes as usual, and I roll my eyes like always, but I notice that Hope's already started wiping down the interior of his car. No expression on her face, she keeps working like a little robot, like this whole conversation isn't happening, and . . . her dad's digging out his wallet, smiling and stuff, like I'm the one who did all the work.

I glance at Hope. My hand is practically itching for the handful of singles or the five-spot that's coming. Mr. Carter's always got bank. Every day he's dumping handfuls of change out of his pockets, dropping us a couple of bucks for nail polish or ice cream sandwiches after school. I don't even have to stay on my hustle, with him opening his wallet every time I turn around, but—

It's like this: Foster Lady and Mr. Carter always talk about choices. When Baby's stubborn butt is getting hauled off to his room for one of Foster Lady's "think times," it pisses him off. But come on—ten times out of ten, the little booger-breather brought it on himself. He doesn't actually *think* yet, because he's little and whatever. But he's not stupid—when Foster Lady asks him why she had to send him to his room, he says, "Because I didn't choose to listen." It's hard to put into words, but something isn't right about taking money from Mr. Carter. Not because of Hope—if she runs her mouth at me, I can take *her*. But getting something for nothing—just me—feels less like a hustle *I'm* running and more like something else—something that has hooks and glue to catch my hands and hold me.

When you've got nothing, you've got nothing to be afraid of, nothing to lose. Though I have to force myself to do it, I choose to take a big step back. I'm not taking the money. Nothing can hook me that easy; I've survived being broke this long, right? I'm nobody's good little worker bee—not even Mr. Carter's.

I sigh loudly, rubbing my ear with a wet finger. "Um, Mr. Carter—you know Hope did the van, right? I just started helping."

He nods, even as he's digging out the wallet from his back pocket. He doesn't look in Hope's direction. "That's all right."

I chew the side of my cheek. Do I have to spell it out? "She's in trouble, but I started it," I mumble, quiet, so Hope won't hear. "If you bust her, you have to bust me, too."

Mr. Carter pauses in the act of extracting cash from his wallet. I can see green in between his fingers, and he watches me carefully. *Come on,* I think. *I was honest. Front me some for that. Tell me I'm a good kid and move on.*

"So I pay you both or pay neither of you, hmm?" he murmurs. Abruptly he smiles and shoves the cash back into his wallet. "All right, Dess. You girls stick together. That's good. I'll let you finish this up," he says, waving a hand, and goes to move the van.

Damn it, I am *such* a fool.

Forty-five minutes later, the ammonia we used on the windows stinks so hard, I can't smell anymore. My shirt is wet, and it's cold out here. If Mr. Carter wants his chrome polished, he'll have to do it himself.

"I'm out," I announce as Hope starts buffing the roof of her dad's car *again.* "I'm not going to die of pneumonia out here when a bird's just going to take a crap on the hood first thing tomorrow."

"Fine," Hope grouses, wiping her hands on the rag. "If Dad makes me come out again, though, I'm going to tell him *you* said it was good enough."

"Whatever." Trying to hold my wet sleeves away from my arms, I go into the house. Foster Lady catches up with me as I pass Baby's room.

"Dess. How's everything with you?"

I scowl. "Why? I didn't hit Hope or anything."

Foster Lady blinks. "Of course you didn't. You girls had

165

an argument, and you obviously worked things out yourselves. I just want to check in with you, and make sure we're all doing what we can to prevent future misunderstandings."

I think of Hope talking about my family like she knows something, and I snort. "Wasn't hardly a misunderstanding," I begin, then bite my tongue. *Shut up, Dess.* People don't want to hear nothing bad about their kids. All Foster Lady wants me to say is "Sorry, it won't happen again."

Foster Lady leans against the wall, quiet, like she's waiting for me to speak. "Okay," she says after a pause. "Well, misunderstanding or not, we can talk about it anytime." Her smile lights her face as she reaches toward my shoulder. "Whenever. Okay?"

Her hand will leave a warm spot on my shoulder. She'll probably squeeze like she always does after one of her "serious talks." I almost sway forward, leaning into it—

I jerk back. "Don't touch me." The words come out hard, and her smile blows out. Her hand freezes an inch above my shoulder. "My shirt's wet," I finish in a mutter, but she just steps out of my way.

"Sure." She nods. "It's chilly out. Better get dried off. There's hot chocolate in the cupboard if you want."

Safe in my room, I twist off my wet things and throw them on the floor, kicking them viciously toward the hamper.

I can't be letting Foster Lady get all touchy and stuff. She's just a blip on my screen, a temporary lady getting paid to pass out love like it's candy. If I let her get under my skin, I'll end up like Baby, calling her Mama and crying when I go.

Foster homes make you soft. At the group home, it's a lot of residents and not so much time with staff, and you've got to watch your back. Here, it's easy to get caught up thinking their bullshit is real. Mr. Carter's always telling me facts, making jokes. Foster Lady talks nice, but they don't know me—and no matter what they say or how they say it, bottom line is, it isn't real. Foster Lady's paid to be nice to me, to let Baby call her Mama like that. She can't like me better than my own family. Trish never talks to me that sweet, and she's supposed to be my mother. All that kind of shit does is make you weak, anyway.

Hard shivers shake me. I go into the clean, shiny bathroom and turn on the taps, all the way up. Rena at the group home always says a hot shower will fix almost anything. I pump out a big handful of body wash and smear it over my face. At least now my eyes are stinging because of soap.

HOPE

. . . .

Deep Waters

Hope closed her music folder and slumped as Mr. Mueller called a halt to rehearsal. They'd started learning "A Gaelic Blessing" for the winter program last year, and she was bored with it already, plus stupid Rob Anguiano kept calling it "Garlic Dressing," which stuck in her head, whether she wanted it to or not.

The whole choir was antsy, judging by how loudly Mr. Mueller had to raise his voice over the shuffling, whispers, and murmurs to make his next announcement. "Ladies and gentlemen, the callbacks for the Stillwaters auditions are going to be finished by the end of the week."

Around the room, students gasped. Darcie, the soprano sitting closest to Hope, fingered her dreadlocks and sighed, "Bor-*ing*," but Hope gulped hard in a dry throat. Mr. Mueller had started auditions the previous week—and

Hope hadn't gotten a second audition. If she didn't get one by the end of the week . . .

"Those of you who don't get a callback, you should know that the choices were very, *very* hard this semester, harder than they've ever been. That's all to the good, though—it means we'll get to sing some really great songs this year with the whole group." He smiled at them, and Hope cringed. It seemed as if his smile was especially for her. "We've got some talent in this room. Thursday, we'll jump right in with two new pieces, so come ready to roll. Hope Carter, please come see me after— Oh, there's the bell."

Hope tried to look unworried. Jas caught her eye and gave her a thumbs-up.

"You're in troub-le," Rob singsonged as he passed.

"Shut it, Rob," Jas told his friend, slapping him on the back of the head.

Hope sat rooted while her classmates surged toward the door. This wasn't a callback—she could feel it in her wildly beating heart. This was when Mr. Mueller was going to try to let her down easy.

"Hope?"

She wiped her hands down the front of her blue skirt and wobbled toward where Mr. Mueller stood, bent over the piano. He flipped through his grade book, jotted something down, and closed it, looking up with a smile, his floppy, light brown hair nearly in his bright blue eyes.

"Ah, Hope." He smiled but gave her his Serious Teacher Face. "I have a question for you."

Hope, expecting the words "About Stillwaters—sorry but maybe next year," was caught off guard. "A question?"

"Yes. Now, I understand there are some, ah, circumstances around Dess Matthews being at Headwaters this year, and she's staying with your family this semester. Is that right?"

"Circumstances." That was a nice teacher way of saying "Dess Matthews is a foster kid." Hope shrugged and wondered why Mr. Mueller cared.

"Here's the question. I wondered if you'd be willing to give up your spot in Stillwaters to give Dess a chance this semester."

Hope opened her mouth, closed it, and blinked.

Mr. Mueller's smile was kind. "You had a good audition, Hope—a great one. I have one more space in the sopranos, and it's earmarked for my dependable anchor soprano. But"—he clasped his hands together—"it could also be for Dess. I have a feeling that this could be an opportunity for her. She might never attend a school like ours again, never have the chance to find her voice, so to speak. I'd like for us to offer her that opportunity for as long as she's with us." He paused, and his voice softened. "I know this is a lot of pressure, and maybe you wish I hadn't asked. If you don't want to give up your spot, you can say no. I'll understand—I know singing with Stillwaters is important to you."

No, Hope screamed inside her head. *No, no, no!*

She uncurled her fists. Her nails were poking holes in her palm. "Can I think about it?" she asked, her voice wobbling.

"Of course." Mr. Mueller touched her shoulder lightly. "I know it's a big decision. You have a great big heart, but you love to sing, and this isn't easy. Why don't you take some time? Think about it and let me know on Friday."

Hope could only clutch her hall pass in her sweaty hand and nod wordlessly.

Give up her spot in Stillwaters for a semester? A spot she'd been planning on for three years? Miss the Broadway Night concert and the Christmas Lights show . . . so *Dess* could take her spot? In her most selfish heart of hearts, Hope wouldn't give up a piece of gum she'd already *chewed* for Dess Matthews. What was Mr. Mueller thinking? It wasn't fair. If he wanted Dess in Stillwaters, couldn't he just make a spot? Just because Hope was a foster sister didn't mean she had to give up everything for *her* foster sister. Just because Dess wouldn't have a chance like this again, or maybe attend a school like this, didn't mean that it was Hope's problem. She already had to share her house, her school, her friends, and— No. She wasn't going to give up her chance for Stillwaters, too. *No.* No, no, no.

Dess didn't deserve it. She hadn't earned it. It wasn't *fair.*

By the end of her last class, Hope was in a serious funk, matched perfectly by the sheets of rain pelting the asphalt. Even seeing Aunt Henry's heavy black pickup in the parking lot was only a momentary relief. Dess splashed past and took the shotgun seat next to her idol. Hope sighed and climbed stiffly into the back of the extended cab. It didn't matter where she sat. If Hope had sat in front next to Henry, Dess would have leaned forward the whole ride and butted into every conversation, tossing her hair and fluttering her eyes as if Aunt Henry was interested in her stick-child, juvenile self. Even if Hope asked Aunt Henry to turn up the radio, all Dess would do was chatter louder or, worse, close her eyes and, in a perfect, breathy voice, sing.

Hope glowered. It was Dess's fault Aunt Henry was even at school. Mom had told them the night before that they couldn't ride the bus home anymore. No stopping by the library to see what new books were in, no wandering past the community center to watch the boys play basketball. Instead, Hope was picked up and deposited on her front porch like a baby—exactly like Austin, actually—all because Dess had told her social worker she'd maybe seen some guy from her dad's old motorcycle gang. The man was in *prison* in *another state* and Hope still couldn't catch a break.

"I didn't see any tattoos," Hope had argued later in the privacy of her parents' bedroom. "He didn't even look at us. It was just some guy in a coffee shop, Mom!"

"It's a little thing to do, to help Dess feel safe," her mother had replied. And because it was a safety issue and Mom wanted to let Dess know she took her seriously, Hope couldn't ditch Dess and take the bus by herself, either. She was supposed to keep an eye on her foster sister. Hope snorted. She was sure Dess didn't know Mom had said *that*.

Today it wasn't actually that big a deal. It was pouring, and it was fine not to have to wait at the bus stop or walk down the block and across the street, jumping over the miniature rivers that formed in the gutter. But Hope felt crammed full of sharp, angry feelings, resentment, and frustration. They'd almost reached the middle of October and there were still weeks until Thanksgiving. Weeks of Dess changing the family routine, being in Hope's face, being right in the middle of her life. Hope didn't think she could take it.

Aunt Henry stopped the truck, and Hope blinked. She'd sat stewing and grousing to herself in the backseat all the way home. She gathered up her books as Dess gave Henry a giggling, flirtatious goodbye, then fluttered out of the truck.

"Hold up, H," Henry ordered. "What's going on with you? You're pretty quiet."

Hope shrugged, not meeting her uncle's eyes. "Tired."

"Too tired to talk to your Aunt Henry, huh?"

She pursed her lips. Today the "aunt" thing seemed embarrassingly babyish. Henry, sitting there at the wheel of his big truck, looking interested and concerned, seemed . . . fake. Nosy, really, and probably apt to tell Mom as soon as she talked to him.

Hope frowned. She didn't like this view of the world she had right now. How did Aunt Henry turn into the problem? Was Dess's nastiness rubbing off on her?

"Can I ask you something?" Hope settled back against the seat and closed the door against the rain.

Aunt Henry nodded and rolled his hands in a "Get on with it" gesture.

"If you were asked to give up something for someone you didn't really . . . um . . . *like,* would you do it? I mean, if there was something a person wanted to do, and they had a shot at it, but also could give their chance to someone else?"

Henry rubbed his forehead and frowned. "Why would I want to give up something if I didn't even like the person?"

Hope nodded, relieved. "See? Yeah. Ex-*actly.*"

Henry shook his head. "Oh, no, you don't. Don't make a decision based on me when I don't even know what you're talking about. Who's asking you to give up something you want to do?"

Hope sighed heavily and explained.

"Wow." Her uncle gave her a disbelieving look. "That's crazy! That's the most unfair thing I've ever heard."

"Well, he knows Dess is in foster care," Hope began.

"But still! That's just a ton of pressure. What's Robin say about it?"

Hope snorted. "What makes you think I told Mom?" She rolled her eyes. "Are you kidding? The right answer is 'Oh, yes, anything for Dess!' She'd get on my case for making Mueller wait till Friday to hear my answer."

"No, she wouldn't." Henry stuck out his hand. "Bet me. Five bucks says she'll agree with me. What your teacher is asking you is unfair. Dess is your foster sister, yeah, but you're just a kid. That's too hard a choice for you to make."

Hope blinked. She was *fifteen,* not five. "That's too hard

a choice because I'm just a—" She made a derisive noise. "Whatever, Aunt Henry."

"That came out wrong," he said quickly. "I meant—"

"What. *Ever.*" Hope snatched her backpack and got out. "Thanks for the ride."

"Talk to your mom, H," Henry called as she slammed the door.

Hope's conflicted, restless, and grumpy state of mind continued through the evening and the following day. She ignored Aunt Henry's texts, turned down Jas's offer to split a brownie at lunch, and was just generally out of sorts and uncomfortable.

Fortunately, Mom picked them up after school on Thursday, not Aunt Henry. Unfortunately, she had both Jamaira and Austin in tow and had to make a detour to the drugstore. As usual, Dess took shotgun. Hope slouched in back, wedged in between the car seats. Maira was asleep, but Austin, whose ears were hurting, was whining.

"Mama, I want to go," he said.

"Not this time, Austin," Mom said, putting the van into park. She left the keys in the ignition. "Don't turn up the radio too loud, please, girls. I'll make it short."

As soon as Mom was out and walking briskly through the mist toward the automatic doors, Austin's composure wavered. "I want to *get out,*" he moaned.

"Hang on, little man. Mom will be back," Hope reassured him.

Austin continued his whine. "My bottom is so *tired* of sitting."

Hope had to smother a laugh.

"Baby, shhh," Dess said absently. She had her earbuds in and was scrolling through her phone for music.

Hope glared at the back of Dess's head. Who was she to tell Austin to shush? She was supposedly so into her "Baby," but she wasn't even paying attention to him when he was sick. "You can take off your seat belt, Austin, but when Mom comes back, you get right in your seat, okay?"

Gleefully, Austin escaped from his seat and made for the keys in the ignition.

"Oh, no, you don't, buddy," Hope said, yanking him back toward her. She turned his head toward the rain-spattered windows. "Look outside. See? That store has pumpkins and scarecrows and Halloween costumes. See?"

"Can we go look?" Austin asked, finally interested in something other than his own misery.

"Um . . ." Hope glanced at Jamaira, then at Dess, who was still fully occupied with her phone. Hope tightened her lips and made a snap decision. "Yes. Let's go see. Pull up your hood, though, or your ears will hurt even worse. Come on."

Hope grabbed Austin and smacked the button for the automatic door to close, then splashed across the parking lot toward the seasonal costume shop and the little pumpkin patch adjacent to the drugstore parking lot. Austin clung to her neck and peered around happily.

Behind them, Dess wailed in a panicky voice, "Wait, Hope! Don't— Where are you going? Don't leave me with—"

"Oh, for—" Hope turned, impatient. Dess was standing next to the van, clutching her open coat at the throat.

"Just a minute, little man," Hope said, and headed back toward the van.

"You didn't even ask!" Dess complained as Hope came within earshot. "What if she, like, woke up or something? I don't know what to do with her!"

Hope, knowing Dess was right, shrugged instead of apologizing. "Okay, okay. Take Austin, then. I'll stay with Jamaira."

Dess zipped her jacket. "Fine," she said, holding out her arms. "Come on, Baby."

Austin transferred easily between the girls and pointed in the direction of the scarecrows. "Over there," he directed his mule, who sighed and carted him off.

Hope fiddled with Jamaira's blanket, but the baby was dozing, oblivious to the commotion. Hope slumped back into the seat, arms crossed, and watched a little girl in frayed shorts stick her fingers in the change-return slot on the pay phone and then into every single newspaper kiosk and soda and snack machine. The girl came away with a handful of forgotten change from a soda machine and gave a happy skip as she walked away. Hope wondered idly if the girl ever worried about getting her fingers caught. Maybe Dess had done that, trolling for change in soda machines, those two months she lived on the street. Hope twisted in her seat, looking to see where the little girl had gone, but she had vanished.

Hope settled back into her seat to wait. "Come *on,* Mother," she muttered as the minutes dragged. She stretched her arms toward the ceiling of the van and tapped her heel, transferring all of her nervous energy to her bouncing knee. She considered digging in her bag for her book, but she'd just get started and then Mom would be back, and she'd be at the part where something good was happening and she wouldn't want to quit and it made her nauseous to read in the car. Sighing, she tipped her head back and closed her eyes.

The opening of the door and a rush of cold air jolted her from her doze. Her mother settled into the driver's seat and looked around. "Sorry. Only one pharmacist working, and there was a line. Where's Dess? Oh."

Hope sat up as her mother pushed the button for the automatic door. Across the parking lot, Austin, free of his sister's arms, streaked away, splashing through puddles to get to the van. Dess followed at a less interested pace, still fiddling with her phone.

Hope got out and stood aside to let Austin clamber up to his seat, only halfway listening as Mom scolded him for running across the parking lot. She leaned in to check his seat belt, then climbed in herself as someone called sharply, "Miss!"

Hope turned.

"Miss! Miss, stop! That's not your car! Miss!"

· ·

Somebody's Little Girl

During fourth-period study hall, Rob and James sent me a single from some group called Manticora. First I couldn't find it. Then it screwed up the playlist I already had.

Sometimes I hate this phone.

Trudging across the parking lot to the van, I glance up to make sure Baby didn't do anything else but get back in his car seat. Jeez, he's such a pill when he's sick. First, he's all whiny, then he—

A hand lands heavily on my shoulder, and I jump.

It's the Felon! Oh, God—

My arms flail. My elbow jars into someone's ribs, and I hear a cry as I jerk away. From inside the van, I hear Hope's exclamation, but Manticora is roaring in my ears. I fumble to jerk out an earbud.

Wait, what? It's some old dude in a suit—rubbing his

chest, spitting mad. A Rent-a-Cop from store security? Aw, not this BS again. I didn't even go into the—

Both my earbuds are out now, and I back toward the van. The guy is still talking to me. He grabs my shoulder, scowling. "Missy, that's not your car."

Missy!? "Don't touch me." I jerk away, my heart accelerating. It's not the Felon, but some guy who thinks I'm jacking a car? What is his problem?

Foster Lady is out of the van, and into his face. "Take your hand *off my daughter!*"

Daughter?

God, what is going on? I have an instant, pounding headache as Foster Lady starts repeating, "What do you think you're doing?" and he's saying, *"Miss! Miss!"* and trying to grab my arm. He grips my sleeve and shakes, demanding my attention.

"Young lady, answer me, please! Miss! Is this woman your mother?"

"Get off me!" Ugh, I can see the little hairs growing in his ears. Foster Lady moves in front of me to get right into the guy's face, and I straighten, peering around from behind her. *That's it, geezer, step off.*

"Who's that man, Mama?" Austin's high-pitched voice is curious, innocent.

The old dude is blotchy, red. "Your *daughter?* I see a little black boy getting into a car, and a black at the wheel—"

The nasal way he says "a *black,*" like it's something offensive on his shoe, annoys me. I move from behind Foster Lady to confront him. "I was with my brother!"

The man darts a glance at Austin, then back at me. "Well, I *am* sorry, but you can hardly blame me." He continues, "You don't look— Well." He gives me what he must think is a kindly geezer look and rubs his chest again. "No harm done, right? You had your head in the clouds with those headphones, and I just didn't want you to get into the wrong car, my dear."

Ugh. I am *so* not his dear anything. I hope I broke his ribs.

I met guys like this after I left Granny Doris's house. Guys like this geezer with his oh-so-sympathetic hands, patting me on the head, telling me to go find my mom. Some of them gave me money or a piece of gum if I smiled right. And some of them said I should come and sit in their car, where it was warm.

They thought I was stupid, just like this man does.

"I appreciate your concern, sir, but I advise you to keep your hands to yourself next time," Foster Lady says in a low, cold voice. "If you'll excuse me, *my children* and I will go home."

Ten or twelve people hover on the edges of the store walkway, taking in the drama wide-eyed. They murmur audibly as the man stomps off toward the supermarket. His splotchy face and the skin wobbling under his chin make him look like a pissed-off turkey. Foster Lady gestures me back toward the van. She still looks . . . intense.

I rub my arms. I hate it when strangers touch me. But he didn't leave bruises or nothing, like the time mall security caught me when I was eleven. It could have been worse, I guess. Hope is full of *Are you okay?* and *That freaked me out* and a lot of other things. Baby just wants to tell Foster Lady about the scarecrow and *Can we have one, Mama, please?* Foster Lady's barely paying him attention. She'll be surprised later when he tells her she promised him two.

My head is full of static. Buzzing. I'm not Baby. I'm not shopping for a mom or nothing, but it's kind of funny. Foster Lady thinks of me as her kid. *Daughter.*

That is straight stupid.

In my bedroom, doing my Spanish, I sneeze as the acrid smell of nail polish remover burns my nose. I look up to see Hope at the bathroom sink with a cotton ball.

"Sorry." She tugs the door pull, ready to slide the pocket door between us.

"No, it's fine," I say, and get up from where I've been lounging on the bed, reading about Diego Rivera's murals. "You're done with homework already? Lucky."

"I'm not done, but the chips in my polish were distracting me from finding the area of a polygon," Hope says, and waves a hand. "Manicure emergency."

"Oh, yeah. I'm sure Ms. Mallory will understand." I watch as Hope cleans up the last of her glittery aqua polish and shakes a bottle of dark navy. "I can't believe how long your mom went off on that guy."

Hope twitches her shoulders. "And I can't believe you're so calm. Dess, he touched you. Like, hands. On person. Eww."

"What, he had old-man cooties?" I lean toward the sink

and reach for a cotton ball. Might as well change up my own polish. "You know how sometimes Ms. Aiello sort of directs people into her office with her hand on their backs? It was like that. Old dude thought he was helping me out." I don't tell Hope that I was thinking of breaking his nose.

Hope gives me an odd look. "Yeah, but . . . it would be one thing if you were Austin's age. Nobody should lay hands on you to 'help' you do something. Ms. Aiello shouldn't even do it."

"Try telling her that."

Hope snorts.

I swipe away the last of the silvery Diamond Crush on my thumbnail. "So, does that mean your parents never 'laid hands' on you? Never even smacked you?"

Hope tilts her left hand and admires the deep blue gloss slicked over her nails. "Mmm, not really. I mean, you saw Dad the other day—he was pissed, but he barely even raised his voice." She grins. "He dragged me kicking and screaming out of stores a couple of times because I wanted stickers or some crap, and Mom would've smacked my hand away from the stove and stuff, but . . ." She shrugs and meets my eyes in the mirror. "Mainly she and Dad talked, and talked, and talked—just like they do now"— she sighs—"till I got desperate enough to do what they said, just to shut them up."

I smile a little and toss my cotton ball in the little plastic garbage can on the counter. Yeah, I remember my first dinner with the Carters, when Baby whined. Nobody cared. I mean, not as if Foster Lady plays that whining thing for long—she always tells Austin he can whine in his room—but nobody hollered. Nobody hauled off and popped him one. I remember.

I've seen Baby being talked to until he's stomping his impatience, his fat bottom lip poked out in rebellion. When the Felon was pissed, he didn't talk—he swung. No talking from Trish, just me crying. Crying and ducking and saying, *No, Daddy, please, Daddy, stop*—

I force myself to move again, touching the brush to my thumbnail, thrusting the memory down and away. "Must be nice."

Hope's voice catches. "Oh. Dess—"

Crap. That didn't come out right. I wave my hand in front of Hope's sad face, hoping to distract her with my China-red manicure. "I meant . . . I was just saying . . ." I shrug again. "It's nice they try and explain shit instead of popping you in the mouth, that's all. You have nice parents."

"They are. They're amazing. Who would I be without them, right?" Hope clears her throat and fiddles with her cuticle. "And, um . . . I'm okay about sharing them, you know. My parents, or whatever." Hope gently bumps her shoulder to mine. Our arms, one wiry and pale, one rounded and brown, look alike as they rest against each other.

For a moment, I stand still, then I shrug, discomfort prickling the nape of my neck, my skin both warm and calm and tight and itchy. Right. Enough togetherness.

"Yeah. You think it's time for dinner yet?"

. . .

"He put his *hands on her.*" In the kitchen, Foster Lady's still all revved up. She's talking to Mr. Carter. I eavesdrop from the hall outside of Baby's room. "He put his hands on her, like he had a *right.* It was *that* important to make sure a Caucasian girl didn't get into the same car an African American boy was running to—and he's *only four!*"

A slam—probably the knife drawer. She's been slamming things ever since we got home and chopping stuff like she's decapitating people. At least it smells good, whatever she's making.

Mr. Carter says something in his much quieter voice, and Foster Lady answers him. "No, I didn't report him. He thought he was being a good person, I'm sure, but I tell you, Russell . . ." Her voice drops, and I can't quite hear— something about almost taking a pop? Taking him *out?* I shake in silent laughter, shoulders twitching. Foster Lady *does not play.* She got up in that man's face like a fierce black Amazon, and she was just about ready to slap the crap out of him. I should ask her if she was being *kind* when she got in his face. Heh.

I don't know why I'm skulking around, listening. It's just . . . funny, that's all. She's pissed, *still,* and we've been home for a couple of hours. Not gonna lie—I don't want some stranger touching me, either, but it's not like I'm a little kid who doesn't know better. If he'd kept ahold of me, I'd have bashed his nose in with my head—he'd have let go fast then. I did it when I was eleven. I know not to let some bastard grab me. I wasn't going to let him *hurt me* or nothing. But Foster Lady's like one of those little birds at Granny Doris's house—they make their nests in the carport and then get all pissy and dive-bomb you every time you get in the car. Foster Lady acts like that guy tried to steal me out of her nest.

Drama. Who the hell knew Foster Lady was gonna get all crazy just from some man grabbing me? She would've hit the roof if she'd seen the soccer coach at Stanton. He always was grabbing people.

Granny Doris wouldn't never been able to pinch me, not with Foster Lady around. Foster Lady probably would kick the Felon's ass, too.

I wish.

"Hope! Dess! Austin! Somebody needs to set the table!"

"I'm on it, Robin," I say, coming from around the corner.

She jumps a little and gives me a sharp look. "You're right here," she says, which really means, *How long have you been eavesdropping and how much did you hear?*

Mr. Carter gives me a look, too, but his look has a lot more smile to it, around his eyes. "Prompt and cheerful, Ms. Dessa. You must be feeling all right, then?"

I duck my head from his look. "That old man didn't bother me. I'm good."

"All right." As I go by, he lifts his hands for a high five, like he does when Baby puts his toys away.

Jeez, really? I roll my eyes. Weak. Totally weak. But I slap his hand anyway.

186

Driving home from my dental appointment after school the next day, Mr. Carter pulls into a turning lane. A loud engine makes me look at the turning lane to my right, and as the motorcyclist nods to me, my heart stutters.

It's one of the Brotherhood—one of the Felon's friends.

He's wearing gloves, so I can't see his hands, but I know. I know it's one of his. I've seen that bike.

"Mr. Carter," I blurt out. "That's the guy! The one from the coffee shop!"

And Mr. Carter, thank goodness, doesn't need me to explain. "The motorcycle club guy? Are you sure?" he asks, peering across me and out the passenger window.

"I'm sure he's from the same club," I whisper. I know the motorcyclist can't hear me through the glass, but I can't find my voice. I pull my hood closer to my face.

"Hang on, Dess," Mr. Carter says, signaling a turn. "Breathe, girl. Breathe."

When the light changes, Mr. Carter makes his turn, then turns again into the parking lot of a drive-through coffee shop. The motorcyclist shoots past, and I lean forward to follow his turn into the parking lot of the grocery store down the block, then out of view.

Mr. Carter joins the line for the coffee drive-up and glances at me.

"You all right, Dess?"

"No." My breathing is rough, and I'm shaking worse than Trish off her crank. "I hate this."

"What 'this' do you hate?" Mr. Carter asks as we inch closer to the order window.

I shrug. Right now I kind of hate everything. I even shake my head when Mr. Carter offers to order me a mocha. I smile a little bit when he orders a double-tall latte, a mocha, and a child-sized hot chocolate instead. Hope and Baby will be happy when we get home, anyway.

When we move away from the pay window, Mr. Carter hands me the cardboard container that holds the drinks and pulls around the back of the coffee shop and into a parking space. He leaves the engine humming and looks out at the cars coming and going for a moment before he turns to me.

"Your social worker said your father was arrested on drug charges in Arizona two years ago."

I nod, fiddling with the cardboard handle of the drink tray. "Yeah?"

"They arrested him, and if he escapes, he's got the bounty hunters and the police chasing him. He's already made threats against your mother, and if a hair on your head gets touched because of him, he's in twice as much trouble. That's a lot of risk, just to chase down one little girl he hasn't seen in years." He leans forward to catch my eyes. "I know that when you were small, he—"

Damn it, this again? I jerk to face him. "I don't care if you don't believe me—"

"Wait!" Mr. Carter interrupts. "I know you're taking this seriously, Dess. So am I." His voice gentles. "I know the man is scary. I know he terrorized you and your mom when you were a kid. I just don't want you to let him get to you. He wants you scared. Don't give that to him. Your mom's going to testify, and for once the bad guy is going to be put in jail for good." He takes another deep breath. "Remember when I told you that your name, Odessa, is from the word 'odyssey'? You have a long life full of adventures and experiences to look forward to, just like the Greek warrior Odysseus. Your whole journey is ahead of you, Dessa. But you can't keep moving forward down the road if you keep looking behind you."

I lick my lips and stare at the gray carpet on the floor of the car. It would be so good if I could believe him, if I could stop jumping at every shadow and waiting for—expecting—those big hands with the hard-callused fingertips to grab my arm and yank me away from everything. It would be so easy if I could stop waiting for it all to go to hell.

"Dess?" Mr. Carter's voice is quiet. "I know I'm just an old dude to you, but I'm an old dude with a fast finger. I can have the police here before you know it, and if anything threatened you, I'd have your back. You know that, right?"

I relax a tiny bit. He's old, but I'm pretty sure Mr. Carter's okay. "Yeah, I know."

He half smiles. "Okay. So, would you be willing to do an experiment?"

"Like . . . ?" I raise my eyebrows.

"Like we follow that guy." Mr. Carter jerks his chin toward the road. My eyes widen as the guy on the motorcycle drives out of the store parking lot down the block, turns, and stops at the light.

"I'm right here, Dess, and we're safe in our own vehicle. I would stay two cars back, and he would never see us. We could follow him, see where he goes, and you could let yourself relax a little if it turned out he wasn't who you thought he was. . . . Or we could call the police and report him. Either way, Dess, you'd know. You could act, and you'd *know*."

"I—I . . ." The words I want stick in my throat. He's right there—*just right there!* I could—I could—

I clench my sweaty fists.

The light changes. The motorcycle roars through the intersection and out of sight.

I slump, relief mingling with disappointment. I glance at Mr. Carter out of the corner of my eye. He is watching me, sipping his coffee patiently.

"Sorry," I mumble.

He shakes his head almost before the word is out. "No, no, no," he says. "Don't *you* be sorry. *I'm* sorry that you don't feel safe."

"It's . . . He sent someone after me when I was eleven." The words come out in a lightning-fast blur. I haven't told anyone this—not even Farris. I'm blinking fast, and my mouth feels dry. I pick at a bump on the cardboard tray. "He didn't, like, come after me on purpose, but I was in Arden, after Granny Doris said she didn't want me, and I was living—well, I was in the mall sometimes during the day, but I couldn't always sleep in there. I would get under a bed or something in the furniture department, but you can't always do that. So I was living rough, and this lady had helped me in this one neighborhood, so I was kind of hanging around this little Mexican market, and then a bunch of guys rode up on bikes. And one of them decided to . . . to take me into the market with him. To get me a little something, he said."

The cardboard has twisted in my fingers. I smooth the pulped edges. "He told me to go in and talk to the lady at the checkout and ask her to help me, at the back, and then he'd get me something. And I was hungry. He said he would get me a burrito, so I did what he said. I asked her to help me . . . way in the back. And they all got in there, and they had guns, and they shot the lights." My throat constricts at the blur of memories from there—the sound of breaking glass, the blood on the lady's lip from where her cheek was gashed, the stink of sugar as they tipped soda bottles on the floors, the smell of exhaust and gasoline as the ringleader pulled me into his lap and roared away. And the lady's voice rising. *¡Dejarla! ¡Dejarla! Pobrecita . . .*

"She tried to stop them from taking me on the motorcycle, but they hit her. And one of them had a tat on his hand like Eddie's, but he wasn't wearing the jacket, so I didn't know, I didn't know, and . . . even the lady gave them money, everything out of the cash register. People did that—everyone did. Even Trish did what they said.

191

I knew I had to go with them, because Eddie sent them. I—I— They let me leave the next day."

The terror of those hours returns—being fed candy and treats like a favored pet from a man who bragged what a good little girl I was, how he stroked my hair and touched my face while he knocked back bottle after bottle of some cloudy brown booze. It was almost like being with Eddie, with that gimlet-eyed attention focused right on me. When he had a girl come to brush my hair and "fix me up," I'd told her I was Eddie Griffiths's kid. The girl was scared.

While she and another girl were arguing about what to do with me, I climbed out the bathroom window and hid in a muddy drainage ditch. I ran all night—and I hid every time I heard a motorcycle. I shoplifted in a drugstore with a security guard, just so I could get caught, just so they'd lock me up, so I'd be safe from ever having to be that scared again.

I feel tugging on my hands. It takes me a moment to realize that Mr. Carter is trying to take the mess of the coffee take-out tray from me. He's already taken out the other coffee, which is good, because there's not much left of the holder.

"Shit," I mutter, grabbing the teetering hot chocolate and putting it into the car's plastic cup holder in front of me.

Mr. Carter pushes it into my hands. "Drink it. You need something sweet."

I warm my hands on it a moment, surprised they're so cold, then sip gingerly. He arranges the other cups in the cup holder as I drink down the sweet chocolaty heat and feel my spine start to thaw.

Mr. Carter sits for a moment, sipping his coffee. Outside, it begins to sprinkle. "You know what I think?" he says quietly. "I think your mother is one of the bravest women in the country. I think you should be proud to be her girl."

I blow out a long exhale. What I think about Trish is a mix of stuff, like always, but her telling them she's going to testify and finish Eddie once and for all makes me hope a little. Like maybe she's going to go through with it. Maybe we're going to be okay for real.

She's got to be freaked out of her mind, knowing Eddie could mess her up so bad, but she's going through with it. She's doing it anyway. They say that's courage, right?

Am I proud to be Trish Matthews's kid?

"Yeah," I tell Mr. Carter, after a long pause. "Yeah, I am."

· · · · · · · · · · · · · · · · · · · ·

Party of Two

Thursday at chorus, Hope realized the best person to talk to about Dess taking her spot in Stillwaters was probably Dess.

"I have to talk to you," she whispered as Mr. Mueller moved students around the room for one of his free-form rehearsals.

"What?" Dess whispered over the boys beginning their slow do-be-dos.

"Is chorus your favorite class?" Hope blurted.

Dess wrinkled her face. "It's okay. Why?"

Hope gave a quick shake of her head. "Never mind. Later."

Dess shrugged and went back to her music.

Mr. Mueller rearranged the chorus lineup three times, mixing and listening. Hope was exhausted when the chime rang. As she joined the group returning music folders, Mr. Mueller called out that he'd see the class next week and that the Stillwaters list would be posted Friday morning.

Crap. Hope winced. She'd run out of time.

Hope followed Dess to her locker. "Did you try out for Stillwaters?"

Dess shrugged and fitted the tiny locker key in the padlock. "Not really. I didn't audition or anything, but Mr. Mueller had me sing after chorus the first day. Why?"

"Do you really want to get in?"

"Did you read your text? Are you coming to our party, or what?" Rob Anguiano whined, trying to get Dess's attention. He glanced at Hope. "Hey, Carter."

Hope raised her eyebrows as Dess covered Rob's whole face with her hand and shoved him away, looking annoyed. "I'm talking here, Anguiano."

Rob ducked her hand and crowded her. "Look, just tell me if you're coming to the party."

"Party?" Hope asked. "Whose party?"

Rob barely glanced at her. "Me and my brother Levi's birthday, same as last year." He prodded Dess's shoulder. "You coming, Dess? Say yes."

Dess threw up her hands. "Jeez, Rob, yes. Yes, I am coming to your party. Happy now?"

"Thank you." Rob threw up his hands, too. "Why is it so hard to get a straight answer out of some people?"

Dess turned her back on him and smiled at Hope. "What are you wearing?"

"Wearing? Um, I—" Hope stalled. She couldn't think

about a party. She needed this Stillwaters thing settled. She wished Rob would go away. "I'm not going. Look, Dess—"

"Anguiano!" Dess barked, grabbing Rob's arm and digging in with her nails.

Rob widened his eyes in pain. "Ow! What?"

Hope sighed. Maybe she could catch Dess after school. "Later, Dess," she said.

"No, wait, Hope. Rob, you didn't invite Hope to your party?"

Hope widened her eyes. "Dess!" she hissed.

"Well . . . I didn't text her. But Hope knows she's invited. Everybody's invited. I mean, you came last year, right?" Rob squinted at Hope, rubbing his arm.

She gave him a sick smile. "Yeah, sure. I guess."

Dess sighed loudly. "Moron, say it right."

"What?" yelped Rob, cringing from her nails again.

"'Hope, would you come to my and Levi's party?'" Dess asked in a robotic voice. "Repeat, idiot."

"I'm not an idiot. Hope knows she's invited to our house," he grumbled before stomping toward his locker.

"Dess, why would you do that?" Hope demanded, her eyes stinging.

"Do what?" Dess looked bewildered.

"Why would you force Rob to invite me to his party?"

Dess's jaw dropped. "What? I didn't—"

Hope blinked back tears of anger. "Look, it wasn't a big deal. I've known Rob and his twin brother, Levi, since the first grade. I could go to any party of theirs if I wanted to."

"Yeah, except they didn't tell you about it," Dess pointed out.

Hope opened her mouth to rebut this, then closed it. "Whatever. Forget it."

"Yeah, whatever, fine. I'm going to be late for math." Dess ducked around her and headed for the hall.

Sighing, Hope turned back toward the choir room.

"I'm sorry to hear that, Hope," Mr. Mueller said, his forehead wrinkled. He looked a little confused. "You've been an anchor for the chorus for a long time. Can I get you to reconsider?"

"I don't think so," Hope said, feeling as if a rock was stuck in her trachea. Her hands were shaking. She'd thought and thought, and this was the best thing she could do—for everyone. "I just need a change."

"Hmm." Mr. Mueller frowned. "Well, how about we talk again next Tuesday?" he asked, signing his name on the yellow hall pass and ripping it from his pad with a flourish. "Okay, Hope? I'd really, *really* like you to just take your time with this decision."

"But—" Hadn't she just said she didn't want to reconsider?

"Just take your time," Mr. Mueller repeated. "Don't make a decision today, all right?"

Hope sighed heavily. "Fine," she muttered, and trudged out of the room.

Now Mr. Mueller wouldn't let her drop choir and join

band as her elective. How dumb was that? She'd taken flute lessons and could at least play as well as the worst freshman. Music wasn't a requirement, but Hope needed another elective or she'd have two study halls. First Mr. Mueller wanted her to give up Stillwaters for Dess. Now he wouldn't let her drop chorus, even though doing so would mean she wasn't eligible to be in Stillwaters at all, and Dess could have her spot—as he'd *wanted*. Why were teachers always so *difficult*?

Though she was supposed to go straight to her next class, Hope went to her locker instead. She stared at herself in the mirror, rubbed her face until it tingled, then gave herself a swipe of lip gloss. She didn't want to look how she was feeling, which was depressed and sad and stupid.

C'mon, Hope. Cheer up, she admonished her reflection.

If she didn't want to look the way she felt, she couldn't think about stupid Rob and his stupid birthday party and stupid Dess, who, even though she hadn't even *meant* to this time, had gotten on her last nerve. She couldn't think about Stillwaters, either, and regardless of what Aunt Henry said, Hope *refused* to think about talking to her mother about it, especially now that she'd found the best solution for everyone. It had made total sense: join band, which had separate concerts and separate practices, and she wouldn't have to hear Dess sing her part with Still-waters. Done.

It was the perfect solution. Why couldn't Mr. Mueller just agree with it?

Hope slammed her locker. *I want you to take your time*

with this, she mouthed to herself, her lips twisted in a mockery of Mr. Mueller's "worried teacher" face. He didn't get it. She didn't need *more* time to understand that everyone wanted Dess around more than they wanted her.

At least Dess wasn't in her sixth-period study hall. Hope slouched into the classroom and handed Mr. Nash her yellow slip. She folded her arms and lowered her head to her desk. Mr. Nash never let anyone sleep in study hall, but Hope decided that if he bothered her, she was going to say something about her period, which usually freaked out the male teachers, or that she was seeing black spots and had a migraine. She actually kind of *did* have a headache. Her *life* was making her head ache.

"So, we're doing this party next weekend?" Dess asked Hope as they stood in the pickup area on the sidewalk above the parking lot. Below them the traffic warden tweeted on his whistle as cars threaded through a crazy maze of orange cones and high school students.

Hope kept her eyes on the cars. "Nope."

"You're mad at me because I asked Rob." It wasn't a question.

Hope ground her teeth. "I'm not mad at anyone. I'm just not going."

"I'm not going, either." Dess shrugged and put in her earbuds.

Hope turned her head stiffly to glower over at Dess. "Yes you are."

Dess shook her head, a brow raised. "No I'm not."

Hope sighed, resentment sapping her energy for argument. "You can't not go just because I'm not going."

"Who says that's why I'm not going? Maybe I just don't want to go. You can't tell me I can't."

Hope sighed again, loudly. "Dess . . ."

"Hope . . . ," Dess mimicked, and Hope scowled, her temper igniting.

"Look, don't be stupid, all right? Just go. I don't need you feeling sorry for me."

"I don't feel sorry for you," Dess said reasonably. "I feel *pissed*. Rob was an ass. We should go and be completely hot and not even *talk* to him. Plus, Hope? Jas is going to be there. You like Jas, right?"

Hope ignored the jolt to her stomach and looked back at the lines of cars, pretending she hadn't heard that last question. It was nice that Dess was pissed for her, but—"It's *Rob's* party, Dess."

"Your point? We'll go shopping after school and make outfits, and it'll be cool."

Hope raised her chin. "I didn't say I'd go."

Dess groaned. "Oh, come *on*."

"I'm not the party girl in this family," Hope said, a little bitterly. "Just go, Dess. You're the one everyone wants anyway."

"Oh, jeez, Hope, seriously? That's not even true. Forget it, we're going. *Please?*"

Hope stared. Dess was looking at her, right in the eyes,

a little wrinkle in the middle of her forehead. Her almost invisible blond eyebrows were twisted in entreaty, her pale blue eyes pleading.

Hope bit back the questions that wanted to shoot out of her mouth, like *Why?* and *Seriously?* and *Is it that you need someone to hang with or what?* Instead, she imagined herself and Dess, gliding superciliously past Rob, noses in the air, dressed like the runway models from glossy magazines. Studying Dess's wistful expression, something eased in Hope's chest, and she sighed, feeling her shoulders settle.

No matter what Dess said, Hope wasn't going to look like a model or anything. No matter how glam she got, people would probably not really notice she was there, as usual. But who cared? Hope wanted to go—she wanted to dress up and go and hang out—even if Rob *hadn't* invited her.

"Okay." She gnawed her lip, noting with relief the familiar minivan idling in the procession of cars. "Okay, I'll go. But I don't need to shop or anything. I'll wear jeans."

"Everybody needs to shop," Dess corrected, and added, smiling happily, "I'm glad you said yes. Seriously, we're going to rock that boy's world. Ooh, there's the van. I call shotgun."

Hope gave Dess a dry look. "I don't know why you bother calling it. You always get shotgun."

"If you ever remembered to call it, *you* could have it."

Rolling her eyes, Hope hefted her bag and schlepped across the parking lot behind Dess, pondering parties and boys and worlds that would be rocked. At Dess's startled

"Who's that?" she looked up and squealed, feeling her whole life improve.

"It's Grandma Amelie!"

"Hey, girl! Hop in!"

Hope bounded into the van, and Grandma Amelie leaned across the driver's seat to give her a hug.

Hope beamed. Her grandmother visited frequently from her condo in the city two hours away, but every visit was still a treat. She had a big voice and big gray curls shellacked into a high bouffant. Today she was wearing a big cowl-necked aqua sweater with pink, yellow, purple, and navy geometric designs on it. Except for her height and long, straight nose, Grandma and Mom looked as alike as a bowl of granola and a pile of sequins.

"Well, hello," Grandma Amelie greeted Dess, who hung back, her body stiff with wariness, and her expression sullen.

"Grandma Amelie, this is Dess Matthews, my foster sister. Dess, this is my grandmother, Amelie Larsen," Hope said, reaching out and dragging Dess forward. "Dess is Austin's birth sister."

Grandma Amelie adjusted her red-framed glasses. "And so I've heard. Nice to meet you, Dess. Go on and get in before that parking guy gets to waving his arms at me again and snaps my patience."

Hope fastened her seat belt and leaned between the two front seats. "When did you come? Are you staying overnight?"

"I'm staying until Friday. I've got to see my doctor, and I

thought I should stop by and see my babies." She beamed over at Dess. "Robin's my biggest baby, and Henry's my littlest one, but I've come to see the rest of my babies, too."

Dess finally found her voice. "Excuse me, Mrs. Larsen? Where did you get your sweater?"

Grandma gave a bark of laughter. " 'Mrs. Larsen'? Darlin', my mother-in-law passed on to her reward years ago. I am 'Grandma Amelie' or 'Ms. Amelie' to you, Miss Dess. As for the sweater—I don't even remember where I got this old thing."

"From the 1980s," Hope muttered under her breath. "And they want it back."

Dess turned in her seat. "We have *got* to find a sweater like that," she said, her expression intent. "Hope, you could rock that sweater at Rob's party!"

"What?" Hope and her grandmother said in unison.

"Are you crazy?" Hope whispered fiercely as she followed Dess to her room. As usual, Grandma Amelie had insisted on sleeping in the family room on one of the fat futon couches, so Hope kept her voice down to avoid offense. "How could you tell my grandmother you want one of her awful muumuu sweaters? I'm not wearing that!"

"Well, duh, you're not going to wear it like it is *now*," Dess said, waving her hands. "Don't you like the pattern, though?"

"No! And there's, like, *miles* of it," Hope complained. "It's horrible and *huge*."

Dess sighed. "Okay, so it's a little wild. But with some work, it could be cute."

"A *little wild*?" Hope repeated. The garish clash of colors was burned on her retinas. She couldn't understand Dess's enthusiasm. "Even if you unraveled the whole sweater and knit another one, it wouldn't be cute. And you can't even knit, can you?" She gave Dess a look of slitty-eyed menace. "Look, Dess. I just got Grandma Amelie to start giving me money for presents last Christmas. If you get her all excited about buying me ugly clothes again, I will kill you to death, you evil heifer. Understand?"

Dess snorted and threw her bag on her bed. "If I'm already dead, who cares?"

"Seriously," Hope whined. "You can't tell Grandma Amelie stuff like you *like* her *clothes*. What is the matter with you? The woman wears sequined *sweat suits*."

"So? Sequins can rock. I like your grandma's clothes better than my Granny Doris's." Dess kicked off her ankle boots. "Even when she picked me up from school, all I ever saw Granny Doris wear was those quilted housecoat things."

"Now, those are *super* cute," Hope said in saccharine tones. "I'll wear *my* grandma's sweater if you wear one of your grandma's housecoats, mm-kay?"

"Actually, now that I think of it . . ." Dess trailed off thoughtfully.

"Ugh! Stop!" Hope pleaded. "You're crazy, you know that? I will not go out in public in a grandma sweater! How do I even know you can sew?"

"You have to wear it," Dess pointed out. "Your grand-mother already took 'before' pictures and put them on her online photo album. She says I have to take a picture of you in the dress for the 'after.'"

"Well, that's not going to happen." Hope scowled.

Dess laughed, a surprisingly evil chortle. "Your mom said she'd take it."

Hope's eyes narrowed. She stomped into the hallway. "Mom!"

Dinner was broccoli stir-fry, two kinds of pot stickers, and steamed rice. Aunt Henry was late, so they started with-out him. Grandma Amelie regaled Dess and Hope with stories of Mom's girlhood. Mom rolled her eyes a lot, and Dad tried to keep Austin from imploding with the sheer excitement of having an extra person to play with.

Aunt Henry finally arrived in a burst of cold autumn air, wearing his regular uniform of plain blue work pants and a blue T-shirt with the fire station emblem on the shoulder. He gave Austin a high five, then kissed Grandma Amelie, who was eating one-handed, cuddling Jamaira.

"S'up, Mommy," Henry said, and snitched a pot sticker off her plate.

"Boy, get your own food." Grandma Amelie swat-ted him, then pulled him closer for another kiss. Hope smiled. That was Grandma Amelie all the way through—halfway smacking you in line and halfway smothering you with love.

"How's work? Been busy out there?" Dad asked as Mom filled a plate with colorful stir-fry, a scoop of rice, and the fried and steamed dumplings.

"Thanks, Rob. Not too bad, Russ," Aunt Henry said, taking the plate and shoveling in a mouthful of hot food. He continued, "Getting a lot of overtime, teaching CPR this month. . . . You're awfully quiet over there. How's it going, Texas?"

Hope caught her foster sister's expression. Dess, sneaking glances at Aunt Henry, looked more witless and worshipful than usual. Under cover of the table, Hope kicked Dess's foot. "Aunt Henry says, *How's it going, Texas.*" Hope spoke with an exaggerated enunciation, as if translating from a foreign language.

Dess blinked, turned a blotchy pink, and kicked Hope back, harder. "Everything's great," she said, smiling through gritted teeth. "Thanks."

"This young lady asked if she could buy my sweater," Grandma Amelie said, apparently oblivious to Dess's whisper of "Quit kicking, heifer," and Hope's muffled snort. "I'm going to wash it tonight and give it to her."

Aunt Henry choked, then coughed noisily. Hope slapped him on the back as he blinked. Eventually he straightened and gave his mother's sweater a long, slow look. His voice serious, he deadpanned, "Halloween, huh? You going as a jester, Texas?"

Grandma Amelie yelped. "*Jester?* Henry Aaron, you wouldn't know fashion if it *slapped* you. My sweater is

206

many things, but it is *not* a clown sweater." She gave an injured sniff.

"I like your sweater," Mom said loyally, patting their mother's arm.

"Suck-up," Aunt Henry coughed, and jerked away as Mom swung a fist.

"I'm pretty sure we had a couch covered like that in the seventies," Dad said reflectively. "Could be worth selling as upholstery fabric."

"Anything I make with it will be worth selling when I'm done with it," Dess said, ignoring Aunt Henry's whoop of laughter and Grandma Amelie's furious protest.

"I can't wait to see it," Mom said, laying her hand on Dess's arm. "I have complete confidence in your design sense."

Dess preened a bit, sitting tall in her seat. Across from her, Hope rolled her eyes expressively. Design sense? *Puh-lease.*

Catching Hope's eye, Aunt Henry gave his niece a meaningful glance before setting his plate on the counter. "Thanks for dinner and the entertainment, folks. Mom, I'm off Monday night. I'll come by Tuesday and take you to Good Day Cafe for breakfast." He jerked his chin toward the door. "H, walk me out," he ordered.

. . . .

Do-overs

"I'm sorry I don't have more," Foster Lady says, handing over a picnic basket with a lid. "These days I don't do much but make patches for Austin's play clothes and replace buttons."

"It's fine," I say, digging through the basket to find a stuffed felt mushroom bristling with pins, two pairs of plain steel scissors, spools of colored thread, a tiny foil sheet of needles, and a variety of buttons, hooks, and other odds and ends. This stuff, along with my kit, a black marker, and a roll of masking tape, is enough to start with.

"It's not what you need for a real project," Foster Lady is saying, biting her bottom lip. "If you make me a list, I'll be sure and get you what you need from the fabric store tomorrow—"

"Yeah. Uh-uh, it's fine," I repeat, forcing my smile wide, willing her to go away. "Really. This is great. *Thank you.*"

"I can tell when I'm not wanted," Foster Lady says, finally catching a clue. She wishes me a good night. When the door clicks shut, I wait until I hear her steps fade. Then I hurry to the bottom drawer of my bedside table.

There's a lumpy roll of blue satin cloth nestled behind my socks. It's frayed on the edges, and stained—really, I should wash it. Instead, I hold it close to my nose, imagining I can still smell Granny Doris's hand lotion the day she gave this to me, when I was tiny and believed that Trish would stay forever and that everything Granny Doris said was true.

Carefully I unroll the slick fabric and lay it flat on the bed, frowning over the places it has frayed. My fingers ghost over the little pockets, each with a small treasure. First, the blunt-tipped metal scissors that Granny Doris bought me when I was six, which are too small for my hands now. Then the odd buttons and an old house key filling one little pocket, the flat paper spools of colored thread that fill another pocket, and, finally, the filmy roll of Stitch Witchery, the ribbon of fabric glue Granny Doris taught me to use with a warm iron when I was eight. It's not much. Mostly, there's inspiration in this little seamstress kit. I found picture after picture on the Internet of other people who took old clothes and made them better than new. I taught myself to use my tools to change my dolls' looks. It was only a tiny step to learn to change my own. And now . . . Hope's. And she'd *better* wear it.

I roll up my sleeves, and get started.

It takes just a second to pull from underneath my bed

the T-shirt I stole from Hope's laundry—clean, of course. I'm not trying to get my hands gross and germy. Putting a bath towel down on the floor, I spread out the gigantic sweater, inside out, and lay the T-shirt on top, aligning the shoulders carefully. I pin it down, trying to keep the pins straight along the edge. The sweater sleeves are huge, so I'm extra-careful to make the T-shirt lie flat, so the under-arms of the sweater match exactly. Too much fabric, or a weird cut, and it will be totally jacked up.

Near the middle of the T-shirt I stop pinning. Picking up my marker, I draw a flared curve, making an A-line from the waist to the sweater's hem. I can barely see the line I've drawn, so I take out my roll of masking tape and follow it all the way down. It looks weird, this pieced-together pattern, but it'll do.

Once the sweater and shirt are stuck together with every pin I have, I start the boring part—sewing it all together. If Ms. Amelie wasn't in the family room, I could use Foster Lady's sewing machine for this, but it's no big deal—I'll have to hem it anyway, so I can make the seams really tight later. This is just to be on the safe side, before I cut anything.

Choosing a strong white thread that I can see against the jumbled colors, I sew fast, sloppy stitches through both layers of the sweater, marking a new seam along the pins. No matter how fast I sew, this is going to take forever. I wonder if Foster Lady will let me move the machine into my room next time.

From the bathroom I hear movement and then a tenta-tive knock.

"Hey, Dess? Can I come in?"

"What did I say?" I singsong.

"Dess! Come on," Hope whines. The door creaks as she leans against it.

I laugh, then swear, stopping to suck the finger I've just stabbed with a straight pin. I have to pay attention. "Not until it's done."

"Oh, come *on*. I just need a peek. Give me some proof—" Hope begins, but I cut her off.

"What did Henry want after dinner? Did he ask about me?"

Hope snorts. "You wish."

I do, but I play it off. "You know he wants me. If he's seeing someone, I will track her down."

"Whatever, jailbait. Anyway, how weird would it be if you were my Aunt Dess, and practically the same age?" Hope pauses, and the doorknob rattles. "Come *on*. Just let me—"

"*Hope,*" I mimic. "Go away. Just till it's done."

A huffy sigh. "I'm not going to wear it. I never said I would."

"You're going to wear it, if I have to knock you down and dress you, woman."

A burst of laughter. "You're violent, you know that? They have medications for *Dessturbed* people like you."

"Yeah? Well, you're *Hopeless*. There's nothing we can do about that, but I'm *trying*."

"Hate you," Hope grumbles.

"Backatcha." I smirk.

"If this little makeover dress makes me look bad, I will *end you.*"

I give a gasp. "Violence! Is that any way to talk to a *foster child?*"

A snort. "Bite me."

After a moment the door creaks as Hope removes her weight. I hear the click of the mirror-fronted cabinet closing and then the buzz of Hope's electric toothbrush.

I suck my finger. I have stabbed myself five times on this stupid thing. Hope had better appreciate the blood I've shed into this fabric.

I double-stitch the last bit of thread, double-knot it, and snip off the remnant with my teeth. After sticking the needle into the mushroom, I smooth out the heavy knit fabric, running my eyes along the white outline. Now for the moment of truth.

I pick up my scissors.

"It's a costume party." Natalie scowls, twisting her pale blond ponytail. "Rob says Levi changed it to a costume party. I don't know why—it's three weeks till Halloween. I haven't started thinking about a costume yet!"

"Me neither," I lie, trying to look concerned. Actually, I don't care if it *is* a costume party. Hope and I are going to dress as *hotties.* That's the best costume, anyway.

Of course, every time you have something else to do, school seems to last your whole life. I'm dying to go home, and by sixth period I'm about to fall over. I'm tired, my neck is stiff from bending over on the floor until late, and I want a nap. When we come in, Hope's standing by the piano, talking to Mr. Mueller, and he's shaking his head, smiling. She looks pissed. Honestly, I'm too tired to care, but I try to be nice.

"What's the matter?" I ask as she grabs her folder and heads for her seat in the row in front of me.

"Nothing," she says, her mouth tight.

If that's the way she wants to play it, okay. I shrug and slump down in my seat.

All through chorus, Hope sits stiffly in her seat, barely opening her mouth to sing. The moment the bell rings at the end, she's on her feet with her bag in hand, the first one headed toward the door.

"The Stillwaters list is posted on the bulletin board," Mr. Mueller calls above the rising noise. "Congratulations to everyone who made the cut. See you next week."

I yawn so hard, my eyes water as I put my folder in its slot. On tiptoe, I crane over the crowd by the bulletin board and see that Hope made it in. Good for her. Why's she pissed, though? Then I see it: my name, next to the words "soprano alternate."

Is that her problem—she didn't want me in the group?

I hesitate, eyes on the column of names. Hope's been okay ever since she got all pissy the other day. She couldn't be mad I'm in Stillwaters. I mean, she told me I had a nice voice. I didn't ask her to say that.

Stupid. None of that means anything. I shoulder my way through the crowd toward my locker. I don't care about the stupid list, and I hate the way my chest feels tight.

Hope is waiting for me, arms crossed.

"It's not what I wanted." Her voice is as sharp as the crease between her eyebrows. "He was supposed to put you in."

I drop my bag. "Huh?"

"I *asked* you. Remember when I asked you if you liked chorus? Mr. Mueller asked me— Well, he *said* he was going to put you in. Then he made you an alternate."

"But . . . I . . . It's fine." I shrug. "Doesn't it mean I sing, like, every other concert or something?"

"That's not what it means. I—" Hope looks thoughtful. "On second thought, that's brilliant. We could try that. . . ."

I roll my eyes. "I am brilliant, duh. Recognize."

Hope sounds normal now. "Shut it, blondie. This is a better idea than Mueller's, anyway."

"Great." I yawn and pull my math book out of my locker. "Anything else? I've got to go sleep through math."

"Slacker." Hope shakes her head and tsks.

"Yeah, instead of being a hard worker like you, who's not making her foster sister clothes to wear," I remind her.

Hope gives me a dirty look. "I am *not* wearing a grandma sweater in public."

The rest of what she says is drowned out by the bell, and we take off running.

· · ·

My plan was to just lie down for a little nap before I started my homework, but Foster Lady wakes me with a knock on my door.

"Dess? Mike Bradbrook's here," she says, her voice muffled by the door.

"What's *he* doing here?" I whine, staggering out of bed. I got the monthly social work visit a week and a half ago, and he brought up those letters from Granny Doris again. I don't want to talk to him.

I take my time in the bathroom, running a brush through my flattened hair, slapping cold water on my face. When I finally open the door, Foster Lady is still hovering in the hall. Her face tips me off—it's serious. Somehow, she looks like a stranger, more like Amazon Lady again. As I shuffle down the hall, I can feel my skin tightening and chills prickling up my spine.

. . . .

Crossroads

Bundled in her magenta wool cape and matching faux fur hat, Grandma Amelie looked like a gigantic round berry with a fuzzy top.

"Come walk with us," Grandma Amelie invited as Austin wriggled and stomped into his boots. "We're just going to circle the block a few times till this guy burns off some energy."

"No thanks." Hope waved a lazy hand. "I burned off all my energy at school." She wasn't particularly tired, but Dess's social worker had arrived minutes before, which meant that as soon as Dess came upstairs, Mom might have a few minutes to talk.

"If Austin is good, we might pick up one of those little balsa wood planes from the market by the park," Grandma said in a loud whisper.

"Really? Wow," Hope whispered back while Austin's eyes rounded.

Hope smirked as the door closed behind them. Little kids were so *easy* at times.

Mom wasn't in the kitchen, but Dad's French press was half-full of dark brew and the electric kettle was hissing for tea. Hope heard Dess thunder by and decided to make the Mexican chocolate she loved and see if anyone else wanted some. She was whisking little beads of chocolate into a pot of hot coconut milk when her mother bustled into the kitchen, brow furrowed.

Hope licked chocolate off her spoon. "Hey, Mom, did Aunt Henry talk to you?"

"Hmm? Henry?" her mother said. She braced Jamaira in her sling with a hand on her back. A quick stretch and she grabbed a mug from the cabinet above the sink. "Talk to me about what?"

"Um . . . school stuff?" Hope offered vaguely. If Aunt Henry hadn't said anything, Hope wasn't going to, but it would help to know how much explaining she had to do on the Stillwaters thing.

"I haven't talked to Henry since— Hold on, sweet," Mom said, turning away with a frown. From the living room came rising voices.

Dess, sounding sick. "*What?* No!"

Hope pushed a hand against her stomach. Her foster sister sounded *awful*. Hope took a step toward the dining room door, wishing she could get close enough to hear Mr. Bradbrook's quiet words.

"Oh, *crap*. I can't— Bradbrook!" Dess wailed, sounding desperate. "I have to go!"

Now Mr. Bradbrook's voice rose. "Wait, Dess. Just calm down. Until we have more information, what's best is for you to—"

"You know what would be best? If somebody would make sure Eddie's boys stay off my grandma. I *told* you he was dangerous. I *told you*. He probably sent someone to *push her*. Where is she?"

"Well, the regional hospital for now, but, Dess, her condition is—"

"Is someone keeping watch on her?"

"I'm afraid that's not—"

"Seriously? Nobody's looking out for her, and I can't even go see her?"

"Dess—just wait, please. Listen. I—"

"*YOU* listen to *ME*! Granny Doris needs somebody watching her. She didn't just fall. She's not that old, all right? The Felon sent someone to push her. I don't care what you say. She was pushed. She. Was. Pushed!"

The whisk slipped from Hope's fingers as Dess raced past the kitchen. From the upstairs hall echoed a ringing *slam!* as her door shut.

Hope blinked and turned to her mother. "What's going on?"

Her mother gestured toward the whisk and the pot of bubbling milk. As Hope hurriedly began to stir again, her mother sighed. "Well, obviously, Dess has had some bad news. When you've finished, take her some cocoa and see if she's all right, okay?"

"And have her bite off *my* head?" Hope protested as she

218

gave the cocoa a final whisk. "Thank you, no. *You're* the mom. *You* go see what's wrong."

"I already know," her mother said, pushing an extra mug in Hope's direction.

Hope poured cocoa into both mugs, but her mother turned to tuck a tea bag into her own mug and doused it in boiling water. The spoon clicked against the mug as her mother stirred. Hope waited.

"You're not going to tell me," she said, finally catching on. "You think if you don't tell me, I'm so nosy I'm going to go upstairs and ask Dess myself."

Her mother just made a noncommittal humming noise and rubbed Jamaira's back.

With a grunt of irritation, Hope carried the cocoa down the hall to her room. Of *course* she was going to go upstairs. Her curiosity—nosiness—had won again.

She kicked the door. "Dess?"

"I don't want to talk."

"Fine. Take your chocolate, though."

In a moment, the door slid open. Dess, stiff-faced, her makeup smudged, reached with both hands for the mug with a grudging mutter of "Thanks."

Hope, questions pressing against her tongue, just nodded and took her mug over to Dess's bedside table. Tucking her leg beneath her, she faced her foster sister, and found herself . . . waiting, her stomach in nervous coils.

Dess sipped her drink, then sighed. Abruptly she leaned against the wall, as if she was too tired to stand anymore. "I'm going down south."

"What?" Hope's mug wobbled, and cocoa splashed her hand. She absentmindedly wiped the back of her hand on her jeans as her stomach clenched. "Where? Why?"

For how long? Would she come back?

Dess carefully sat on the floor and exhaled, seeming to fold in on herself. "The old lady broke her hip. I have to go see her."

"Your grandma?" Hope's stomach lurched as she imagined Grandma Amelie's big, tall body falling. "Jeez, Dess, I'm sorry. Is she all right? Do they know what happened?"

Dess shrugged and shook her head. "Nope."

Hope's lips parted in dismay. "Is she— She can't tell them?"

Dess shrugged shortly and glared at the floor over the rim of her mug. "They're looking around, I guess. Social services is involved, 'cause the neighbors found her outside and she was loopy. They're not listening to me, though. Bradbrook says old people fall and break their hips all the time. But somebody probably pushed her." Dess shook her head.

"I heard you say that," Hope said without thinking. "This sucks. I wish you didn't have to go."

Dess's expression went blank and sullen. "I wasn't going to stay here forever."

Hope recoiled. "Well, I know, but . . ."

"It's not like anyone can control when psycho motorcycle thugs attack people."

"Motorcycle thugs?" Hope looked confused.

Dess set her jaw. "It's what happened. *I* know it, even

220

if nobody believes me. It was one of the Felon's Notorious Brotherhood guys. Eddie always got away with this crap. But this time, Trish is going to make sure he gets nailed forever." Her voice rang with conviction.

"Well . . . good. I guess," Hope said lamely. She picked at a bubble in the mug's glaze, a mess of confusion. Dess was a pain, but Hope had finally gotten used to her. And now she wasn't going to be around to hang with her at the Anguianos' party, or complain about the fluff from Hope's faux fur bathrobe, or use all of her crackle-coat nail polishes. She glanced at Dess's nails, and sure enough: red with yellow crackle glaze. Hope shook her head. Just when she'd gotten used to things, everything changed. Again.

It would be weird to have access to the laptop anytime she wanted it, and she'd have to start watching *Jeopardy!* with Dad again or he'd be all depressed. And Austin—

"Wait, what about Austin?" Hope asked, her pulse fluttering in her throat. "That's his grandma, too, right? Does he remember her? Will he be upset?"

Dess froze. "I—" She shook her head wordlessly.

"Well, good he won't be upset, but . . . Austin's going to miss you." Hope decided not to mention again that she'd miss Dess a little, too. A little.

Dess hunched as if she'd been slugged in the gut. "That— It's—" She cleared her throat, and her voice splintered as she said, "Baby doesn't need me. Y'all take good care of him. He'll be all right. I've got to see about Granny Doris."

Hope sipped her cocoa, then licked her lips. "Look,

Dess. You could tell Mr. Bradbrook to bring you back. It's not fair you have to be with only your grandma and you don't get to be with Austin. You just got him back."

"I don't want to talk about Bradbrook," Dess said, rubbing her arms. "And Baby doesn't need to be mixed up in Trish's drama," she added. "Farris shouldn't have moved me here with him, anyway."

Hope gave her a shocked look. "But Austin loves you. You love him—and he should get to know his own sister, don't you think? Your social worker should think about that—moving you might do psychological damage or something. I mean, Austin's only four. He can't keep losing his sister. People—people can't keep losing people." Hope rose, brimming with determination. "I'm going to talk to him. The two of you should stay together."

Dess looked up, her eyes filled with something Hope couldn't name. "No," she said quickly. "Look, Hope—just leave it. Bradbrook won't listen."

"Yeah, he will," Hope said, firming her jaw.

"I'm glad to hear Dess has an advocate," Mr. Bradbrook said a few minutes later. He smiled over his coffee at Hope, but his eyes were tired. "This placement is working far better than expected. Of course Dess and Austin *should* be together. They're family."

Hope was confused. Didn't Mr. Bradbrook disagree? Wasn't that what Dess had said? "Yeah. They should be together. And if you think any motorcycle guys are going

222

to come here now that they beat up Dess's grandma, they won't. They don't know where Dess lives."

"Hope—" her mother murmured. She'd put Jamaira down and was leaning against the wall in the dining room, her arms clasped around her waist. She looked—worried.

Hope turned. "What? Mrs. Matthews didn't tell where Dess lived, did she?"

"That's not it—" Mr. Bradbrook's mouth tightened, and he glanced at Hope's mother. Hope turned to her as well.

"Mrs. Matthews was unconscious when she was found, Hope." Her mother looked hesitant. "She was able to say Trish's name when the EMTs brought her out of the house, but she hasn't said anything more."

Hope's stomach lurched. *"Oh."*

If Mrs. Matthews had known where Dess was, then she could have told, Hope realized. A shiver skittered up her back. The old lady could have given her attackers a hint, or even told them everything. The social worker and Mom had no way of knowing.

"We have to get Dess out of here," Hope blurted, panic racing through her nerves.

"There's nowhere to go."

Dess's voice startled Hope, and she turned. Dess was in the hallway behind her. She pushed past Hope and stood in front of Mr. Bradbrook.

"The Felon always found us. Trish moved us to three different houses in Houston. We moved to Arizona, then to a trailer park in San Diego. He found us anyway."

"Stop, Dess," Mr. Bradbrook said, his voice firm. "First,

Hope, Mrs. Matthews simply fell—we have no evidence that she was pushed. Second, yes, your father followed your mother, Dess, but let's not give Eddie Griffiths power he doesn't have. She remained in contact with him. This time, he and members of his gang are in prison, where he cannot hurt you. I don't have concerns about the rest of his motorcycle club finding you—"

"They will." Dess's voice was lifeless. "They found Granny Doris, didn't they?"

"Dess, you're not listening, babe," Mom interrupted, moving to put an arm around Dess's shoulders. "No one knows how she fell. It was very likely something like a slick sidewalk or a cat twining around her legs when she was getting the paper or picking up the mail. Older bones sometimes break when people fall. People slow down and become fragile as they age. It *happens*."

"Your grandmother hasn't had much contact with your mother in the last five years," Mr. Bradbrook added. "When there were threats made against your mother, Mrs. Matthews wasn't concerned for her own safety, and she felt she didn't need to change where she was living."

"You guys asked her?" Hope worried that Mr. Bradbrook wouldn't answer her, but he gave a slight nod.

"Mrs. Matthews wasn't concerned about anything, that I can promise you."

Hope looked back at Dess, who stood stiffly next to Mom, staring at the floor. Dess's face was a funny grayish shade, the same color as Jamaira's powdered formula. "I need some privacy," she muttered hoarsely.

Hope blinked, then realized her mother was gesturing to her. "Oh, okay." She glanced at Mr. Bradbrook and tried to smile. "Thanks for talking with me."

"You're welcome," he said.

Hope glanced back at Dess. *It's going to be all right,* she wanted to say, but the little polite, bogus words of comfort were worthless, and held the bitter taste of a lie.

DESS

. . . .

For Old Times' Sake

Four years. For four years I told them to shred every letter. For four years she kept trying to talk to me, and for four years Farris, now Bradbrook, has kept every one. A letter a month.

I stare in silence at the folder full of letters as Bradbrook blah-blahs on at me about something. Why the hell did she keep writing?

She's always hated Eddie. When Trish got sick of Eddie or one of her other men beating her up and came crying to her mom, Granny Doris used to say that the Felon was like those nasty roaches, the kind that survive even after you spray everything at them, the kind that will be here just fine when they bomb us and end the world. Roaches never die. He knew Granny hated him, and if you mess

226

with him, Eddie Griffiths *always* gets you back. If he found Granny Doris once, he'll find her in the hospital.

I'm not going to have that old lady's dying be on me. I *told* them somebody's got to look out for her.

As soon as I can, I leave the table. The couches in the family room are rough against my face, but I like sitting here in the dark, pressed into the fat, scratchy pillows. It feels like I'm sitting on a thick old woman wearing an ugly housecoat.

In the dim afternoon light, I pretend that I'm still little, sitting on Granny Doris's lap. I pretend that she's here, and not laid up, broken and bruised in some hospital. I pretend that I'm small and sweet like Baby, and still believe everything she says.

"Your daddy loves you all, but he's got things to do," she used to tell me when he would leave Trish and me on our own in the little house. At first, we'd be fine, but then he'd stay gone. Trish would run out of drugs and cry for days, and then she'd pack us up and we'd go stay with Granny Doris in her trailer park for a while.

Your mama and daddy love you, but they need some time to work this thing out. Trish would go to find him, and I would wait with Granny Doris. And wait. And *wait.*

Your mama loves you, and she's going to get herself straightened out this time.

Like Bradbrook said, Trish stayed in contact with the Felon. Sometimes Trish went looking for him, and we found a motel close to where he was. Sometimes when she needed crank and she didn't find him, we moved and we moved, and she kept looking. Sometimes, she left me to look for him, and didn't come back. Sometimes, after she found him, Trish was so messed up on crank that she didn't think about coming back for me until she was broke and sick, or he'd beaten her up, and she was in jail. I'd call Granny Doris to come get me, and months later, after Trish did her time, she would find some tatted-up loser to drop her off, looking like a human skeleton, on Granny's front porch.

And it would all start over. No matter how many times he beat her up, no matter how many times she ran from him and hid, he'd hunt her down or she'd go back. Again and again Trish would choose my father, the Felon, over Granny Doris and me. Until it stopped.

Until the day I called Granny Doris to get me, and instead a social worker came.

I don't know why I wish for the days when I used to believe anything. I don't think a lie would help, even though that's what I want to hear right now. I just want somebody to say they can fix this, that I don't have to.

"Family is important," Bradbrook keeps telling me. I hear that, but Granny Doris sure didn't. She left me and Baby hanging, the racist hag, and now, when she needs somebody, there's nobody. Trish is in lockup again, and other than Baby, Granny's all I've got. I'm all *she's* got.

Damn.

After the first few, the envelopes aren't even open. I pick up the one with the oldest postmark, tilt the yellowy notepad paper toward the light, and read the spidery script.

Dear Odessa,

I am so sorry that I couldn't take care of you this time. When you left up out of here mad today, I know you didn't believe it when I said it was best you stay with that lady from the state. Thing is, doctors told me I had no business trying to raise nobody's baby anymore, not with my blood pressure like it is. You're a big girl now, Odessa. Look after your brother. When you get over your mad, you write me and tell me how you're doing.

Your grandma,
Doris Lee Matthews

Some of the letters are just cards—for holidays; for my birthday, with a limp five-dollar bill enclosed; for Valentine's Day, showing a cross-eyed poodle with a glitter-covered bow; for my graduation from the eighth grade—and that one has a whole ten dollars inside. Some are just notes scrawled briefly on her little yellow notepad, and most repeat the same last line, *Tell me how you and your brother are doing.*

I read quickly, grabbing the next letter and then the next letter in the stack, the pressure mounting in my head. The spidery handwriting has, over the past several letters, grown loopier and larger, the swooping capitals not as steady anymore.

Dear Odessa,

Today I am seventy. Your mama has been my only child now for just under forty years, and you have been my firstborn grandbaby for fourteen years.

I got a call from your social worker, telling me how proud she is of how you're doing at that high school. I am proud of you, too, no doubt about it. You keep it up, girl. When you got nothing else, you've got your brain to keep you going.

You come see me sometime, and let me know how you are doing.

Your grandma,
Doris Lee Matthews

I scrub my face across the tweedy fabric, my stomach twisting. I promised when I was eleven I'd never run away again. But Bradbrook isn't listening, and I've got to see Granny Doris. I owe her.

On the bus, it's about eight hours to Rosedale; I checked the first week I got here. With the money from Granny Doris and my allowance, I have enough to get me on a city bus to Arden, and I can walk from there to Granny Doris's trailer park. In my sewing kit, I still have my key. Farris will know where to look for me once Bradbrook tells her I'm gone, but I'm hoping Mr. Carter will think I met somebody at Rob's party or something. If she wouldn't run her mouth, I'd tell Hope the truth, but that girl's *Hopeless* for real. She couldn't keep a secret from Foster Lady or Mr. Carter to save her life.

I won't miss anything—except Baby. But it's not like this place is home, so walking away doesn't matter. I walked in this house with one bag, and that's what I'll leave with. You can't lose what you never had.

I'm lying, but it helps.

It doesn't take too long to make my plans. I have two pieces of picture ID, and time to myself online. It's easy—too easy—to point, click, and leave.

My stomach boils with nerves, so I set up Foster Lady's sewing machine. I'm not feeling it, knowing Hope is going to hate me for everything the day after she wears it, but there's no point not finishing her dress now that I've got it this far.

I center the bulky fabric across the machine and line up the needle carefully. The only thing I can really do with a sewing machine is sew a straight line, but that doesn't matter— all I need is a line right now, to tighten up the seams I've already sewn. I've got fabric glue for everything else.

By the time Hope's grandmother comes in, the shoulder seams have two lines of stitches—just don't look too close at the threads hanging out all over the place—and I'm cutting the dress loose from the machine. All I have to do is fold down the cowl part and maybe glue some leftover fabric on some big buttons or something to make a cool neckline. One big, ugly cowl-necked sweater plus time, thread, and glue equals one cute off-the-shoulder mini–sweater dress. I didn't even have to shorten the sleeves that much.

"Well, look at that!" Ms. Amelie crows, holding it up. She prods the seams, and turns it carefully right side out, examining it closely. "Girl, you are an artist! Is this what you're going to school for? You're going to be a dress designer?"

I give a half smile. Ms. Amelie is funny, how she acts like everything I do is such a big deal. "Nah—I just make stuff like this for fun," I say, picking up a piece of thread off the floor. "People who design dresses have to be able to draw. I can only do stick figures."

Ms. Amelie clicks her tongue. "Just for fun—*pfft*. You don't need to draw if you can see the design in the clothes already. You could make good money opening a dress shop with clothes like this, Dess. Don't sell yourself short, now."

I try smiling, but my face feels mannequin-stiff. Yeah, I'm sure all the big-shot designers have their moms doing time for using meth and their daddies doing time for selling meth and guns while riding with the Notorious Brotherhood. I can't imagine myself, in any kind of "someday," growing up to open a dress shop. How can I, when I can't even imagine myself past this week?

Ms. Amelie seems like she reads my mind.

"It's not always going to be like this, Dess," she says, and squeezes my shoulder. "You've got a lot going on right now, but this is gonna pass, and then you'll go on and there will be all kinds of possibilities opening up for you."

Now my smile is real. She sounds like Rena, talking about "limitless possibilities."

232

. . .

"Aren't you still working on Hope's costume for the Anguianos' party?" Foster Lady asks when I've sat on the
floor in Baby's room for too long, watching him play.

"Nope."

For the past hour, Austin has been scribbling out neck-
less, noseless people on sheets of scratch paper—Foster
Lady, Mr. Carter, Hope, a floating rock with eyes that's
supposed to be Jamaira, and me—with bright green hair
and a pink mouth. Baby's drawn us all with orange and
green crayons and given us all pink mouths. We look as
alike as peas and carrots, but he asked me to spell "family," so the word marches up the page in his backward,
giant print. It matters very little in Baby's head how "real"
families look.

Foster Lady sinks to the floor next to me, her thick legs
bent, ankles crossed, in one of her yoga moves. She watches
me in silence for a moment. "Dess, I hate to see you just
give up."

"I haven't given up," I say with a frown, nudging a piece
of crayon toward Baby. He draws so hard, he breaks them
in half. "There's nothing to give up on."

"I know you're worrying about your grandmother, but I
hate to see you sitting here with the kids like you have nothing else to do," Foster Lady says. "It's Thursday night—no
movies, no homework, no phone, you're just . . . here."

I shrug.

"Well, what are *you* wearing to the Anguianos' party tomorrow?"

I'd forgotten that *I'd* need something. I shrug again. It doesn't matter anyway.

"Have you decided not to go?"

I scowl. Hope would love to skip that sweater. Not *even*. "Oh, I'm going."

"Well, then, let's go shopping. Let's find you a costume better than anybody's."

"I'm not going in a costume. I'm going as myself."

Foster Lady rolls her eyes. "Fine. Then let's get your 'self' something nice to wear."

I shake my head. I can't face the idea of the mall—stores full of strangers. "Nah. I'll wear jeans."

Foster Lady looks at me for a moment, her eyes narrowed. Then she digs in her pocket, and dangles a set of keys. "Okay, how about this? We *could* go shopping . . . in my brother Henry's closet."

Henry's— I choke on my words and cough. It would be *amazing* to wear something of Henry's. I wouldn't even cut it up. I'd take one of his blue button-up dress uniform shirts and wear it with the sleeves rolled over my nubbly crocheted tank, belted, with skinny jeans, or—maybe Liesl's red miniskirt? Or maybe I could—

Foster Lady just watches me, a grin widening her face, making her eyes crinkle.

I press my hands to my hot cheeks. Foster Lady's cackle is straight *evil*. Whatever. She can laugh if she wants to.

234

"Are you serious? We can go to Henry's house, and pull stuff out of his closet? For real?"

Foster Lady nods. "We'll take some of his old clothes. He'll never miss them."

I'm on my feet. In spite of everything, a party sounds . . . interesting. "Let's go."

HOPE

. . . .

Casa de Anguiano, 6 p.m.

Hope touched her hair—flat-ironed and unfamiliarly smooth—with the back of her hand.

Dess growled. "Don't."

"I'm not even touching my face," Hope objected.

"Don't," Dess repeated shortly, peering out from under the tilted brim of Aunt Henry's fedora. "Don't touch your face, don't smudge your lipstick, and don't keep pulling that!" Dess slapped Hope's hands away from where they tugged futilely at the hem of her sweater dress.

"It's too short," Hope hissed, darting a glance at the front seat. Her father was driving them, and his raised brows and long exhalation had been *his* statement on Hope's outfit.

"It is not," Dess argued for the nth time. "When you

stand up, it's just above the knee, which is fine. And anyway, you're wearing boots *and* tights. It's not like you're flashing your backside at anyone."

"You'd better not be," Dad muttered from the front.

As Dess glowered at her, Hope smiled to herself. At least the party had distracted Dess from the hole she'd dropped into after her social worker came. Hope had asked her mother if she believed the story about the motorcycle gang, and Mom had said, "What's important is that *Dess* believes it." Dess yelling about the dress was a lot better than Dess sitting in the dark, too depressed to move and too scared to stand by the window.

Hope's father braked as they turned and approached the security gate. The guard in his little house waved them through when he found their names on his list. The gate slid back silently.

Dad cleared his throat. "Okay, ladies, let's go over the rules again. Stay with the group. If somebody spikes the punch, both of you drink some water and tell an adult. We're leaving at fifteen minutes past ten o'clock, on the dot. If I have to—"

He slammed on the brakes, and they all strained forward against their seat belts.

"Hey, Dess. We're here," Hope said unnecessarily.

In silence they stared at the line of stop-and-go traffic from the car to the split-level ranch house up the wide road. The house and porch were lit with spotlights, revealing a circular drive and a three-tiered fountain.

"Jeez. That *pink* thing is Rob's house?" Dess stared, stunned, as they slowly approached the sprawling coral-and-cream stucco with the terra-cotta tiled roof.

The house always made Hope think of a gigantic frosted cake. She laughed. "Yep. That's Rob's house. Remember when you thought *we* were rich?"

Dess gaped. "The Anguianos are rich? *Rob?* But ..." She trailed off, her brow furrowed. Hope half expected her to say something dumb, like the sorts of things she'd said about black people when she'd first come, but Dess just sputtered. "He doesn't even act rich!" she finally managed.

"How do you know?" Hope asked. "Maybe Rob's how real rich people act."

Dad tapped on the horn and waved at someone crossing the street, who waved back. Hope leaned across the car toward Dess and peered out the window. There were tons of cars and tons of people walking up the path to the house. The Anguianos knew everybody. And *everybody* was going to see her dress.

She looked at it and gulped. She kind of liked it—mostly. Instead of bright bands of neon-aqua blue at the hem and sleeves, Dess had replaced the knit with wide black ribbon she'd found somewhere. The original, oversized neck Dess had folded flat and decorated with a pair of big black buttons, turning yards of stretched, sagging knit into a cute off-the-shoulder cowl neck. With the rest of the sweater tight enough to hug Hope's body and not just hang, the dress didn't suck. Hope just wasn't sure it was *her*. It was short, tight, and bright. Could she, Hope Carter, wear a slightly-longer-than-usual, off-the-shoulder sweater with black tights and tall black boots in public, in front of Jas and God and everybody? Her sweaty hands said no.

"I'll have to drop you girls by the door and find somewhere to park," Dad said, frowning at the lines of brake lights along the road ahead. "We should have gotten here earlier."

"Sorry," Hope mumbled. It was her fault they were late—Dess had had to practically drag her away from the mirror. Then Mom had taken about a hundred and sixty pictures while Dad fussed and muttered, until he finally hustled them out to the garage. He was cranky tonight, for sure. Hope thought it was partly how much makeup she had on, and the other part was the length of her dress.

"Ten-fifteen," Dad repeated as he braked in front of the house.

"Ten-fifteen," Hope echoed. Slipping out of the backseat, she grabbed her gift bag with one hand. With the other, she yanked on the hem of her dress.

"Would you leave that alone?" Dess slapped Hope's hand, then turned to look around. "Who the hell are all these old people?"

Hope delicately touched her hair again. "Headwaters parents. The Anguianos always invite the whole family to their kids' parties."

Dess's eyes widened incredulously. "Parents other than Mr. Carter are staying?"

"Yep. But don't worry. We're going to be in the back. The adults stay in the front, mostly."

"They're going to make us stay *outside*?" Dess wailed. "Nobody's going to see our outfits with coats on."

"It's a sunroom, in the back. It's not really outside—it's got glass walls. There are all these plants and a pool table and Ping-Pong and air hockey." Hope grinned and dragged Dess up the path with her. "Trust me—everyone's going to see your outfit."

"And yours," Dess reminded her, which made her wince.

It would be fine if they looked at Dess. She'd borrowed an old brown-and-cream bowling shirt from Aunt Henry and belted it over a black tank and a pair of black legging capris. "Henry" was embroidered in brown thread over the chest pocket. Hope didn't have the heart to tell Dess that the shirt had belonged to Grandpa Hank, whose real name had been Henry, too. Wearing Aunt Henry's fedora and Hope's stack-heeled brown boots, Dess looked adorable—not too dressed up but *right*. Hope tugged the dress, which seemed to shorten with every step. She was a mess. And she was probably flashing everyone, too.

"Hopeless," Dess sighed. "If you smear that eye shadow, I'm going to kick you. Don't try and pull up the cowl on the sweater. Your shoulders are *supposed* to be showing, and it's supposed to be short. Pretend you have style, all right?"

"I know, I know, I *know.*" Hope swatted at Dess's hand and prepared her company smile for Mrs. Anguiano, who was wearing an apron over her ruffled pink dress and was giving a hug to the woman in front of them. Hope wiped her sweaty hands on her hips, her pulse pounding in her throat.

"Don't cross your arms. And remember, don't talk to Rob until he apologizes," Dess bossed in a loud whisper.

"We *brought a present,*" Hope hissed through her toothy smile.

Dess whispered, "So? Give it to his mom."

"*Bonitas!*" Mrs. Anguiano smiled, holding out her hands. "Hope Carter, look at you! You look just like your mother!"

"Really?" Hope couldn't remember ever seeing her mother wearing makeup, especially not as much as Dess had smudged around her eyes tonight.

"What a stylish dress, young lady. Love that hat!"

"Thanks." Dess, who wasn't too shocked to be polite, beamed. "This is our present for Rob." She pushed Hope's arm forward and offered the gift bag.

"Oh, you can give that to him. Roberto?" Mrs. Anguiano called to her son, who was standing in the high-ceilinged entryway, talking with a crowd of people from their class. His jeans looked as if they'd been ironed, and his thick dark hair, usually a freestyle mess of tufts and cowlicks, had been firmly and definitely gelled back from his forehead like Elvis's. He lit up when he saw the two girls and came eagerly to the door.

"Rob owes Hope an apology, so we're not giving him his present," Dess said clearly as he came toward them. "We'll just give it to you, Mrs. Anguiano."

Hope winced.

Mrs. Anguiano whipped her head from Dess to her son. "Beto? What's this?" she asked, her voice dangerous.

Rob was sulking. "Dess, come *on*. You are *not* still making a big deal over this—"

"*Ro-bert-o.*" His mother's tone sharpened all three syllables. "What did you do?"

Rob widened his eyes comically. "*Nada!* I forgot to invite Hope to my party, Ma. That's all. She knew she could come, though." Rob flung up a hand to gesture at the crush of people moving from the entryway deeper into the house. "Everybody else knew."

Mrs. Anguiano sighed and took the bag from Hope with a slight grimace. "Thank you, *bonitas*. I will take this until Roberto decides to work a little harder. Welcome to our home."

"Thank you, Mrs. Anguiano," Hope and Dess said, almost in unison.

Hope choked back a laugh as Dess made a big show of walking *around* Rob to go in, her nose in the air. Hope followed, amused and slightly embarrassed.

"See?" Dess whispered as Rob trailed after them, complaining at the injustice of not receiving his gift. "I told you we were going to come and rock that boy's world."

"Yeah, I'm sure he'll never be the same." Hope giggled.

The house opened up into an entryway, with a big living room two steps down. The girls found their classmates in the den off the living room. Almost everyone they knew was camped out around the food table, which looked like a good place to go. Hope dragged her feet as Dess bounced up to the group, but Dess turned back and tugged her into the circle of eyes.

"Check it out, people," Dess announced over the gasps, "You like?"

"Look at your hair!" Ronica, her own natural hair cropped close for her gymnastics competitions, gave Hope's sleeked strands an admiring glance. "That must have taken *forever*."

"Hope, I don't think I've *ever* seen you wear makeup!" Liesl exclaimed.

"I wore makeup for class pictures," Hope mumbled, embarrassed.

"Lip gloss doesn't count," Dess informed her, and batted her eyes at Hope's glare.

"So that's the dress you 'upcycled,' Dess? It's amazing!" Natalie, wearing a sparkly red dress and matching horns on her head, circled Hope and touched a sleeve. "I can't believe that's the same sweater!"

"It looks good on you," Wynn assured Hope, giving her two very positive thumbs-up. "You look older—like a senior."

Hope admired Ronica's costume, which was her brother's old basketball uniform, and Wynn's outfit, which was halfway between Lara Croft and Indiana Jones. She admitted she couldn't tell who Liesl was supposed to be, in her white turtleneck, navy jacket, skirt, and heels.

"I'm CEO Barbie," Liesl said, lifting up a briefcase. Her jaw-length black hair was stiff with hair spray. "This is the same outfit as on my mom's Barbie doll, except Barbie's blond. And white." Liesl laughed.

"Liesl's mom collects Barbies," Natalie said when Dess looked confused.

"Oh." Dess looked horrified. "That's . . . cool."

Liesl laughed, but before Hope could hear her reply, a hand touched her shoulder.

"Hope? Hi!"

She turned, a goofy smile blooming as she saw Jas in dark-washed jeans and an orange T-shirt that read "This *Is* My Costume." Hope clenched her fists behind her to keep from pulling, smearing, tugging, or fixing anything at just the wrong moment. "Hey, Jas! Did you just get here?"

"No." Jas was staring at her oddly. "You look . . . taller," he said, taking in her outfit.

Taller. Hope lifted her foot, and they examined the heel on her boot. "It's three inches. That's tallish," she offered. *Tall? Was that all he had to say?*

"Oh. That would do it," Jas said after a pause. "That's weird," he mumbled.

Hope clutched her middle, her smile sliding. "What?"

"Well, now that you're taller, I feel like I should be . . . taller. Or something," Jas said, looking confused. "Forget it—just a thought." He cleared his throat. "Have you played air hockey yet?"

"I'm going to eat first." Hope wished she had pockets in which to hide her hands.

"Oh. Well, I'm up next." Jas looked toward the sunroom awkwardly.

"Maybe I'll come watch when I'm done," Hope suggested.

Jas nodded and shrugged. "Yeah, sure. Come play winner."

Hope gave a deflated sigh when Jas disappeared. He was being awkward, but it was okay. Hope had been crushing on him long enough to not feel too bad. At least no one had gasped or pointed or laughed at her outfit. After a time, Hope realized that no one was really even *looking* at it. Relieved, she began to relax.

The house was packed—the Anguianos knew just about everyone and had invited what seemed like the whole town. Levi's and Rob's friends attended either Headwaters, St. Kateri Academy, or Cardinal Newman High School across town, and almost every stranger was an Anguiano relative—a first or second cousin.

When Hope had circulated for a time, Rob found her and muttered a completely incoherent apology. Hope accepted, because she knew Mrs. Anguiano's eagle eyes were watching and also because, even though Rob was dumb, he'd probably suffered enough.

At one point, Hope drifted toward the front of the house to admire the chocolate fountain in the dining room and saw her father. He raised his glass in her direction, and Hope raised her chocolate-covered marshmallow. Her father made an *"Eww"* face and went back to his conversation. Hope went back to her marshmallow.

She played two games of air hockey against Grayson and then played winner when Jas beat Micah. She was sweaty when she grabbed a water bottle from the bucket of ice on the bar and stepped out onto the back porch. Micah was standing close to one of the sophomore boys, the two of them squinting at something on Micah's phone. Someone had brought out badminton rackets, and there was a game going on between the pool and a strip of lawn, mostly in the dark. Hope watched idly, knowing someone was going to fall in, eventually, or lose the birdie thing at the very least.

One of the freshman girls pushed out onto the porch and looked at Hope. "Hey. You know Dess, right?"

"Yeah." Hope straightened from leaning against the wall. "What about her?"

"Some guy is looking for her." The girl's gesture was vague. "Out front."

"Really?" Hope wondered who. "I saw her, like, five minutes ago. I'll tell her."

Was it only five minutes ago? Putting her water bottle down on a wrought-iron table, Hope went inside. The crush of people seemed to be thicker now, and the noise level louder. Hope pushed for the dining room, where she'd last seen her father, but couldn't find him. It was warm in the living room, with the gas fireplace that cut the room in half, and though she circled both sides, Hope couldn't find him—or Dess, either.

She poked her head into the room full of guys playing

video games and glanced around quickly. Dess had probably already found the guy by now.

Another circuit around the front room, and Hope stopped for sustenance. "Have you seen Dess?" she asked Ronica, who was dipping banana pieces at the chocolate fountain. In the stuffy room, Ronica's sleeveless basketball tank and long shorts looked more comfortable than anything.

"You know, somebody else just asked me that," Ronica said, frowning. "She was just here a minute ago."

Curious now, Hope grabbed another marshmallow. As she moved into the entryway, the cooler air from the front door, which someone had just opened, tempted her. She opened the heavy door a crack, and slipped out onto the front porch.

The cool air was a relief. She sagged against the door and squinted into the dimness as the breeze leached the heat of too many people from her. It was quieter here, too, which was nice. Now that Rob and Levi had had their cake, everyone had spread out. Some people were playing air hockey, but many were wrapped up in their phones, no doubt texting someone's hot cousin, and most of the boys were playing stupid video games. Hope moved to the edge of the yard and sighed. It was much better outside, but since she didn't see Dess out here—

"You seen Dess?" Jas poked his head out of the door and looked around the porch.

Hope shook her head. "You're looking for her, too?"

"Yeah." Jas frowned. "She was supposed to meet me at the pool table." He rolled his eyes. "Probably with Rob. Again."

Hope straightened. "Well, did you want someone else? I'd love to play—"

"Nah, that's okay," Jas said quickly. "It's a grudge match, and James has money riding on it." He grinned. "I'll find her," he said, and disappeared.

Hope sighed a little. Jas was . . . completely oblivious, as usual. Dess said the thing to do to get his attention was to pay attention to someone else. "Boys are not that serious," Dess had lectured. "You could have a lot more fun if you loosened up and let yourself. Jas isn't the only boy in the world." But Hope wasn't like Dess—she didn't need some revolving door of guys coming and going. Hope had seen her foster sister with Jas, Rob, James, Micah, and two other guys she didn't even know, all at one party. All Hope wanted to do was find one nice guy—just one—and be happy with that.

Why was that so hard?

Behind her, the door opened, and a gust of warm air touched the back of her neck and made her shiver.

"Hey," someone said.

Hope looked up into a stranger's face and stepped back, startled. He wore a red cloak draped over one shoulder and belted over a woven orange tunic and baggy orange pants, and he was carrying a broom. Sunglasses were perched atop his close-cropped dark hair, and he was looking down at Hope with a tentative smile.

"Um . . . hey," Hope said, swallowing.

They stood in awkward silence. Hope dug into her bag and checked the time, then dabbed on a little lip gloss, wondering how much trouble she'd get in if she blotted her face. Was her makeup melting? Beside her, the guy cleared his throat. She resisted the urge to pull down her dress but gave in to the need to cross her arms. The cool air outdoors was suddenly not cool enough.

"So . . . nice party, huh?"

"Yeah." Hope's voice cracked. *So awkward.* She shot the tall boy a sidelong glance, then did a double take. "Nice costume. You're the Sweeper from Pratchett's *Thief of Time,* right?"

The guy blinked, shock showing on his face. Then a wide grin brightened his face. "I'm Cal Rhodes, and you've got to tell me your name, because you're the only person who's gotten my costume, and we book nerds have to stick together."

Hope laughed. "True. I'm Hope Carter. You go to Cardinal Newman?" she asked, surprised she sounded normal.

He nodded. "Senior year. I'm also taking a couple of classes at WHCC, just to get a jump on things," Cal said, tilting up his chin. "You?"

Hope blinked. He was a senior *and* taking college courses? She felt awkward and young. "Um . . . I'm a sophomore. You have your major picked out already?"

Cal shrugged. "I like philosophy and math, and programming, so I figure I can do computer science or something. I'll figure it out."

Hope's phone buzzed. It was her dad, wondering where she was. She tapped out a quick reply. Hope slipped her phone in her pocket and stood uncomfortably. She thought she ought to go in and say something to Mr. and Mrs. Anguiano, but she was paralyzed by indecision. Were she and Cal done now? It seemed to be a little rude just to vanish, but he wasn't *saying* anything. . . . The door opened behind her, ending her conundrum.

"Hope!" Dess's exclamation nearly deafened her.

"What? I'm right here," Hope snapped as her foster sister stepped onto the porch.

"Sorry. Your dad—" Dess broke off, taking in Cal's robes and his broom. She looked from the boy to Hope and back again. "I'm sorry, but are you supposed to be Gandhi or something?" she asked.

Cal just looked at Hope and rolled his eyes.

"Cal, this is Dess. Dess, this is Cal. Um . . . Cal, nice meeting you."

"Did they hire him to sweep the porch?" Dess whispered loudly.

"Shut *up*," Hope groaned.

"Hey, wait!" Cal grabbed the door. "Hope, would you give me your phone?"

Dess jerked to a stop, turned, and gave Hope wide eyes.

"Um, sure." Hope scrambled for her phone and shoved it into Cal's hand, tugging surreptitiously at the hem of her dress.

"There's this book club you might like," Cal said, tapping rapidly as Dess glared and mimed slapping her hand.

250

"Drop me a text and I'll let you know when we're meeting. We're reading *The Goblin Emperor* right now, but—"

"I just finished that," Hope burst out. "It's amazing."

"Goblins." Dess rolled her eyes. "Of course, the guy with a broom likes goblins. And probably dragons."

"Give me your phone," Hope instructed, ignoring Dess entirely. She tapped her number in quickly, and returned it to Cal with a smile.

"It was really nice meeting you." She said the words sincerely. And it had been nice. Even if he didn't text her about the book club, she could text him—or not. For a little while, it had just been fun to talk to someone new. Hope hadn't even thought about Jas. Maybe she was getting to be more like Dess than she'd realized.

As they dodged through the crowd to search for their hosts, Dess asked, "So, seriously, Hope. Why was he holding a broom?"

· · · · · · · · · · · · · · · · · · ·

Last Dance

Hope, even all sweaty, looks really nice. I hope she remembers tonight when everyone is saying shit about how I'm just like all the other foster kids, stealing and running away. I hope she remembers that I did this for her—that I fixed her an outfit, that we went to this party, and that we had fun.

Before we go, we have to find who invited us, so I find Rob again, which is pretty much what he's wanted all night.

"You're leaving?" His brown eyes glint in the low light from the backyard. "For how long?"

"My grandmother's sick," I say, wishing I hadn't let him corner me in the gazebo. He'd given me some crap about a "house tour"—*so* obvious—and then he'd made his move. It was fun, right up until we started talking.

One minute we were kissing and the next, *blurt,* it's all out there, how I'm leaving tonight and don't know when I'm coming back. I can't believe I told him I'm going to see my grandma. Stella calls this kind of thing "sabotage."

"You're gonna come back, though, right? You'd *better,* Dess." Rob's a decent kisser, but his hands stroking up my sides right now feel more like cages than cuddles. I duck under his arm, and give myself breathing room.

"I don't know, all right? Jeez, Rob, she's *sick.* Unless you've got a magic wand or something to fix that, don't keep asking." I rake my hands through my hair and re-adjust my hat so it tilts over my eye again.

Rob sighs loudly. "Yeah, all right, fine." He grabs my hands and pulls me closer. "Glad you came, though. You're really hot, Dess."

I roll my eyes. He wants more kisses after telling me what I'd "better" do? Please. He's got a nice mouth, but it's not *that* nice. "Whatever. I've got to find Hope."

"Dess," whines Rob, still pulling my hands. "Don't leave."

Don't leave. If he only knew how much I wish I wasn't leaving. I crack a smile. "Dude, don't make me call your mom. She'll take *all* your presents."

Rob jumps like someone hit him in the butt with a Taser. "You're mean."

"Yeah, you're right." I grin at his pout. "I'll be back. Maybe."

As much fun as Rob is to mess with, I've been out here

too long. Last time I saw Mr. Carter was an hour ago, and he was watching me put Grayson Cho in his place—the little poser accused me of cheating at air hockey. The puck went down the hole. So what if it bounced off his shoulder first? A point is a *point*. Anyway, I know Mr. Carter wasn't playing about us leaving at ten-fifteen on the dot. I hurry my pace. The warm, loose feeling I had from being with Rob cools. Too soon I'll be walking in the cold dark, downtown to the bus station.

Levi's friends are playing video games with the lights off in the game room, so it's dim on the stairs. The slider is open, as is the screen, and I almost plow into Mr. Carter in the dark as he's heading in my direction, his phone in hand.

He squints at me. "Dess? There you are. It's after ten."

"Already?"

"Five after. Hope's in the bathroom. Both of you wait at the front door, all right? I'll get the car." He melts into the dimness.

While we wait, I hug people—Liesl, in that bad wig, Wynn, Natalie, Ronica, who smells like chocolate, even Jas. We find our host and hostess, and while Hope smiles and charms, I put on manners I didn't know I had. "Thanks for inviting us," I say, even though Rob never did officially invite Hope.

"We're so glad you came," Mrs. Anguiano says, patting my shoulder.

I go into the front room and wave at all the adults, people I don't know. "Good night!"

Hope looks at me like I'm crazy. "Are you *on* something?" she asks finally.

"No," I snap.

" 'Cause I heard Levi and his friends brought some stuff. . . ."

My face heats and I am seriously, *seriously* pissed. "What, I do drugs now? Jeez, Hope, what does it *take* with you? Just because I'm—"

"Shut up. Nobody brought any drugs to Rob's *birthday party* at his *house* with all our *parents here*!" Hope's shoulders are shaking, and she leans against the wall, weak with laughter. "Dess, you're too easy."

I glare at her, torn between punching her and hugging her. Jeez, she drives me crazy. "Let's go, *Hopeless*."

"I'm coming, *Dessturbed*."

Rob meets us at the door, giving me Sad Face. "See you when I see you, I guess?"

"Yeah," I say, hands in my pockets. Hope is watching with interest, and I wish I could be anywhere else.

"Sorry your grandma's sick," Rob adds lamely.

I nod, throat too tight to speak. *Me too.* I've left before. Why is this so hard?

"Text me when you get there," Rob continues, and a panicked flutter fills my chest. "I just—"

"Aw, sweet," Hope croons, then rolls her eyes impatiently. "Seriously? Text you when she gets *home*? You guys are going to see each other at school. Get a grip!"

"There's Mr. Carter," I say quickly, running over Rob's words. Leaning forward, I give him a hard hug. My lips skate off the corner of his mouth, the best I can do with everyone looking. "Bye, Rob."

I haul Hope out of the house, practically at a run.

"So, you and Rob are a thing?" Hope asks as we head down to the van.

"No . . . Well, yes. No. I don't know." I shrug, feeling like my skin's too tight. I'm jumpy. I've only bailed once, but I remember this feeling, this nervous energy.

Hope shakes her head. "'No, yes, no'? You are *so* messed up."

Blood rushes to my cheeks. "I am not. Shut *up*."

"Have a good time, girls?" Mr. Carter asks as we get in the van.

"I did," I say with a grin.

"I definitely did not have as much fun as my girl Dess." Hope smirks.

"Zip it," I whisper, shooting a glance at Mr. Carter.

Hope whisper-chants, *"Roberto and Dessa, sitting in a tree . . ."*

"What are you, eight? Shut up!" I fight the urge to laugh hysterically. "It's not like that. We just messed around."

Hope grins and elbows me gently. "Rob's nice, you know. When he's not being a total guy. He can be really sweet. And bonus—if he's not? His mom will kick his butt."

"I don't—we just—" My shoulders sag. *Jeez,* I'm so stupid. Why did I start up with Rob when I'm leaving? Staying and cuddling up is *not* my jam—that's Hope's thing. I was never going to stay. That's not what this was about.

"I'm not going to mess with you about him anymore,"

256

Hope says, watching my face. "I was just teasing. You guys make a cute couple. Seriously."

I hold up a hand and razor-wire the words. "We. Are. *Not*. A. Couple."

Hope doesn't jump back, as she would have a few weeks ago. She isn't afraid anymore. She narrows her eyes, like she does every time I yell at her now. "Jeez, all *right,* Dess. I get it."

We sit quiet all the way home. The silence goes up the stairs, down the hall, and to our rooms.

I wash off the party gunk and dress down as fast as I can. I need to pack a few more items from the snack pantry, but I'm mostly done. Once I get that squared away, I head for the nursery. Baby's already asleep, but I kiss him good night like I always do—like it's any other night.

"Did you have a nice time?" Foster Lady stands in the doorway of the office.

"Yeah, it was all right. That house is crazy big."

"The Anguianos are generous, lovely people to share what they have with the community. That Roberto's a sweet boy, isn't he?"

I give her a narrow look. *Hope.* That heifer has a big mouth. "Good *night,* Robin."

She grins. "I see we're not going to talk about him. Good night, Dess."

"Make sure and ask Hope about *Cal,* why don't you." *Take that, Hope.*

"Cal?" Foster Lady's eyebrows rise. "Hmm." Smiling, she goes back into the office.

I stand in the hallway, looking at the lighted square in the dim hall. *Peace out, Foster Lady. You're the weirdest granola hippie black Amazon chick I've ever met. But you're all right.*

Mr. Carter's already in bed when I pass their door, and I don't knock. We said good night when we came in the house, and though I will miss him, he's too good at clues to risk talking to. I head into my room and hesitantly tap on the bathroom door.

"Come in," Hope sings out.

I don't want to come in, but her voice—loose and friendly—draws me like a moth to a light. She's in another pair of her nasty, baggy, I-don't-give-a-crap sweats and a ratty pink T-shirt, and I swallow hard, looking at her jacked-up outfit paired with her sweet smile.

"Hope? You had a good time for real, right?"

At the sink Hope is wiping makeup from around her eyes. She pauses. "It was okay. I probably wouldn't have gone if you weren't here, but it was fine. And . . ." She ducks her head. "Cal was nice."

I frown. Hope is—jeez, *Hopeless.* "You should go to parties by yourself," I tell her, scowling. "Meet other guys. I'm not going to be here forever."

"I know that." Hope leans in and peers at her lashes.

"If you'd actually *say* something to Jas, you guys could hook up."

"I don't know if I like him that much." She shrugs. "Why all the advice?"

I back off immediately. "I'm not giving advice. I'm just *saying* you looked nice tonight. You could make a little effort and step up your game. You'd get Cal, Jas, Clayton—anyone you want."

"Clayton?" Hope looks startled. "He needs to grow up first."

I roll my eyes. "So not the point, Miss Maturity. I'm going to bed."

"Wait. Thanks again for the outfit, the makeup, everything, Dess." She's moving from the mirror toward my door. She hesitates, then squeezes my arm. "Even though my butt was hanging in the breeze all night, I really, really love that dress."

I wave her off. "You are way too paranoid about your butt!"

"I am not. Anyway, thank you. I—I'm going to return the favor." Hope gives a shy smile. "I found out Mom has some boxes of Grandpa Hank's clothes in the attic. . . . You want to go up there tomorrow and look? I found this pattern for a shirtwaist dress out of a man's dress shirt that you might like. Grandma Amelie says if we do more sewing, she'll send us some more of her clothes, so I thought, what the heck." Hope shrugs like she doesn't care, but her eyes are shining with plans and expectation.

"You did? Cool." I plaster on a smile that hides the cracks in my expression. "Sounds cool. Tomorrow." I yawn widely. "Much, much *later* tomorrow. I'd better get to bed. See you in the morning."

Hope nods and picks up her dental floss. "Night."

If I didn't have to do this, I wouldn't. I really, really wouldn't.

The buzz of my phone under my pillow jerks me back to consciousness. It feels like I just fell asleep. Silently I roll out from beneath the covers and feel around for my jeans. I slept in half my clothes to make this go faster. My backpack has been packed since before the party, and I check my snacks one last time.

At least it's easy to get out of this place—I left the window open a crack in my room and in the family room. Mr. Carter sets the security alarm before he goes to bed, but he pushed in an override code when he saw there were two windows open—I told him I'd close them. Now all I have to do is open the window in the family room a bit wider, and pop out the screen.

The last Hilltrans bus downtown stopped at 11:30 p.m.— not much help at 4:50 in the morning. Still, it isn't that long a walk out of the neighborhood and to the gas station at the bottom of the hill. I'll call a cab to the transit station, where all the buses go, and take an intercity bus to the commuter ferry. The 6:32 Bolt Coachline will take me to Rosedale, and my ticket's at the will-call window.

This is it.

I pull my dark sweatshirt hood up and put my arms through the backpack straps. . . .

And then I take it off again.

Baby's not going to understand this. I just . . . I have to see him one more time.

I ghost up the stairs. This house, so quiet, seems full of sound. The pipes under the floor make tiny ticking noises as water rushes through them, making them expand the tiniest bit. I can hear Mr. Carter snoring a little—at least I assume it's him and not Foster Lady—on the other side of their bedroom door.

As I walk down the hallway, the refrigerator kicks on, and I freeze, then silently count to ten, walk forward again, down the hall, past the night-light, into Baby's room.

As usual, he's out cold, his body twisted and his arms flung wide, as if he's leaped into a wild dream.

I smooth my hand over his round, Charlie Brown head lightly. Baby takes after Trish; you can't wake him up with an explosion. But if you do get him back to the land of the living before he's ready, he's cranky like a dog you took a bone from. He whines and tries to bite you. It's not cute.

I lean over and kiss his forehead. "Bye, Baby," I whisper. I try to walk away. If I don't get going, I won't find a cab to the transit station in time. I exhale and turn to the other crib, where Jamaira is awake, as usual, making her little squeaky noises. Poor thing, with all those seizures. I heard Foster Lady telling Mr. Carter last week that her swallowing has got so bad, they're going to put a feeding tube in her. She'll probably die before long. I force myself to walk to her crib.

"Hey, Maira. . . . Whoa."

She's awake—but still. Not shaking with little shakes,

like her seizures give her, or kicking her little legs, but stiff like a plank, and still. Her little back is arched, and I reach for her without meaning to.

My hand touches her face, and I know instantly. She's sick—like, fever sick.

God. I can't—

I sprint into the kitchen and rip off a paper towel. The tiniest stream of tap water wets it, and I fold it in a square. Back by her crib, I touch it to her face.

"Here, Jamaira, here—stop that. You're going to kill yourself. Shhh, baby."

It's not stopping. I don't know why I got her face wet. What was I thinking? It isn't enough. Oh, God. *God.* Help.

I look down the hall toward Foster Lady's room. I can't—

Damn.

With a sharp sigh, I hurry down the hall and knock sharply.

"Hope?" a sleepy voice inquires.

I open the door a crack. "Jamaira's making funny noises," I whisper loudly.

Mr. Carter's voice. "Who is?"

Foster Lady murmurs, "Is it the baby? Let me turn up the monitor—"

Into the humid silence come little mewling choking noises. I hear the rustle of bedclothes as Foster Lady rolls out of bed. I back into the hall, and she pushes past, practically running, not even turning to look at me standing in the middle of the hallway in my black jeans, black hoodie, and black shoes.

But Mr. Carter does.

"Dess?"

I move from the door as he comes closer. "Good night," I whisper, backing away.

"Thanks for waking us," he says, peering at me, a little frown between his eyes. Will he ask me what I'm doing out of bed?

"Welcome," I whisper, stepping back farther. "Good night."

"Wait. Dess—"

"Russell? Russ, I'm going to the ER." Foster Lady's voice is low but breathless, panicky. Mr. Carter turns, for just a second, and I melt away into the hall and out of sight.

I listen a moment. Voices. A light goes on in Foster Lady's office.

It's the perfect scenario. A commotion at the other end of the house, all the loving, careful faces turned toward the littlest one, who needs them.

I'm out. Hell, nobody will even miss me.

HOPE

· ·

After

When Hope finally dragged herself out of bed, Mom was at Children's Hospital with Jamaira, and Austin was keeping company with Dad on the family room floor, leaning on Dad's knees as he did crunches.

"Hey," Hope said listlessly, and plopped, yawning, on a recliner.

"Hey, yourself," Dad said, slightly out of breath as Austin chose to sit on his stomach. "About time you got up."

"I got hungry." Hope sighed. "I tried to send you mental messages that I needed breakfast in bed, but you didn't pick up."

Her father snorted. "Wish *that* was going to work. I made waffles. There's a couple left. If you want more, all you have to do is pour the batter, and *voilà*."

"Meh, too lazy." Hope looked over at Austin, who was

untying his father's shoes. "Hey, Austin. Go wake up Dess."

"Now, that's just cruel," Dad said as Austin obligingly wandered off.

"It is, isn't it?" Hope said cheerfully. She gave a luxurious stretch and sighed her contentment. "I think that makes up for her getting Mom nosing around me about Cal."

"What?"

Hope smirked and shook her head. "Never mind. You had to have been there."

Her father looked affronted. "Well, I thought I *was.*"

Austin came back into the room, looking annoyed. "Where's Dessa?"

"She's not in her bed?" Hope settled deeper into the recliner. "She didn't go with Mom, did she?"

"No. Your mother left just after five." Her father sat up with a frown, then rolled to his feet. "Dessa!" he called loudly. "Odessa Matthews!"

Hope blinked. Dad *knew* how Dess felt about being called by her whole name. What was he thinking? A flutter of unease forced her to her feet. Maybe Dess was outside?

Hope padded over to the slider and peered into the yard. It had been frosty earlier, and even now it was cold—too cold to be out in the yard doing nothing. Hope glanced down as she stepped away from the glass and stilled, her eyes on a square of black screen propped neatly against the side of the house.

"Oh, no. Are you kidding?" she whispered. "No . . ."

She headed for Dess's room at a gallop. When she reached the door, her father stood in the room, an awkward figure in the midst of the bleached pine and posters. He held up Dess's phone to Hope's inquisitive face.

"Well, she's here, then," Hope said, relief coloring her tone. "She must have gone for a walk or something."

Her father shook his head slowly. "Not and leave her phone," he said, his voice tired. "Look around, Hope. Everything she came here with is gone."

Hope turned, wordlessly taking in the neatly made bed, the small pile of clothes folded on the dresser, and on the bedside table, the crackle glaze nail polish Dess had borrowed just yesterday.

Her father sighed. "I wonder . . . Tell me, did Dess seem all right to you last night?"

"Well, yeah, she—" Hope broke off, remembering Dess towing her through the Anguianos' house as she said her goodbyes. *Are you on something?* Hope remembered, with a sick feeling, Dess's almost angry retort. *I'm not going to be here forever.*

"She wouldn't do this to me," Hope blurted. Then her hand hovered over her mouth. Dess would do what she wanted, to Hope or anyone else. She darted a quick glance at Austin, who was lining up Dess's colored pencils from the cup on her desk. "She wouldn't do it to Baby, I mean."

Her father wordlessly extended an arm, and Hope buried her face in his chest. Her ribs seemed to squeeze her lungs painfully as feelings ricocheted through her chest.

Dess had *bailed*? Just like that? When they'd finally become . . . something like friends? Why?

Her voice muffled, Hope asked, "What are you going to do? Call the police?"

Dad sighed. "Well, yes," he began. "Or Mr. Bradbrook, who will take a report and then call the police." He sighed again and shook his head. "We should have expected this. The girl's been worrying about her grandmother, and I thought she was too dressed in the middle of the night." He sighed again, a long exhale, by now a familiar sound. "Well. Let me get on the phone. I—"

"Dad, wait. Can't we just find her?" Holding him in place, Hope wrapped her fingers around her father's wrist.

"Where?" Dad shook his head. "Hope, no. We don't know when she left, we don't know what direction she went. She could have had a friend help her out. We need to call this in."

"Wait. I'll—I'll call Aunt Henry. We can just drive around for a while, can't we? You don't have to tell anyone yet, Dad. It'll go on her record, won't it? If she runs away, don't they put her back in Juvenile Hall?"

Her father's face seemed old. "Hope, Dess is a ward of the state, and we're her guardians. We *have* to call this in. Do you understand? That's our job."

"Well . . . call her social worker. The old one, the one she likes. Tell her we'll look for her first. And . . . and if we don't find at least what direction she went in two hours, then we'll call the police. Or her other social worker."

"Hope." Her father's expression was kind.

"Please, Daddy." Hope caught her bottom lip between her teeth. "It wasn't fair that she couldn't go see her grandma. We should have— Hey! We could drive her to her grandma's. If *we* drive her, it's not like she's running away, right?"

Her father blew out a hard breath and scrubbed his hands over his face. "Sweet, you're not making sense. It's almost eleven o'clock on a Saturday. Rosedale's a seven-hour drive, on a good day. We're not showered, you haven't eaten, you're not dressed—"

Hope headed for the bathroom at a dead run. "Five minutes, Dad!"

It was more like twenty-five once Hope had tied up her hair and jumped into a pair of jeans and a sweater, and once Dad had cleaned up and wiped down Austin. His wireless headset screwed into his ear, her father discussed the situation with her mother, who was still at the hospital. From Dad's responses, Hope could tell that her mother was frustrated.

"No, you couldn't have known," her father repeated as he bundled Austin into his car. Mom had taken the mini-van with Austin's usual car seat, so Hope was strapping in his spare. "She likes to raid the snack cabinet at night— you couldn't know this was the night she wouldn't go back to bed. Yes, I called the bus company. I know—she's got a four-hour jump on us, but—uh-huh. . . . Yeah, babe, I know. I understand. . . . Well, we'll just have to take our chances."

"Do you have your truck, Austin?" Hope asked tersely while checking that they had extra training pants in case they couldn't find him a bathroom in time.

Austin nodded solemnly, seeming to sense the importance of his cooperation. "I have my backpack."

"Good man." Hope ducked back into the house. Next to the door was a bag into which Dad had thrown what looked like the entire contents of the snack cabinet. Hearing the garage door open, Hope tossed in a couple of bottles of water, grabbed her impromptu waffle-sausage-egg-cheese sandwich, and closed the door behind her.

"Ready?" Dad looked at her from the driver's seat.

"Ready," Hope agreed.

DESS

· · · · · · · · · · · · · · · · · · · ·

Homecomings

Visiting hours for a lot of hospitals are 24/7, unless you're trying to get into the Critical Care Unit. Then they get all picky with you, especially if you're carrying a fat backpack full of what looks like everything you own in the world and if you look like maybe you slept in your clothes, and like some little kid at the Kaffee Haus down the road where you had breakfast spilled his mother's coffee on your shoes. And if you look younger than, like, twenty, they get real nosy.

The receptionist tip-taps her manicure on the keyboard as she types. "Matthews . . . okay. Are you a relative? Immediate family only in CCU." She looks me over.

"I'm a relative." I give the lady a close-mouthed smile. At the Kaffee Haus, I washed up, brushed out my hair, and did the best I could to get the coffee smell off me. I should have put on more makeup.

"Name?" An over-plucked brow rises.

"Tricia Matthews," I deadpan.

She scribbles my name down on her clipboard and takes out a black felt-tipped pen. "And you are—"

"Her daughter."

"Uh-huh, thank you."

She hands across the counter a square name tag that reads "MATTHEWS 4505c." "The elevators are just down the hall to your right. Fourth floor, room 4505, by the window."

"Thanks." I peel away the backing and slap the tag on my chest.

I slept on the bus but find myself yawning as I stand in the stale air of the elevator. One of the hard things about traveling is not bathing. And the food . . . This morning I ate jerky and granola bars and splurged on a container of yogurt when we stopped for gas. I've been using hand sanitizer on everything. I need a shower. I miss having as much fresh fruit as I want, and also Mr. Carter's good coffee.

Weak. I've been gone, like, ten hours, and all I can do is whine. Foster care has made me soft.

I sigh as the elevator chimes. Time to get this over with.

The "hospital smell" hits me as soon as I set foot off the elevator. My stomach heaves at the noxious aroma of drugs and sick people, alcohol swabs, old coffee and cafeteria food, too-strong disinfectant, and fear sweat. I've smelled this before, in the emergency room with Trish when she got the flu real bad one time. Without meaning to, I raise my hand to my face but remember not to touch it, just in time. Man, the *stench*. I don't see how people in here can stand it.

"Hi. Can I help you?"

I turn toward the nurses' station. In better light, the guy might be cute, but it's dim, and all I see is a coffee cup and scrubs. I don't want him looking at me, anyway.

"I know where I'm going, thanks," I say, and edge away down the tiled hall, reading numbers. It's not far from the nurses' station, and when I step in, the room is white, white, and that pale hospital green. *Blah*. Curtains are drawn around the bed by the door, and the second bed is empty. I head for the window, relieved that it's not quite as dim by the third bed. Maybe there will be more air there.

"Granny Doris?"

The woman's face is wrinkled and pale, with a mass of purplish bruises down one side. Her eyes are closed, and a needle is taped into the bend of her arm, with another machine connected to her index finger. Only the stripy white-orange of her wiry hair lets me know for sure that this is Granny Doris, whose bold hair color I used to look for in the crowd at Mass when I lost track of her. She looks different now—caved in, almost, and really, really old.

When did she get so old?

Maybe she wasn't lying about being too old to take care of us. She's too old to look after Baby, that's for sure.

My stomach flips again, and I grab a paper cup from the

stack next to her water jug on a little table and pour myself a drink. When I'm sure I'm not going to heave, I pull up the brown visitor's chair and settle my pack over the back before I sit.

I stare at her a moment, then lick my lips. "Well, I'm here. I didn't bring Baby because hospitals are *crawling* with drug-resistant germs—I read it on the Internet at the library. You didn't think I'd come, but I'm here—till they kick me out. Okay? And they might kick me out—I just want to warn you. You don't have to talk if you don't want. I brought some stuff to read."

I unzip my backpack, pull out my little bottle of sanitizer, and squeeze out a clear blob on my palm. I rub my hands together until they're freezing cold and germ-free. It's temporary, but it makes me feel better. I don't know if she can even hear me, but I read on the Internet about how people in comas can hear you. Granny Doris only got a bad concussion, so she can probably hear me all right.

"I guess I could say sorry for not answering your letters, but . . ." I shrug. "You pissed me off, not taking Baby and me when we needed somebody. Anyway, I'm with Baby now. He's been staying with this one foster family for all this time, and when they finally decided I wasn't going to be a bad influence or whatever, Farris got me put with him. Actually, I guess Trish decided she wanted me moved—"

"*Trish.*" The voice is a weak whisper, and behind blue-veined lids her eyes move. I freeze, my pulse pounding. That answers my question about whether or not she can hear.

"Yeah, Trish," I repeat. Pause. I glance at the door and

lower my voice. "Your daughter. She's the one who got me moved back with Baby—her and Farris, my old social worker." I drink more water. It's too weird to talk to Granny Doris without her talking back. Usually she made me be quiet. She used to say I talked so much, she couldn't think.

"So, anyway . . . You know they moved Trish down here to Ironwood? I probably can't see her. They put her in solitary, since she's . . . um, since she's doing some stuff for the police. Anyway, later, I might use your shower. I came all this way down here on a bus, and I probably smell like fast food and diesel." I clear my throat, and a nervous laugh pops out. "Hope says I'm obsessed with smells, and with germs. Hope—she's the real daughter of my foster parents. My foster sister, I guess. You'd like her." I rub my chest with the heel of my hand. "She probably hates me right now, though. They were nice—really nice—and I ran away anyway. That's going to make them look bad, you know? Like they didn't do a good enough job with me. You know what people say about foster parents.

"They don't do it for the money, though. Granny Doris, they've got a swimming pool, and a big old house. Me and Baby and another little—" My voice dries up, and I rub my chest again.

"Trish," Granny Doris whispers.

For the next several hours, that's all I can get out of her: "Trish." She thinks I'm my mother, which tells me she hit her head a lot harder than I thought.

Trish. Man, I wish she was here to do this instead of me.

Even though Granny Doris doesn't answer me, I talk to her. I tell her about the Anguianos' house, Rob, air hockey, Stella, the souvlaki that Kalista shares with me at lunch, and how much *Jeopardy!* I watch. When the volunteers come and bring us magazines and cookies, I sanitize my hands again and tell her about the snack cabinet and all the celebrities I read about, and how Ms. Aiello works my nerves.

I talk until I get hoarse, till I get sick of the sound of my own voice.

I'm gulping water when I hear the curtain swish back from the first bed. Twisting in my chair, I see a small Asian woman in a patterned blue smock over her scrubs and sensible shoes.

"Hi there. It's time to do vitals on Mrs. Matthews. Can I have you step out for just a minute?"

I blink. "Oh, yeah. Sure. No problem."

I check the clock in the nurses' station and stretch. It's almost six. I should probably go down to the cafeteria and see if there's anything decent to eat, but I can't bring myself to go anywhere farther than the bathroom, where I wash my face and hands again and press my cool, wet fingers to my skin. As I think about how hot Jamaira was, my stomach lurches. I guess she's all right—Foster Lady got up and took care of her. But it's stupid how bad I want to pick up the phone—the phone I don't even have—and ask.

The nurse is out of the way when I step back into the room. Behind me, I hear the chime, and the elevator doors open. And then I hear a voice.

"Hi, excuse me. I'm looking for Doris Matthews's room."

The nurse's voice is quizzical. "I'm sorry. They should have asked at reception—are you family?"

I dart into the hallway. "Yes! She's family," I insist, skidding to a stop next to Hope. I'm blinking fast. "She's my sister."

"Yeah." Hope shifts so that her arm is touching mine. My throat tightens up, but we stand shoulder to shoulder, daring the nurse to say something.

She looks us over and clears her throat, eyebrows raised. "Ah, okay, then. Great. Well, no more than two visitors for our CCU patients at a time, and visiting hours are over at eight," she begins, but Hope shakes her head.

"I'm not going to stay," she says, eyes on mine. Her sunglasses are perched on her head, and her ponytail is a little more subdued than usual—like she's been leaning against the car window or hasn't brushed out her hair since I flat-ironed it. "I just came to bring you your phone," she continues, putting the familiar sleek rectangle in my hand. "Dad got a hotel—when you're ready for bed or to get something to eat, just text, and we'll come pick you up."

"We?"

"Me and Dad and Austin." Hope smiles a little at my expression. "Mom and Jamaira were still at Children's when we left, so it's just us."

"Come here." I haul on Hope's arm and drag her toward Granny Doris's room. When the nurse is out of earshot, I turn to Hope, eyes wide. "What the hell are you guys doing?"

Hope shrugs, keeping her voice to a whisper. "Giving you a ride home?"

"Seriously? I—I can come back?"

Hope scowls. "You *do* remember we have a Constitution test Monday."

"But—" I can't find the words. Isn't anybody going to blame me? Isn't anybody mad? "Is Maira okay?"

"Maira?" Hope's expression saddens. "She's . . . Well, Mom says they're helping her eat, and she's comfortable. She . . . Mom says she smiled for her a couple of times."

Without meaning to, I look toward my grandmother's bed and swallow hard.

Comfortable. Is Granny Doris comfortable? She might not even wake up. She might still think I'm Trish.

Hope leans half against my shoulder, half against the wall, and yawns. Her breath smells like fruity purple gum. "Sorry. Long drive. Look, Dad's going to yell at you, all right? And then Mom will. Then probably Mrs. Farris and Mr. Bradbrook and probably Austin. But what else is new? Let's see your grandma and then go home, all right?"

Home. I thought home was where I was—with Granny Doris, doing what Trish would maybe want me to. I thought that since Granny Doris needed me, I was in the right place. Family is important, right? Me and Baby aren't going to stay with the Carters forever. Trish—eventually—and Baby and me are going to try and make some kind of life. Maybe.

But if Trish can't make it? If Granny Doris kicks off? What then?

"Dess?" Hope straightens. She flails a self-conscious

hand. "If you're not ready, we can wait for you or whatever. Just don't rush, okay? I know she's part of your birth family. The rest of us can wait."

The words loop like a rope around me, pulling me into the herd. *Mom. Dad. Home. The rest of us.* Hope talks like I'm supposed to be with her—like "home" is real, not foster care. No wonder I got soft. Foster Lady and Mr. Carter got Baby and me believing it, too.

"No, don't wait. I'm coming." My throat is achy and sore, but my shoulders are straight, like a weight has been lifted off my back. I move to the bed and bend over Granny Doris.

"Granny Doris, it's Dessa. I'm back," I announce. "This is Hope. She just . . . showed up. So I'm going to go now and let you rest, okay? I'll come back and check on you later."

"That's it?" Hope hisses, turning to me.

I shrug. "Yeah. What do you want?"

Hope rolls her eyes, then bends close, and pats Granny Doris's hand. Her voice is a whisper. "Hi, Mrs. Matthews. Um . . . nice to meet you. I'm Hope Carter. I hope you feel better. We're taking good care of your grandkids, and . . . um . . . everything's fine. Just get better and stuff. Everything's fine." Hope pats her hand again.

Everything's fine. I roll my eyes. Seriously? Does she have a magic wand now? *Jeez,* this girl. Granny Doris might never write me another letter. Trish might flake on Baby and me. Nothing is "fine." But as I follow Hope out of the hospital room, for the first time in days it kind of feels like, eventually, things might be.

Author's Note

Foster parents, foster care, and foster families sometimes get a seriously bad rap. In some cases, it's totally deserved—I had myriad students with whom I worked in group homes who were justifiably bitter about the emotional and sometimes physical damage they sustained in some horrific foster-care circumstances. On the other end of the spectrum, I've also known multiple amazingly loving, supportive, and giving foster parents—my own mother included. Like anything else within the scope of human nature, foster kids and foster parents run the gamut from notable to notorious. When it works—when kind people can be there to help a young person get to that point in adulthood where he or she can navigate independently—it can change both the foster parent's and the foster child's world.